Praise for *H*

"Fresh, haunting . . . In her rol[...]
novel, Monica Brashears upen[...]
—*The New York Times Book Review*

"*House of Cotton* is dazzling, full of surprises, and told with a voice
that's unpredictable and, more important, that lingers. Fans of
brave fiction would be remiss to skip this one."   —NPR

"A lush and lyrical debut."   —Shondaland

"Brashears offers a fresh new perspective on Appalachia and the
American South, and Magnolia's rich voice will echo with read-
ers long after the pages are closed."   —*Shelf Awareness*

"A haunting and macabre debut . . . Magnolia is a wonderfully
complex character."   —*Publishers Weekly*

"Delightfully morbid."   —*PopSugar*

"A haunting and sly Southern gothic with plenty of things to say
about race, gender, and appropriation."   —*CrimeReads*

"A novel for anyone who loved *Salvage the Bones* by Jesmyn Ward."
—*Debutiful*

"A lyrical fever dream of a novel."   —*Kirkus Reviews*

"Mythic, agile, and alluring all at once."   —*Bustle*

"Startling, vivid, and impressive . . . Brashears has written a lush, pictorial, and often steamy novel with an indelible heroine."

—*Booklist*

"Lush and gorgeous . . . Brashears employs language like a knife, cutting and shaping with remarkable dexterity, and the result is a wonderwork of a first book. This is a novel that sweats and broods, a story where something fretful is always boiling just under the surface." —*Nashville Scene*

"A beautiful book about the strange contours of grief."

—Raven Leilani, author of *Luster*, winner of the John Leonard Prize

"An incredible work of harsh beauty and a novel you won't forget."

—Nana Kwame Adjei-Brenyah,

New York Times bestselling author of *Friday Black*

"Monica Brashears is an immense talent, and her enchanting, strikingly original prose will astonish you. Magnolia is such a vivid, tender character: whip-smart but deeply innocent, traumatized but also joyful and funny. Magnolia's complex voice is nothing short of miraculous. *House of Cotton* is a powerful, seductive, and subversive novel."

—Dana Spiotta, author of *Eat the Document*,

winner of the Rosenthal Family Foundation Award

"Mystical, carnal, and written in fire. *House of Cotton* ushers Monica Brashears straight onto American lit's main stage, which she should grace for a long time." —Jonathan Dee, author of

The Privileges, winner of the Prix Fitzgerald

HOUSE

OF

COTTON

*MONICA
BRASHEARS*

FLATIRON
BOOKS
NEW YORK

HOUSE OF COTTON. Copyright © 2023 by Monica Brashears. All rights reserved. Printed in the United States of America. For information, address Flatiron Books, 120 Broadway, New York, NY 10271.

www.flatironbooks.com

Designed by Donna Sinisgalli Noetzel

The Library of Congress has cataloged the hardcover edition as follows:

Names: Brashears, Monica, author.
Title: House of cotton / Monica Brashears.
Description: First edition. | New York : Flatiron Books, 2023.
Identifiers: LCCN 2022037012 | ISBN 9781250851918
    (hardcover) | ISBN 9781250903860 (Canadian edition,
    sold outside the U.S., subject to rights availability) |
    ISBN 9781250851925 (ebook)
Subjects: LCGFT: Novels.
Classification: LCC PS3602.R3855 H68 2023 |
    DDC 813/.6—dc23/eng/20220815
LC record available at https://lccn.loc.gov/2022037012

ISBN 978-1-250-85193-2 (trade paperback)

Our books may be purchased in bulk for promotional, educational, or business use. Please contact your local bookseller or the Macmillan Corporate and Premium Sales Department at 1-800-221-7945, extension 5442, or by email at MacmillanSpecialMarkets@macmillan.com.

First Flatiron Books Paperback Edition: 2024

10 9 8 7 6 5 4 3 2 1

To House Mountain,

whose location I change at each story's insistence,

for looming over my life and

hosting so much strange beauty

Oh, if I do not get some rapunzel from the garden behind our house, I shall surely die.

—Brothers Grimm, "Rapunzel"

I don't want to make somebody else. I want to make myself.

—Toni Morrison, *Sula*

And from a little girl I had been taught that you don't waste your time telling people things you know they won't believe.

—Gloria Naylor, *Mama Day*

It tasted so very good to her that by the next day her desire for more had grown threefold.

—Brothers Grimm, "Rapunzel"

HOUSE

OF

COTTON

1

I ain't ever felt as trapped and choked as I do right now. When I get this way, when I feel like kudzu is wrapped tight around my rib cage and I'm bleeding a bright heat, I like to slip inside my head. I can forget about this hard-backed pew and all the silk, wide-brimmed hats bobbing to the mourning gospel. I ain't here. I ain't in Mountain Bend Baptist. I ain't even in Tennessee.

I am a little black bean. I am a little black bean in England, 1734, and a boy is carrying me home. When we get to his cottage, his mama says: *Boy, I just know you ain't sell the cow for some beans.* Before she whips the white off him with her slipper, she throws me out the window, but I ain't hurt. I am a little black bean landed in soft loam. I sleep deep in the cool ground. When the morning comes, the sun don't wake me. The boy wakes me. His skinny fingers grip my sides. I am a stalk: thick, and green, and healthy, and tall enough to touch heaven. But the boy can't let me be. He wraps his legs around me and pulls up his milk-fed body. His bones dig into me. I say, "The fuck you climbing up me for?"

A smooth palm rubs my shoulder, tugs me back to the eulogy. "Magnolia, baby. Your granny got peace, now." The dusk-colored woman next to me must have mistaken my laughter for sobbing. She traces loops on my arm, soft as a whisper, with her acrylic, until Pastor Wooly strikes something in her. "Hallelujah!" She claps. Mama Brown and me, we only came to church twice a year. Easter and Christmas. I can't remember her name. But she loved my Mama Brown. Unlike most people.

They sure didn't love her enough to know she'd hate the flowers clustered around her casket: fluffed carnations, limp roses, tongue-colored peonies. Mama Brown would have wanted something like home: garden tulips with sprigs of baby's breath. They got her face all wrong, too. Her foundation is two shades too light and Bible thick. And she wouldn't want this rambling sermon. She would want music and happy dancing.

"Now, what the Good Lord say?" Pastor Wooly taps the head of the microphone on the back of his hand. He is a dark and wrinkled man, with a tuft of dandelion seed for hair. Every Sunday, he starts his routine by hobbling up to the altar with his cane. This funeral ain't no different. When he catches the Spirit, Pastor Wooly throws his arms up. The sound of the cane smacking against the hardwood floor always results in a resounding *Hallelujah*. The individual voices of the congregation—the throaty old women; the young men with fire under their toes that make them jump, jump; the sinners that find bits of glory in their mouths—become a uniform voice, strong and deep. When I was little, I thought in these moments he was conjuring up the voice of God. Now I know that ain't true.

"I'll tell you what the Good Lord say," Pastor Wooly says.

"Yes, Pastor!" a man in the back shouts.

"He say, 'I am the resurrection and the life. The one who believes in me will live, even though they die.'"

"Hallelujah," the pretty woman next to me says.

"Y'all hear me?" Pastor Wooly jumps, loses his breath. Every other word is shot into our ears with a wavering inhale. "He say, 'I am-uh the resurrection-uh and the life-uh!" The cane smacks the floor.

"Hallelujah!" The congregation rises in the fading spirit, churning out a low hum of funeral's-done chatter.

I can't stand the thought of standing around, being strangled by hugs and White Diamonds and Old Spice and condolences. All the God Bless Yous the church plans to gift me can't take away this hurt. Can't take away me knowing that the only person who would have an answer to my problem is stiff and mute in an oak box.

I slink out the side door that opens to the edge of the cemetery. The horizon ripens with red; it'll be dark before they lower Mama Brown.

"Miss Magnolia," a voice calls from the headstones.

Sugar Foot saunters from the cusp of the open grave, puffing on a wrinkled roll-up. He grins when he reaches me. "Ain't this some bullshit?"

I didn't see Sugar Foot during the funeral. He sure ain't dressed for one: mahogany suit with a gold tie and a slanted fedora to match. I been knowing this man my whole life, and I ain't ever seen him out of his deacon clothes: white shirt and slacks. He tosses a disk of butterscotch.

I catch it. He been feeding me sweets since I was little. "Sir? What you mean?"

He waves his lit cigarette in circles at the door. "All this. Your granny would hate this."

"Mama Brown'd be fine with it," I say, "Church has done their best."

He takes a drag, blows a fat cloud of smoke in the space between us. "I seen a miracle in there."

"A miracle?"

"Yes, Miss Magnolia. I seen about ten women in there crying with dry eyes. Not a damn tear." He chuckles.

I smile. "The Lord works in mysterious ways."

The church's side door opens. "We been looking for you all over, girl," an usher says.

"You drive?" Sugar Foot asks as I step in.

"No, sir. I walked here," I say.

"I'll take you after."

"Yes, sir."

The usher leads me back to the front pew; the pallbearers lift Mama Brown like she's light as a wish.

I follow the shuffling crowd out to the dirt, this tiny fenced-in graveyard. How would I feel if I could weep? Silly. Wetting the earth with tears ain't ever made anybody sprout. The last light of the day sinks into the ground with her.

Sugar Foot finds me before the repast, his arm snaked around the small of my back, and walks with me to the church's basement, to the banquet hall. On the long white folding table made for fellowship are aluminum foil trays. Baked spaghetti, fried catfish, angel eggs. Yeast rolls, green beans, fried chicken, potato salad with mustard. Off to the side, a pound cake. I ain't got a hunger. There's a polite wait for me to fill my plate, so I do, then walk to a table near the exit and nurse my soda. Someone fires up the sound system, and Lauryn Hill starts singing, and I know Mama Brown would at least be happy with this part.

Sugar Foot joins me in a dance-walk, only some potato salad and a small roll on his plate. He waves his plastic fork over my food. "I wouldn't eat that if I was you." He stabs at his salad, looking like a damn fool eating before the blessing. "Miss Wanda cooked that fish. Last time she 'bout gave the whole congregation cholera."

"Ain't that from water?" I ask.

"Ain't that where they live?" He jabs me with his elbow, chuckling.

Everyone finds a seat with loaded plates. Pastor Wooly, standing at the head of the serving line, says, "Let us bow our heads."

Sugar Foot sets aside his fork.

A stomach-growling prayer, an echoed amen.

For an hour and a half, I sit through it all, this parade of good intentions. People trying to remember Mama Brown in a way they should, ending the same way: calling a woman an easy heifer with kindness. For an hour and a half, I bite my cheeks.

Pastor Wooly stands, signals the end of the feast.

Sitting in the front seat of Sugar Foot's car, I still got gospel ringing in my ears. How can they sing about freedom, about flying away, when they covering somebody with dirt? We ride slow in the humid black, down the road, down House Mountain, this forested knob separating North Broadway from the East Side.

"How old you now, Miss Magnolia?" Sugar Foot asks.

"Nineteen," I say.

"No disrespect intended here, and I sure do hate to bring up business on a day all riddled with grief, but I ain't made my money being worried about kindness." He lights a roll-up. I crack the window.

"What business?"

"Well, you nineteen and work at a gas station. You ain't got your granny around no more to pay me my rent."

"I'll have it to you on time. Always do." I poke my arm out the window and let the breeze cool my wrist. We pass a patch of honeysuckle, and the sugared scent fills the car.

I cling to it when he asks: "Where your mama at? I ain't seen Miss Cherry in a minute."

"Me neither," I say.

His thick-bodied car lumbers down the gravel driveway to my home. "It's a damn shame she hooked on that shit. You pretty like your mama. Got them light eyes."

"Thank you, Sugar Foot." I force a smile and open the door. He grabs my wrist.

"Now, I know it's hard living alone young as you are, making ends meet. We can work a little something out when you ready." He licks his lips like they sticky with molasses and drives off.

This house got a hollow feel. The puzzle we ain't get to finish on the coffee table: half a donkey in a flowered pasture. We must have glued hundreds of puzzles together before the dementia got her and chewed her brain.

I sit in her scarlet recliner, where I can smell her memory most—peppermint lotion, her occasional cigar, and the humidifier she let puff out stale mist. Growing up, the only time I sat in this chair was on Mama Brown's lap. The velvet arms pocked with charred craters from her cigar. In the end, she'd forget she had lit up and would crush the embers almost anywhere. Mostly on the furniture. Twice, her thighs.

Before the dementia, she breathed and talked like a June thunderstorm. If she'd been around to see Sugar Foot in his cheap suit, and the way he wet his lips like he was parched for my spit, we wouldn't have to worry about rent. She'd have his dry tongue slick with grease, frying in the skillet. And if she seen that funeral! Pastor Wooly sounds like he got the answer, like a car salesman or one of those jeweled psychics on TV. But he don't. Mama Brown do. But she's gone.

I ain't bled in a month and a half. Maybe it's stress, dealing with this love carved out of me. I could believe in loss messing up my tide. Maybe it ain't stress. Maybe I got a lump of life growing in my belly, no bigger than a sweet pepper seed. Pregnant. I don't like that word. It's got a swollen sound to it.

Then again, maybe Mama Brown wouldn't have helped. I was fifteen the last time I saw Cherry. I was in my bed. My body ached and was heated by a virus. Mama Brown had just brought me scalding boneset tea, a pink tablet of Benadryl. I gulped it and cuddled up to a notebook to write poetry about a boy I can't remember. There was a muffled knock on the front door. We never got visitors, unless it was Sugar Foot dropping by for rent and a cigar or one of Mama Brown's boyfriends—but they knew to come only if she called. I heard a woman's voice weighed down with rasp and knew it was Cherry. Their conversation started cool, unheard, but then grew rowdy as church.

There was a moment of silence. I remember because I could finally put my pen to the paper. My eyelids drooped, even though I thought the medicine hadn't had enough time to sit in my stomach. I wanted to drift off. I wrote instead because ain't love best written when it's sleepy and fevered? There were footsteps on the hardwood, three knocks on my door.

I shoved my half-finished poem beneath the quilt. "Come in," I said.

Cherry crept in, shut my door. She wore rags too big for her gaunt self. Skeletal in all the shadows. Her white skin: jaundiced. A wilted tulip.

"Maggie," she said. I ain't ever liked her calling me that.

"Hey." I made sure to strain my voice through my throat so she knew I was sick with no patience.

She sat on the edge of my bed. I could smell her: an alleyway next to a fast-food joint. "How you doing?"

"Sick," I said.

"Just thought I'd pop in." Cherry had a boyfriend, potholed with acne scars, named Quarry Jones. A white, scrawny man. He beat Cherry sometimes, but mostly he watched TV. The way she shuffled her feet and eyed the door, I knew his pickup truck waited on our driveway. I knew he was sitting and scowling with impatience in the idle. "I've missed you."

"You, too," I said.

"Maggie, could you do me a favor?"

I closed my eyes.

"Could you ask your granny if she'd give me a loan? She won't do it for me. You're her baby."

"Mama Brown said no?" I asked.

Cherry tilted her head, expectant. "Come on, now, Quarry's out there waiting, and we're low on gas."

"I ain't doing it. I don't feel good," I said.

"I've done so much for you." She shook her limp hair. "You know how young I was when I had you?"

"I don't feel good."

"Should've known I wouldn't get no help. Last time I asked her for money was when I found out I was pregnant with you." She stood. "But, apparently, a woman wanting to be free goes against God."

"Why she got to help you? She ain't even yours. She's Daddy's."

"Your daddy been dead so damn long. Who else she got to be a mother for? Can't count on nobody in this motherfucker." She slammed my door.

I wasn't there to hear her footsteps retreat, or the *fuck you* she probably muttered to Mama Brown. I wasn't in bed. I wasn't even in the house.

I was a loaf of baked bread. I was a loaf of baked bread in a wicker basket, and a girl was carrying me to her granny's cottage. When the girl neared her granny's cottage, just when I got lulled by the sun and the smell of cinnamon cookies beneath me, a wolf sauntered in the path from behind a pine tree. That fur-cloaked beast said: *You fine, Little Red Riding Hood. What you doing after this?* The girl carrying me tight in the basket said: *Thank you, Big, Bad Wolf. I'm going to my granny's.* I was only a loaf of bread, but I still knew danger. When the wolf pretended to leave, I said: *Bitch, are you dumb?*

That probably made me laugh then. It don't seem so funny now. Anyway, if Mama Brown didn't help Cherry with her problem, she probably wouldn't have helped me with mine. I wish I had time to think. I wish I had time to sit in this hollow quiet and let all my sadness curdle in me. But I ain't got no time. I got to go to work.

2

I lean against the register, floating somewhere between awake and asleep, when in walks a whistling man with blood-smeared hands. I straighten my posture and look at his glossed knuckles. I like summer music when it comes from bullfrogs and cicadas and fat warblers. Hearing a man whistle when he walks in a place he don't own ain't natural. Like finding a chipped tooth on concrete. An omen.

He looks at me and stretches his smile, says, "Ma'am, do I need a key for the restroom?" in a sap-thick drawl. He goes back, no key needed, and he better not leave that mess on the doorknob for me to clean. Before this, it'd been a typical night at work.

It's a weeknight, so I'm by myself. The place sits in the middle of Halls Crossroads and stays steady until ten. After ten, I get maybe one customer every half hour; that's when the men in this area eat pages of the Old Testament, tuck their bodies in bed, and sleep.

There's a sharp clanging outside. It's midnight. Cigarette Sammy, the only other Black person I see on this side of town. He's rummaging through the trash cans next to the pumps for cigarette butts, muttering and laughing with the angels that flutter in his head. The plastic bag next to me, already full with our nightly routine: L&Ms, a chocolate MoonPie, apple juice. When I got extra money, I'll key in a fake birthday and throw in a Pabst. Tonight ain't one of those nights.

I take the bag and a wood-tipped wine Black & Mild, going outside. That bloody man still ain't come out the bathroom. I know I shouldn't leave him alone in the store, but whatever he's up to can't be holy. If he wants to take, let him take. I won't shed nothing for it. Maybe if he sees me outside smoking, he'll understand the store is his until I kill the ember.

Cigarette Sammy, elbow deep in the can, don't look up at the sound of my footsteps.

"Hey," I say. I smile, reach my hand to him, bag swinging from my wrist.

He stops searching and sits on the pavement next to me, nurses his apple juice. Ever since I've known him, looking at the sky and laughing: his way of saying thanks.

It took a few months for me to get these midnight bags to Cigarette Sammy's liking. My coworkers trade rumors about him: before the synthetic weed fucked him up, he was a good man, they say. Like he done up and died. Told me after that bad blunt, he got on the hard stuff, and now he touches children. When I first saw him, I knew it wasn't true. The night of our meeting, I noticed him scavenging the garbage. He pulled out a ketchup-coated Styrofoam cup and chugged. I rushed outside with a bottle of water, but he wouldn't look at me. I said: *What is it, Cigarette Sammy? What you like?* He kept shifting his feet on bits of torn straw paper, eyes on his toes. *You want a Coke? Milk? Juice?* He stopped his shifting. I came back with apple, orange, and fruit punch. He picked apple. After that, I paid attention to his feet and obliged. But he ain't ever stopped digging in those cans, and because of that, I know he a little too used to being left alone.

I light my cigar and lick my lips. The first puff always sweetens my mouth. I can only smoke half of these, though, before my tongue and throat and lungs feel like they been doused in cleaning chemical and fire. Awful, but if there's one thing I can be proud of, I don't crave the nicotine. I can pick up a cigar any time I want and put it down any time I want. I ain't nothing like Cherry. Ain't an ounce of addict in me. Still, I know it's awful for me. Awful for the baby that might be in me. I got enough apologies to last my life, and the might-be baby's, too. I should buy a pregnancy test. Not knowing is what's killing me most but also the only thing comforting me.

"I went to a funeral today," I say.

Cigarette Sammy crinkles his MoonPie wrapper, points to the neon sign on the roof: People's Gas Station. Maybe his way of asking, *Why you working with this hurt?* White moths flock to the neon-red glow. Mama Brown had it in her mind that if a white moth landed on someone, death was soon to follow. She had all kinds of superstitions she believed. One time, she strung glass bottles on the branches of the maple in our backyard to protect our home from evil spirits. She'd say: *My nose itches. Somebody about to visit.* And she wouldn't ever put her pocketbook on the floor because she thought the lower it sat, the lower the income.

She must have let it slip once or twice because in all her careful-
ness, what we got to show for it?

Cigarette Sammy crinkles his wrapper again, points to the
storefront. The man with now-spotless hands stands at the
counter with disinfectant wipes and Twizzlers in his clutch. I
don't want to go in. When he whistled his way into the bathroom, I kept my eyes on a crushed beetle on the terra-cotta.
I could feel his eyes on my skin, knew by the slow drum of his
shoes that he was taking his time drinking me up.

I look back at Cigarette Sammy. Graham cookies and marsh-
mallow and chocolate sit in the corners of his mouth. Most im-
portantly, he got still feet.

"See you around," I say. I take one last puff from my cigar and
head inside.

I shuffle behind the counter. "Sorry," I say, "Figured you would
be in there awhile."

He grins, and I look at his face for the first time. Milk skin.
Pine-green eyes, deep dimples, and a sandy freckle on his nose.
Ringlet curls and good cologne. I'm guessing late thirties, early
forties. His fingers rest on the counter. Manicured nails.

"Sorry for the way I came in," he says. He sounds like he's from
here, but he don't dress like it. A nice, dark suit with a silk blue
tie. I can tell by the look and smell of him—he got money. Maybe
he's a businessman downtown. Maybe he makes laws and writes
checks. I bet he sells something with those pretty teeth. Maybe
he's a pastor at a castle-church, a mortician for famous people.

I been looking at him too long without speaking. "The way
you came in?" As if I ain't see him and his gruesome waltz. I scan
the disinfectant wipes and Twizzlers.

"Some jackass hit a dog on Raccoon Valley. I had to pull over and move it off the road."

There was no car in the parking lot. He opens his wallet on the counter while eyeing the cigarettes, then flips it shut. I think I saw a New York driver license, too quick to be sure. He sounds like he's from here, but he can't be. "It's damn near impossible to find a gas station this late. My steerin' wheel . . ." He shifts his attention from the tobacco to me, bunches his lips like he's got something to say, and eyes my name tag. "Magnolia. Can I get a pack of Virginia Slims, too, please?" He don't look like he smokes Virginia Slims.

I scan them. He taps his card against the chip reader. "Josephine Baker," he says.

"Huh?"

"I was tryin' to figure out who you remind me of. Josephine Baker."

"Thank you." I smile. I don't know who that is.

He inserts his card in the chip reader. "You know what, you could be a model." He punches his PIN into the keypad.

A polite chuckle. "You are funny." That pause between "you" and "are" is careful. I try to avoid contractions at work. It don't sound or feel natural, but the customers seem to like the way I talk.

"I'm serious. Would you model?" he asks.

"Sure. If people made careers modeling in Knoxville, I sure would."

He reaches in his pocket, flips a card between his fingers, and places it on the counter. I touch the card, almost thick and white as bone. The dimples in his grin make him look a little younger.

"Think about it." He takes his items and walks to the door. His shoes make music on the tile. "Y'all have a good night."

After tossing his receipt, I peek out the windows to watch his exit; he's vanished.

When my shift ends, I consider walking thirty minutes out my way to a different gas station where I could buy a pregnancy test, where I'm faceless and nobody knows my name. Angie's at the register now, counting cigarettes, and she'd twist her mouth in that oh-I-didn't-know-you'd-been-fucking way. As if she ain't near sixty and in a relationship with a man who gives her a high school type of drama. It's three in the morning, the world is dead, and my feet ache. I can do all that tomorrow. If I know now and realize I either got to pay for two people to keep breathing or I got to be okay with really being alone, how could I sleep after that?

The bus rides from Halls Crossroads to the base of House Mountain. Halls turns into Fountain City—tanning salons, boutiques, and spas. Farther up Broadway—title loans, pawn shops, Taqueria La Herradura with the good fish (bones and all), tattoo parlors, and more title loans. Everything closed this late.

Off the bus, down the side street, through the woods. Up the driveway, my steps feel too heavy, like walking through water. One-story white house and its little porch, the lights off because nobody's home. Shadows of night dulling the yellow door.

I don't think about the business card until I get inside. I'm sitting on the recliner, buried under a quilt, blunt lit. A jazz radio station shuffles. Santo & Johnny's "Sleep Walk" plays. I ain't heard this before, but it matches something in my chest. I inhale fake grape and weak weed and take the card out my pocket. It don't feel like card stock. It feels like suede. A swirling script in dark gold letters: Cotton and Eden Productions. There's a phone number, email, mailing address, but no description or website link. Thinking of that white man conjures up a new want. He had a mystery about him: the way he talked, the smokes he picked, and the steady, good-soled shoes. But I ain't going to contact him. The only modeling jobs in Knoxville would end with my hair stiff and teased in a bad revival of 1980s glamour shots. Or my body diced and stored in cardboard boxes on the floor of a dank, abandoned warehouse. I take another hit of the blunt, scratch my nose, toss the card on the coffee table. Who that white man say I look like?

My nails hover over my laptop's keyboard until I remember. The photos tell me I don't look nothing like Josephine Baker. She had pouting eyes and a pet cheetah. We might got the same skin tone. She looks like a different person in every picture: jezebel, then businessman, then jungle goddess. My favorite picture is the one with bananas roped around her waist. I wonder if I'd look good in a skirt of fruit. Damn this itch. I scratch my nose.

Time don't mean nothing. It's four in the morning, and I ain't in bed. My only sun is the reading lamp and the dimness of my laptop. I'm swimming in darkness or the darkness is swimming in me, and Mama Brown's life still smells strong here, and my nose won't stop itching. All the windows and doors stay locked, but it feels like the harsh summer leaking in. A good balm is what I want. I rise, slide my laptop in the recliner seat. Let Louis Armstrong sing about green trees to an empty room. In the bathroom, cold water runs on my wrist. What I need is to cool. Maybe it's being high, but all my life seems to flow down into this sink. And when I see this little dip that is my sink, and mine alone, I realize I ain't ever saw a sink this small on TV. Not even in shows and movies where the people supposed to be poor. And the tub—I got to fold my legs a little if I want to take a bath. This room ain't for bathing and scrubbing teeth—it's for being real small.

The only sink I ever saw smaller than this one was in Cherry's trailer. When she first started dating Quarry, I was five. He still had his teeth and a head of hay-colored hair. And in the early days of them knowing and loving each other, he tried to love me, too. The day after he moved in, he came home from work. He had a box of Pizza Plus and a pink cowgirl hat. *I got it with my tips,* he said. I put it on. He got on all fours, and we laughed until we cried: me with my legs wrapped around his neck, him horse-trotting across the living room, Cherry snapping pictures with a disposable camera. My bladder was full, but the fun couldn't stop. I let it go; piss streamed. We laughed harder. I jumped off, and he ran to the bathroom, doused his neck and skull with pump soap and water. In that tiny sink. Yes, places like these made for small living.

How Mama Brown live her whole life hunched down, cramped? I want room to fill my lungs all the way up, room to exhale real slow. Maybe Mama Brown did know how suffocating our life had been, not having nothing but walls and a thumping heart. If she knew all my bad thoughts, she'd say: *Magnolia, why you sitting in pity when we got a pearl in the sky, shoes on our feet, and love in our bones?* I can't see the moon as a pearl. If I'm sitting in pity, let me sit.

Three knocks on the front door.

I stop the stream of the water and listen. I don't hear nothing other than Louis telling me how he thinks the world is wonderful.

Three knocks on the front door.

I creep into the living room, and before I can bring myself to squint through the peephole, I stay real still and listen. On the other side, a light whistling. And for a moment, I'm a child scared by what could lurk—a banshee who's come just a little too late, a man who pretends to need the phone only to make me into a pile of bones. If I don't look now, I won't. Eyes pressed against the little bulb, I see him. Sugar Foot stands in his suit, chomping pink gum. He looks at the peephole like he can see the whole of my self and smirks.

I tiptoe to my room and press the door shut, crawl into bed. His own bed is where he should be, missing that empty space of his wife who he stuffed in the old folks' home—missing the sleepy scent of whatever night cream she uses, her dream mumbles. Not knocking on my door. The house falls quiet except for the stifled saxophone. When I'm sure he's given up and gone home, I slink back into the living room. The lock turns—a quick chatter of teeth—and he walks in my space.

"The hell—"

"Miss Magnolia," he says.

I rub my eyes. "I was just coming to the door."

We sit on the yellow sofa with sunken cushions.

The silence stretches. Sugar Foot bobs his head to a wordless song while scanning the room. He look like he's taking inventory. And it's late. Too late for this. But he don't smell like closing time.

Finally, he speaks. "How you holding up?"

"Best I can."

"I wanted to dip in and check on you." He blows a bubble. The pop—a flat smack. "You ain't seem to be yourself earlier."

He got his legs sprawled, eating up all the space.

"Mama Brown died." Those words falling from my lips make me feel like I'm speaking in tongues. Those words make me wish I believed in ghosts. Haunt me, Mama. Even if you a tiny puff of smoke. Slide down this man's throat. Make him cough. I'd tell him we ain't got throat lozenges. He'd have to go out the door, into his car, on down to the pharmacy. Haunt me like you ain't ever left me at all.

"I wanted to say my sorries for earlier," he says.

"What you mean?" As if I ain't feel the rocking of my stomach when he licked his lips.

"Talking to you 'bout the ways of the world." He pauses, scratches his stubble as if the right words hide somewhere beneath. "You sheltered, Miss Magnolia."

"I wouldn't say all that." He must not know all about Cherry's attempt at raising me. And I wasn't sheltered in the last months of Mama Brown's existence. Swiping through Tinder. Finding warmth in the musk of men. Splaying my body in littered parking lots, in beds of strangers, in the ribs of a breathing forest. If my problem really is a problem, this baby won't know its daddy. But knowing a daddy and knowing a mom don't seem to make much difference in living. "I pay bills. I work."

"You know what your granny was doing at your age?" The way his eyes soften, he's deep in remembering. He giggles, and for a moment, he don't sound like an old man. He sounds like a child. "She was walking around town with a soda bottle cap pinned to her shirt."

I laugh. "What?"

He smiles. "You really, really sheltered."

"Why a bottle cap?"

"She was letting the men know——" He purses his lips and studies my face. "She was selling sugar."

"That ain't none of my business or yours, either."

"But it was."

The broken sofa swallows my weight. I don't ever sit on this thing——more a funny and sad decoration than a place to rest. Why didn't I sit on the recliner? It'd feel rude to move. It'd feel like asking for a fight. He scoots a little closer. His scent is loud: bubblegum and sandalwood.

"I ain't saying she wrong for what she did. She made ends meet." He blows another bubble. "She was built different."

"Everybody know Mama Brown was built different." I yawn. "I'm sleepy."

"I'm a little worried 'bout you making it, is all. Your granny had backbone. She had grit." He touches my thigh. "You soft."

"No," I say.

3

I am crumbs of rye bread. I am crumbs of rye bread in a little boy's pocket. He walks with a girl, and every step they take in this log-jumbled forest makes me bounce. The little girl whispers in a sad voice: *I want to go back.* The boy don't speak. The little girl says: *Brother, can you take me back?* He drops bits of me on the ground. It's okay because it don't hurt. I am crumbs of rye bread. I don't mind being scattered. She says again: *Brother, let's go back.* He drops the last of me in the yard of a candied cottage. There's disks of butterscotch and peppermints and soft caramels. Sassafras sticks and root beer drops and strawberry bonbons. There's swirled lollipops and jawbreakers and so much bubblegum. I ask the wind to lift me and my crust. *Let me have candy*, I say, *Let me go back.* The wind don't hear me, which is natural because the wind is the wind. A fat crow swoops, lands. He pecks at me with his stony beak. I say: *Get off me, you crow.* I say: *Your breath smell like the dead.*

4

I know I should cry until my eyes puff. I should track down Sugar Foot and draw blood. Make him ask God for life. Sadness and anger don't come easy for me. Instead, I take a shower and gauze the small bathroom with steam. I scrub and scrub and scrub. Scouring myself to the moaning of old pipes. After, I salve my skin with cocoa butter. When I slide into a sundress—no bra, no panties, not even a thong—I am a fearless woman. I am the name I use on Tinder. I am Carolina Nettle.

It feels good to be out the lonely gloom of home, away from my newest bad memory. If I'd stayed inside, with all those reminders of Mama Brown, with all those in-the-flesh truths that she ain't here to protect me anymore, I just know I'd get to sobbing. The kind of sobbing where I panic because my lungs won't do their damn job and balloon. But I ain't there, anyhow. No, I'm in this forest throbbing with heat and light. Humidity clinging to my skin. This good weather and all the life make something pump within me. Green, reaching fingers of sycamores and cottonwood. Spread palms of scarlet bee balm. Sparrows and yellowthroats singing, woodpeckers tapping along to a tumbling drumbeat inside me, matching the rhythm.

I was tired, tired when I clawed out of sleep. I stayed up until the sun peeked through its purple veil; I woke up around noon and knew I needed out.

The sun lulls me, cooks my damp skin. I sit on the baking wood of the porch. The warmth spreads to my thighs as I wait. A cherry-red car pulls into the driveway. A new one. I never see the same man twice.

A dark-skinned man steps out, walks up to me. He flashes a river pearl smile. "Carolina?" He heads for the door.

"No, follow me." I take his hand, lead him to the garden. We stand in the center, closed in by snapdragons, ripe tomatoes, squash, basil, tangles of mint. Monarchs and honeybees suck nectar.

He kisses me. I slip my tongue past the fence of his teeth. My hand slides down his chest, down the ridges of his abs, fumbles until his buckle clicks undone, until his pants fall to his ankles. At our feet: curls of honeysuckle. He leans into his kiss, and we float down to the soft soil like we forgot about gravity. I hike my dress up, and he pushes between my thighs, goes deep. I let him think this is how it goes until he's hard, and I push him over and straddle. Even after all that bathing, an unseen filth settles in my skin. I can feel it—seeping down, brewing meanness. My nails twisting his shirt. And this man's touch ain't any different than Sugar Foot's. No sweet wanting, only a hunger. My hands grip his throat; my nails pierce, but only a little. What right's he got to crave my pussy, to need my pussy like he went to bed without supper? My eyes start to pool, but I pull out my tits so he don't notice. He twirls his fingers on my nipples, and God, I don't want it to make me sing, but it does, and I do. I feel sweat dewing on my inner thighs, trickling down, joining all the wet. His arms limp, his face wearing that childlike, slack-jawed look of goodness. He looking too comfortable. My hands scramble to his chest and scratch and scratch and scratch. When it looks like he got fear in his eyes, I say, "Yes, Boy, it's me you afraid of." I say, "You stay still." I cum.

When my screaming and whimpers die down, his eyes get fat. "I'm gonna——" I hop off and shove him in my mouth. The bitter heat hits the back of my throat, suffocates the anger inside. I swallow and stand.

He stays on his back, breathless, shaking. "Can I use your bathroom?"

"I got someplace to be." I walk on, wiping dirt from my dress, cum from my lips. Leave him buckling his pants in front of all the flying things.

The Walgreens on the East Side ain't far. I trudge out the crowded patch of woods onto Magnolia Avenue where I have service and check my bank balance on my phone. I got nineteen dollars to last me the rest of May, until my next check. Two weeks. I guess I don't got to pay this month's rent. A cheap pregnancy test will have to do.

I walk by the apartments, teens kicking it on the side porches, kids playing chase in the ryegrass. This side of town feels like love and lust. Booming bass from passing cars, rolled down windows. Days feeling this good, I know there's a full wait at Tammy's Fried Green Tomatoes, and the flea market nearby probably crowded and haggling. Next to Wok N Roll, pretty women step in and out of Q Nails. Up to Asheville Highway, by the smoke shop, there's always a cluster of old heads outside.

I welcome the cool kiss of the air conditioner inside Walgreens and take slow steps by the makeup aisle. I shouldn't spend money I don't have, but it don't hurt to look. I like the eyeshadows that shimmer like fish scales. I probably get that from Cherry. When I was little, five or six, and still lived with her and Quarry, she'd do my makeup as she did hers. Everything was soft then: her vanilla perfume, our glossed lips, Ashanti's voice coming out the radio. I'd sit in the softness, allowed to be little, and I'd say: *Mommy, make my face gold.* Cherry would say: *Maggie, I'll make you so gold, people will think I robbed Fort Knox.* I'd sing along to the songs and pretend I was in the station, holding a microphone, eyelids heavy with glitter. I wanted to be famous: a feather boa diva with fans and limos and skinny champagne flutes. Cherry promised I would make it. And we'd sing together before she went to work or as she made supper. We sounded pretty as windchimes. But Quarry always made me wash my face when he saw what she did.

I don't wear much makeup now. I pluck a tube of red lip-stick from its snug place on a shelf. A bloody shade—the shade of someone who bites off the pinkies of men and spits them in ditches. A shade for Carolina Nettle. I turn to the price sticker and place it back on the shelf. Got to do what I came for and leave. I reach the aisle with the pregnancy test.

"Magnolia?"

Before I turn around at the voice behind me, I hear the click-ing of a cane.

"Pastor Wooly," I say.

He limps to me. "How you doing?" His black bean eyes wander to the tests on the shelves.

He squints, and I wonder if he can smell the cum on my breath.

"I'm good. I'm fine," I say.

"You know, Mama Brown got peace," he says.

"I know." I wait in the brief silence and hope the pharmacist pages him to pick up his prescription or that his wife will call and ask him to get a Debbie cake or that he will remember it is time to talk to God.

"Sugar Foot told me," he says.

If I had anything in my stomach, I'd vomit on his shined shoes.

"What you mean?"

"Spoke to him this morning; told me he had plans on letting go of this month's rent." He nods to some beat in his head. "You take comfort in us, now. The church is your family. We here."

"Thank you, Pastor." I give him a smile that feels too plastic. The minute Mama Brown's heart stopped is the minute I said no more church. Seeing the funeral only confirmed that for me. And Sugar Foot taking my body and being a deacon. If this is what family is now, I don't want it.

The pharmacist pages his name in a sterile voice. I shuffle away.

"You be good now, hear?" I feel his eyes on my back.

I circle around to the red lipstick in the makeup aisle. Yes, this a bold shade of a woman whose sharp-heeled footsteps demand attention. When a woman paints a color this mean on her lips, nobody, not even Pastor Wooly, tells her to be good. I bounce the tube in my hand and wander until I see a case of perfume. Body Fantasies in vanilla—cheap and smells like the past.

I kill time.

In the candy aisle, I scoop a bag of suckers. I ain't going to spend money on this stuff. If he saw me with the test, I'd get a soft-spoken fire-and-brimstone lecture. Everybody in the church would know I'm fast. Sugar Foot would know I ain't going to have money. He'd probably come by more often.

I peek in the pharmacy. He ain't here. I stalk to the edge of the registers. There he is, scanning the newspaper, leaning more into the fresh print than his cane. He must feel my gaze because before I can dip into the aisle, his attention rests on me.

I walk to him, holding the innocent products in clear view.

"You checking out?" he asks. He continues to eye the newspaper.

I place the lipstick, perfume, and candy on the counter. "Yes, Pastor. You?"

"God's wrath cuts us deep, don't it." He fans the paper in the air, drops it to the wire stand.

My phone number beeps onto the keypad. No reward points. "Yes, sir. It sure is hot outside."

"Cuts and cuts and cuts." He leaves the store after my transaction processes. Damn, ain't that something? I could have bought the pregnancy test, and he wouldn't have even noticed. All swaddled in his thoughts. I don't got to know the truth just yet, anyway. I'll come back to Walgreens and get a refund, but right now, I'm hungry. Or maybe I'll just buy the test with my next paycheck. Ain't like I can do anything about it right now if I am carrying.

I glance at the newspapers as I step away with my purchase and see something about a tribute to Prince.

At the McDonald's next door, I gobble up a cheeseburger and milkshake. McDonald's was a treat growing up. When Quarry got paid, he'd take me and Cherry. We'd feast on the dollar menu in

the truck. I liked when we went during storms. He'd play something with slow guitar, and I'd watch the raindrops race down the
window with knots of meat stuck in my teeth. Sometimes after,
he'd take us to Walmart and let us pick out one thing. Cherry always got CDs or more makeup. I always wanted a doll. My party
of dolls grew in a couple of months: blonde, brunette, glittering
dresses. Some dolls came with brushes. Some dolls were scented
like fruit. Quarry made me stop getting them after my toy bin got
full. He said I needed to make some friends.

The bathroom here reeks of stale piss, and my belly, all bloated
with grease and cream, churns. I spray my body and hair with
perfume, then unwrap the plastic from the tube of lipstick and
smooth red onto my pout. In the mirror, my lips say: *I eat blood*.
In the mirror, my lips say: *Listen*. If my pretty as strong as it feels
right now, why can't I be something to see?

I slide that suede business card out my pocket and type
the address into my phone: only a thirty-minute walk, north
from here, at the end of Broadway. The address on the hem of
downtown—close enough to the banks and firms to have people
with fat wallets around. It can't hurt me none to see the business
from the outside. If it's stained with spray paint and rust, I'll walk
on home. If the windows too tinted to see inside or there's a big
van parked in the driveway, I'll walk on home. And if it's near
an interstate on-ramp, which I don't think it is, but if it is—I'll
run on home. That's sex trafficking waiting to happen. In some
pocket of my mind, I hope the building will be sleek and steel
and bustling with pedicured women.

When I leave the clang and chatter of the McDonald's, step
into the dying heat of the afternoon, I strut. This lipstick doing
something to me. Hair's spritzed with perfume. I read online that

the scent lasts longer that way, reaches out to everyone you pass, so I let it sit in my dense curls. Other than my screaming lips and drowsy fragrance, nothing about my look today says model. I should have worn one of my church dresses, or at least my laced skirt. My outfit: a sex-soaked, sweat heavy sundress, worn flip-flops. Maybe he'll see a good vision in me. I'll pass through the sliding door of the deep gray building, and I'll say in a radio-smooth voice: *Hello, I am ready for the summer.* No, I'll say: *Hello, I am ready for the summer shoot. I am a beach girl.* And he'll smack his palm against his thigh, beam, and say: *Yes, you are right on time,* and *Are you ready to be paid?*

I only spent four dollars on my meal, but my haul at Walgreens cost me twelve dollars. That leaves me with three dollars in the bank. While I wait at a crosswalk, I check my bank account to be sure. Those red numbers push my heart down to my belly, down to my undigested meal. Fuck. I should have cancelled my Netflix account.

I don't even care what the building looks like. It could be mostly swallowed by termites, and a rat could answer the door. The red hand, held up at the other end of the crosswalk, blinks to a white walking man; the flat beat of my flip-flops on asphalt gains speed.

Through the woods that swallow my house, to Broadway, buildings in the distance caught in webs of kudzu. I pass plazas, littered underpasses; the traffic's pace quickens. Near the historic district where well-dressed people live, my phone dings: *The destination is on your right.* I cross from the bubblegum-blackened sidewalk to the parking lot. The building seems promising: a white plantation-style house with columns that look like they made of fondant.

Three floors. The towering sign bolted into the flattened area of sidewalk where cars can pull in reads Weeping Willow Parlor, not Cotton and Eden Productions, but I like the sound of that. "Parlor" gives me the image of thin women smoking long cigarettes, silk gowns hanging loose from their shoulders.

I shuffle across the parking lot to the area where it narrows into a wraparound driveway. Up the sloped pavement, I notice a wax-slick hearse parked near the entrance. Maybe this some kind of cruel joke played on me. Maybe what that white man meant by handing me the card: *You ugly as a corpse.*

I want to go in, but I don't. It's a public business, but I don't want to parade on in there and ask for the suited man. What I look like, asking a mourning family if they know where I can find a modeling job? I'll just peek in the windows and maybe I'll see him.

I crouch behind a bush heavy with roses by the door. Fat bumblebees hum. My heart thuds in all my secrecy. Maybe this is something like how Sugar Foot felt when he stood at my front door, blood flow rushing to his zipper, waiting—just waiting—for me to answer.

The heat and my nerves dizzy me. At the edge of the window, I peer, half-expecting to be met with a face pressed against the glass, words pushed out with a knowing grin: *Aha, I caught you.* Nodding in disgust: *Aha, you like to creep on sad people. Want to see them chest-clutching, bag-eyed mourners, you sick bitch.* Nobody's in there. A black velvet curtain blocks most of my view: a sliver of hardwood tile and, up high, a crystal chandelier. Spying at places like this don't end with a pistol's warning shot at the sky. It ends with a spit-sprayed confrontation, a phone call, and handcuffs.

Behind the window, a flicker of movement. Before I can stand and run—run back to Broadway, back into the forest at the base of the mountain, back home—the door opens.

A woman steps into the sunlight: silver bob, yellow-and-white blouse, wrinkled lips matte with mauve. She must be the one who smokes Virginia Slims. She shuts the door behind her without noticing me.

My phone dings: *You have arrived at your destination.*

"Who the hell are you?" The drawl in her voice lets me know she's a hard woman, chewed and spit out of a Tennessee valley. The woman removes her sunglasses, steps down from the brick stairs, onto the mulch.

I rise, dust the hot dirt and wood chips from my knees. She looks like somebody I know. "I was, well, really what had happened was—"

She tilts her head, smirks, and because of the rise of her cheekbones, I say: "You look like Meryl Streep."

"Who the hell are you?" She don't seem as threatened now. My stammering must have relaxed her. She takes the small pack of Virginia Slims out of her pocketbook and lights a cig.

I show her the business card.

"Lordy. He really reeled one in." She opens the door, shouts, "Cotton!"

While we wait, the woman studies me, smiling. She exhales a tuft of smoke. "Secret's in the contour."

"What?"

"Meryl Streep is in the contour."

Cotton pokes his head from behind the door. The woman, who I guess is Eden, looks at him. She gives him a smile soft as cream, pinches his cheek. "Dumbass," she says.

He don't step outside, just chuckles and watches her drive away in the hearse. When the end of the hearse pulls onto the road with a scrape, his floating head gives me a too-big smile. My name comes out his mouth high-pitched, like I just caught him dancing in the mirror. "Magnolia." He clears his throat. "Hi." He's only wearing boxers. Calvin Klein. Green and blue paint splattered on his hands, his chest.

I follow him into the amber glow of the place. The lobby is bare: a desk with a vase of virgin-white lilies. No receptionist. A chandelier hangs like a skirt from the ceiling, and some part of me wants to smash it to glass crumbs. There's a hallway that must lead to a viewing room. We climb the stairs.

"Where are the dead folk?" I ask.

"Basement usually." The stairs whine under our weight. "Business is slow."

I sit on a plush, purple couch and he disappears to get drinks. What the hell I got myself into? There's a fireplace; silky flames waver in the dark. Above the old hearth, a painting looms. I ain't scared, not really, but I do feel nauseous when I study the art. In the center, a bare-breasted woman with a bloodied mouth, lying on a couch. Near her, a man gazes into a gramophone. By the entrance of the room, two men wait unnoticed: one with a club, the other with a net. From outside the room, three men stare at the gore through the window. Beyond the room, the people, the window, snowy mountains slope and cross like tangled thighs.

Cotton returns in a pink robe holding a platter with wine glasses filled to the brim with a liquid that looks like melted candied apples. I hoped for a contract—I don't see no papers or a pretty fountain pen. But the bass in his Southern voice sounds like business: "You like Magritte?"

I look at the drinks and almost say: *Never had Magritte*, but the bottle between the glasses reads Campari. He nods to the painting.

"It's fine art," I say.

He hands me a glass, raises his in the air. "That fabric draped over the woman's collarbones, you see that?" He sits by me on the couch, country voice rumbling. "Magritte's mother killed herself when he was thirteen, just cast herself into the river. And Magritte was there when they found the body." His eyes, directed at the painting, bulge with too much passion—he sounds like pastors at white churches. "When they found her, her dress covered her face. He put that image in a lot of his work. Cloth over faces." He looks at me, that strange passion exiled, and chuckles. "But enough about context. What do you see?"

"I see a man who ain't, isn't, aware." I sip the alcohol. It ain't as sweet as it looks. "You don't look at music. You listen. His senses all warped."

"But you're aware, aren't you?" He sits by me on the couch. "Go ahead, pick apart our encounter."

"You seem nice." I trace my fingernail along the rim of the glass, dancing around the print of my lipstick.

"Oh, I'm giddy. No, really, come on."

"Eden, I think is her name, didn't seem happy that I'm here, I don't see a contract, and you're from New York." The words spill out my mouth. And I want to add: *You real happy when you speak tragic*, but instead, I say, "I mean, I think you're from New York." My face all flushed with heat. Maybe models are supposed to be a little rude.

He drops his Southern accent, switches to a clipped, neutral voice. "I spent a few years in Manhattan, yeah. I moved back two weeks ago."

"Why fake the accent?" This Campari makes me feel light, like I could float from this couch with a puff of air.

He smiles. "There was this exclusive modern disco club in the city. Get this: there was always a crowd at the door, and I tried every weekend to get in. A wig, a cane. I bought the most expensive suit I could find. Magnolia, every time, without fail, I was turned away. Then one night, I came dressed in jeans and a white shirt, like I was fucking Matthew McConaughey, and I walk right up to the bouncer, and I say in my most Tennessean voice: *I'm here for Piggy.*"

I sip, wide-eyed. "Did that work?"

He nods. "I walked in, and I had the best night of my life."

"Wow," I say.

He laughs and shakes his head, shoos me with his paint-stained hands. "No, I made that all up. I have a propensity for perfor-mance." He places the bottle on the glass table, still grinning. "I'm hoping you do, too."

I can't tell what's in his eyes—if he's peeling the dress off my body in his mind or taking up a genuine interest in me. "You worked with models in New York?"

"Oh no. I was a clairvoyant." He shifts his weight on the cushion. "I loved the setup. I even had a wacky moniker." He bends in a half-bow. "The Seer." His face firms with a serious look. "I helped a lot of people. Everyone wants answers. I only came back be-cause my uncle died, and I inherited this business. I mean, really, isn't it the most lachrymose building you've ever seen?" He nods in agreement with himself. "Lachrymost."

"I don't see how this has anything to do with modeling."

He jabs his finger with a "you got it" smile. "Right. Aunt Eden is so caught up in such trivial matters: like what direction I should take with my life, whether or not I should go to therapy, am I properly mourning the loss of my uncle. Anyway, I can't say her preferences—"

I rise, place the empty glass on the table. "You a con man."

Rage creases his eyes. I've gnawed on his soft spot. "What, do I look like I need to con?"

My body stills, planted, stuck in his gaze.

"I'm old money, sweetheart."

"Good for you."

"I could buy your family."

I head for the staircase.

He stammers. "I didn't mean—shit, I didn't mean like that."

I make my way down the stairs, gripping the handrail so I don't tilt. I drank a little too fast.

"I deal in death," he calls from the top of the staircase. "Is that what bothers you?"

"Not getting paid is what bothers me."

I'm halfway down the parking lot when Cotton yells my name from the door. I take longer strides. Stupid, I'm so stupid. And I used the lipstick and perfume, and now I can't return them. His footsteps thunder behind me. I don't turn around. Before I step onto the sidewalk, his voice is close enough that I can feel the air from his throat on the nape of my neck: "Look."

I turn around. He's breathless, pink robe sliding off the left side of his body. Car horns blare as they pass. He waves a hundred-dollar bill in the space between us as he steadies his breathing. I want to run away, but that crisp money got my knees locked.

He says, "I'll admit it. I'll admit it right here. I was a little underprepared. I didn't expect you to come without calling."

"I ain't expect you to live in a morgue." I resist the urge to spit on his feet.

"A funeral parlor, but never mind semantics." He gasps for air slow. "Come here for dinner. Day after tomorrow. Can you swing six o'clock?"

I lie. "I got to work."

He holds out the money. "Aunt Eden will be here. We could have a nice time." I grab the money. I feel sick. "I have contacts. Contacts in New York."

"Fine." I slip the money in the pocket of my dress. "You don't tell me you can buy my family."

He got shame weighing down the corners of his mouth. "Right. Right, I know. Sorry, right."

The pissed-off heartbeat switches to easy fluttering in my chest, nudges me down Broadway. Maybe it's the alcohol or maybe it's the money I got pressed against me. The sun floats low; a crescent moon, skinny as a nail clipping, hangs in the sky. Daylight will drain before I get home.

I take advantage of my good mood and go into a Dollar General, buy two pregnancy tests. Strut up Broadway, through the mossy forest, down my driveway's night-cool gravel. My mood and thoughts stay feathered until I walk in and notice the puzzle on the coffee table. I guess with all the thrashing, Sugar Foot bumped the table. The donkey and flowered pasture's all scattered. It's probably just in my mind, but I swear his sandalwood cologne haunts this space. I hope he ain't been in here since I been gone, but I wouldn't be surprised. I don't think I locked the door when I left. What's the point in that? Ain't nothing left to be violated.

I pick up the puzzle pieces that fell to the floor, place them on the coffee table, and light my second Black & Mild. Mama Brown probably wouldn't give me roots or herbs to push this life out me. She took all her secrets with her into the earth. It takes courage to peek into Mama Brown's room. Ain't had it in me to go through her things, aside from the quick trips to her dresser to steal her weed.

On the nightstand: water rings from her late-night beers and a velveteen ballerina box. Mama Brown kept her change in a compartment beneath the spinning slippers. I'd steal from it every day before going to school, and every morning there'd be more to take. She must have known. She must have put more there for me. I'm mad I didn't think of this before.

Inside the box, in place of new quarters, is an envelope with my name penned in a shaky hand. Touching the paper, my finger pads feel a static. Mama Brown's life strong here, with whatever's folded inside. I crease it, slide it in my pocket. The ballerina box shuts with a click. I shuffle out, close the door. All the grief I been swallowing down threatening to leap out.

In the bathroom, I pee on the stick and place the test on the edge of the toothpaste-caked sink. Yes, my life come down to this little room, to this rusted faucet, to this drain. My life come down to the pink-and-white stick, to the soaked-up piss, to the two faint lines christening me Mommy.

5

A cloud of white moths, all scrambling for the red light—as if they could scoop it up with their tiny mouths and take it back to wherever they nest. I know how they feel: wanting peace is a lot like that.

Cigarette Sammy sits next to me, sipping his Pabst and smoking an L&M. I light my cigar, suck the sweet burn deep in me.

"I'm pregnant," I say. He don't look away from the glowing end of his cigarette. "I found out yesterday. I ain't got it in me to be a mother." Where is Cigarette Sammy's mom? Is she alive, wondering where he goes? She know he's wearing a coat in summer, finding soggy treasures in trash? When he was little, did she slather his rolls with baby lotion, spoon-feed him cake frosting, whisper prayers at night? Cherry did that for me when I was a child, for a little while. Where my mom, where his mom, where all these wandering women? Maybe they all live together in a damp cave, talking under geodes and sleeping bats about the joys of freedom, of separation.

He inhales smoke, shuffles his feet, makes a beat with puffs of breath.

"I'll figure something out," I say.

The ember of my cigar crushed on concrete. Cigarette Sammy throws away his emptied goods, hobbles on into the darkness. He mutters to himself as he leaves. We ain't ever on the same plane, but I'm glad our friendship works. Without him, I'd have nobody. I go inside, into the stale air. Time ain't passing quick enough. I lean against the register. This quiet makes me want to pace. Ain't nothing to be heard but the buzzing of the coolers holding tubs of pimento cheese and containers of bologna. I shuffle music on my phone. Frank Ocean begins: *Too many bottles of this wine we can't pronounce. Too many bowls of that green, no Lucky Charms.*

The bell rings as the door opens. A woman in a dingy hoodie and cargo shorts walks in. Her sandy hair hangs in matted clumps. She approaches the register, places a wad of sweat-heated cash on the counter. "Cheapest pack of full-flavored 100s." She reminds me of Cherry—all that beauty hidden under the cracked surface of rough living.

I hand her the pack of smokes, take her cash.

"How's your night?" I ask.

"Some bitch bit me." She rolls up her sleeve, peels back a muddy bandage. "In the parking lot of the bowling alley." The congealed wound rises to my face.

"That is crazy." I act like I drop my pen and bend. When I straighten my posture, I'm two steps back from the counter. I can't say I'm surprised. I don't get many people on my shift, but they usually wild-haired with a story to tell. Once, a woman came before my shift ended. She said she beat bone cancer, but before she did, she lost her leg. Anyway, she was broke, and could I give her a hot dog? I fished a wiener out the murky water with tongs, plopped it in a bun. Gave her a few ketchup and mustard packets. She raised her jeans and knocked on her knee before she left. Told me before she lost all her money, she could afford a realistic prosthetic. Mama Brown always said the Devil is a liar, but I guess hungry people are, too. Until then, I ain't ever seen a fake leg with ashy skin.

Sometimes, though, I get people passing through who seem to live in a different world: women with structure gifted by scalpels, men in tweed suits with elbow patches. After my two years here, despite working the slow shift, it seems ain't nobody alive who can avoid going to a gas station. If things work out at Cotton's dinner tomorrow, will I leave this place? I can't say I'll miss the gross boredom: sore feet, MAGA hats, mint dip spit on the tile.

After my long walk home, I vacuum the carpet, shower the broken couch with my perfume. Mama Brown's kind scent has been ate up by Sugar Foot's cologne. In my room, I feel a little less heavy. My closet don't have much to offer. Got to look nice for tomorrow. No, not nice. Got to look beautiful and mean. The black dress I wore to Mama Brown's funeral. It falls to my ankles. The shears by my bed a little dull; it takes a few tries. I cut the dress to above my knees, enough to hint to the world I got thighs.

All these nerves I got over dinner—my hands won't keep still. My fingers find their way to Tinder and type a message. The blue car pulls into my driveway a little after three in the morning. A short white man steps out, arms inked up with tattoos, followed by an empty Mountain Dew can. He picks it up off the ground, tosses it back in his car. I lead him into the black night, to the sleeping flowers.

"We can't go inside?" he asks.

"My mama is in there."

"Carolina, can't you just sneak——?"

I snicker. "What is it, Boy, you afraid of the dark?" I undress. He reaches to cup my tit like he owns it; I put my hand up before he can. He drops his pants instead and strokes himself, thumb massaging the head. By my ankle, a potted majesty palm. I rip a frond and cover my chest. I give a taunting grin and move like water to the back of the garden, where darkness dominates. He follows, wrist moving in and out. The shadows eat us up, give me a good set for drama, the frond my only prop. I slide the frond aside, let it graze my nipples. In a sweet voice, I ask, "Do you like what you see?"

His answer's a groan, mouth open and ready to devour.

I trace the frond down my belly, then reach out to him, tickle his shaft with the frilly green. That closes the space between us, draws him in. His hardness presses against my wet: a shared heat. I kiss him soft. Treat him like he might break. In his ear, I whisper, "Tell me I'm pretty."

His tongue's a slug down my jawline. "Carolina, pretty. So pretty."

I drop the frond and rub my clit. My words come out moaning and secretive. "Tell me I could model."

He hesitates, a swollen pause. "Fuck, yeah, baby, you could model."

He lies on the earth, and I slide him between my legs, up inside, fake surprise with big eyes like I've never been full. Men like that untouched innocence, no stains. And he soaks in the pleasure. But he seems afraid of the dark. "Yes, Boy, you dumb as hell for coming out here with me." Stuffed. Up, down, up, down, looking at his growing fear. Until my body shakes. I stand, ball up my clothes, walk barefoot to the edge of the garden.

"I didn't finish," he yells.

I go inside with power in my walk and drift off.

In the morning, I fry up breakfast as if I were Mama Brown: over-easy egg, charred Spam. Waste daylight smoking the last of Mama Brown's reggie and listening to old Britney. I shave my legs, color my lips, and slip into the revived funeral dress. At the warm dusk, I set out, heels clicking together in my hands, an apple sucker nestled in my cheek. When I reach the door, I toss my flip-flops behind the rosebush and climb into my heels. Mama Brown bought these heels for me. Three knocks on the funeral parlor's door.

Squeezed inside a snug-fitting turtleneck and corduroy pants, Cotton steps out with an eager smile. "There you are."

"Here I am."

We go up, past the fireplace, into the dining room. Lit taper candles line the walls. The look of the long table demands I eat without spilling a crumb: a royal purple silk tablecloth, a plump, roasted chicken. Honey-glazed carrots and potatoes, a lightly sea-soned soup with jutting chunks of cabbage. Three crystal glasses and an open-mouthed bottle of Campari. The forks and spoons might be real silver.

Beside the table: three black-and-white family portraits blown up, propped on easels.

I take my seat. Cotton pours my glass to the brim.

"Help yourself."

I load my plate with a fist-size cut of breast, lumps of sticky vegetables.

Cotton looks at the ceiling, nods, leaves the room.

That odd white man ain't out the room long before I've gulped the neon-red drink, swallowed every bite, and licked the neck of my spoon clean. When Cotton and Eden join me, I've got my second plate half-devoured.

"A girl after my own heart." Eden chuckles as she sits. She ain't got the Meryl Streep face anymore. Tonight, she look like Geena Davis. She wears a green dress with a plunging neckline. Her chest's covered in sun freckles. She pours brown liquor from a flask into her glass.

Cotton sits and serves himself a small bowl of soup. "Sweltering day."

"Blistering," Eden says.

"We worried you wouldn't show." Cotton chews softened cabbage.

I study Eden to see if that's true. She seems more concerned with sawing off a chicken leg.

Cotton shakes his spoon in the air. "You know, I finished a painting today, and I was thinking—"

"What did you paint?" Eden asks.

"A vagina," he says.

Eden nods. "A vagina."

"It has personality." He swallows his soup. "I looked at my fingernails, and they were stained pink. And I thought, huh, all the times I've had stained fingernails and never noticed. So, when I clipped them, I saved them." He wiggles his fingers. "It's a mosaic in progress. Like a tattoo, but more . . ." He looks up to the ceiling, drums his fingers on his arm. "Visceral?"

Drink swirls in my mouth. They work away their hunger. The scrape of silverware on milky china. How long I got to listen to

Cotton slurp and Eden gnaw on gristle before we talk about my modeling? Eden finishes the whiskey in her glass and switches to eager swigs straight from the flask. Cotton places his spit-glistened spoon on a cloth napkin. He clears broth from his throat.

"Death creates a chasm of want. I saw that every day in New York. People want answers—where is the missing little girl with the blue ribbon in her hair?" That curious drama building in his throat waters down when he catches Eden's eye roll. His voice switches with effort to cool party chatter. "Is she alive, deceased? Is there life after death?"

Eden takes from her flask a squelching swallow.

Cotton's pine eyes focus on me. "You've lost someone, and it's bothering you."

Eden snorts, then downs her flask.

"You don't have to answer," he says, "if you aren't comfortable."

"Who'd she lose?" Eden asks.

"I'm talking to Magnolia," Cotton says.

"Who'd I lose?" I ask.

"So, you did," he says, "I told you I was clairvoyant."

That satisfaction in his words eats my wonder. Mama Brown knew there was power in dreams. She dreamed every family birth and death, marriage and divorce before it happened. I ain't buying that magic is what he's touched by, this fumbling man. But that faraway talent of seeing beyond did make Mama Brown fumbling, too, and in the end, her memory fuzzed with mold. No, whatever makes this man strange is as present as the teeth in his mouth, and he must got some kind of cavity.

He continues. "So, you know with wanting answers comes an itch for closure. Can you reach the missing little girl with the blue ribbon in her hair? Can you send my message to her, to the other side?"

Eden switches to Campari. I pour another glass. Guess his talk makes sense. Mourners needing to heal a pus-leaking wound, feeling like a stranger with pretty words might help. But I ain't sure it's true for me. If I read the last of Mama Brown's words—that hidden letter—all that's left of her would be used up, heard before. Closure ain't nothing but a bolted door with a broken key.

Cotton flails his hands. "How do these people heal? The ones who, for whatever reason, were robbed of a proper good-bye? The people with abducted or missing loved ones? The people who find the remains decades later—dust and bones scattered by scavengers?"

He tilts his head, waits for my reply. When I don't give one, he says, "They never do. They seek help from yoga or bundles of sage or folks in incensed alcoves with crystal balls and tarot cards. They grasp, and they grasp, but they always leave with that chasm."

I nod in agreement as if I been holding his ranting in my heart but ain't had the right words to speak it.

"What do you think of the people in these pictures?" He points to the portraits on the easels.

"They look like the 1800s," I say.

He leans into his words. "What else?"

I squint. "That girl got bad posture. Some of the people ain't as blurry."

He grins. "The cameras back then, they took awhile to capture the picture, so you had to be still to get good results. The people that stand out—their posture, sharp focus—those people are dead."

I look at their eyes—unknowing, unfeeling, staring right at me.

"I want to create a way to help people in particular circumstances find closure in a particular manner. With Aunt Eden's help, of course."

She pours her drink down, refills.

"I called old clients in New York. As of now, two are interested." He wiggles his shoulders. "We're at the fun bit. You ready?"

I press my lips in a thin smile, nod.

He lets out a deep breath. "The people will send pictures and personality descriptions of their missing loved ones. And by personality descriptions, I mean the real meat of who they were. No guff. Eden will transform your face, with her ethereal skill, to match those of the deceased. You'll Skype with the mourners while they send their final message. Think of it as a performance—and I do think you can perform—but you won't have to speak. Only nod in agreement occasionally, smile when appropriate, and if at some point, you can cry, fuck, that'd be really great."

I hold the alcohol in my mouth, roll my tongue around in the bitterness, trying to think of what to say. Mama Brown would cackle at this proposal and say that I was born for this job. When Cherry found out she was pregnant with me, she and my daddy moved into a trailer. He started working construction to save money for my coming. But then, Daddy got hit with a loose cinder block. Dead on the spot. I always thought it was cruel, the building he was helping create reaching out and taking his life. Cement, beat of sun, nail guns, all of it: ungrateful to my daddy.

Anyway, Mama Brown didn't want Cherry coming to his funeral with me in her belly. She said: *Cherry, you'll mark that baby for life.* She said: *Everybody know you don't go around the dead when you pregnant.* Cherry hated her for this. According to Mama Brown, she said: *You don't want me to go 'cause you can't stand the thought of your son loving a white woman.*

Mama Brown thought that was funny. She said: *That ain't true. You go to that funeral, death will follow that baby. Wait and see.* Yes, Mama Brown was right.

"Will you be the lady palimpsest?" Cotton asks.

Eden flashes a smile wide enough to show the pink of her gums, her face blushed from the liquor. She must got Irish in her blood.

"You'll get five hundred dollars per case," Cotton says.

Five hundred dollars is more than I make in two weeks. And he got two people already interested. I stare at the portraits. The families wanting to make more memories, looking in the eyes of someone lost and gone—I know that feeling. A camera flashes.

"Moments of hesitation translate well to film." Cotton returns the camera to the floor beneath his chair.

"Okay," I say.

Cotton's pleased. "This is beautiful."

"Why me?" I ask.

"Actively searching for a muse seemed garish to me." He drinks. "And even if I felt inspired to actively search, most of the women I've encountered here are victim to, um, how to put this"—He rakes through his brain, hunts for the unoffensive—"victim to rural tragedy."

What he means by that: pregnant or addicted to pills. By the time I finish the two cases, I should be able to afford an abortion. I hate that word—makes me think of latex gloves and cold stirrups and hell. Only my hell wouldn't be an open burning cave, it'd be a pantry with closed-in, scorching walls. I won't let him know since he got a problem with pregnant women. I'll keep this secret inside me.

"Meeting you was natural, and something about you just screams . . ." He looks up, taps his arm. "Ambiguous? Wait, no, it's more than that. It's . . . well, it isn't really important."

A stuffed-down secret at the end; whatever he got to say, he won't. So he wanted to scout me because I look like a question. I'll be clay if the check comes easy. "What's Eden think about all this?" I ask.

Eden tosses her French manicure in the air, chants in her slurred drawl, "C'est la vie! C'est la vie!"

"She's agreed to the arrangement, granted we maintain the affairs of the parlor. But I assure you—" He leans across the table, whispers, as if Eden ain't right here. "People will really want this. We'll devote our time to the art."

Eden claps her hands. "C'est la vie! C'est la vie!"

Cotton rises from the table, returns with green bottles of sparkling water. He forces Eden to drink.

"I almost forgot dessert," he says.

His footsteps click on the hardwood. This got to be the first time in a long time I don't feel like a struck tuning fork. One thousand dollars. If Cotton gets more cases, I can save up. I can get a nice apartment on the West Side. I can fly to Paris. I can buy a banana skirt.

"I like your dress," I say.

Eden places the nearly empty bottle on the table. Her grin: sloppy, dripping water. "Half off."

All that product on her face, something different got to be underneath. I've watched YouTube videos where makeup artists give tutorials on how to change their face into celebrities. The transformations are fun to look at, but I never thought I'd meet someone who did it this often. In the videos, it takes patience; a steady wrist; shining, expensive brushes.

The woman with the changing face clinks two of the sparkling waters together. "Pretty, pretty things," she says. She finishes her water, belches. "C'est la vie."

Cotton ushers in two vine-patterned saucers with thick slices of Mississippi mud pie. He places a saucer in front of me, the other in front of Eden. He sits with a bag of Twizzlers and chews.

I finish another glass, and then the pie makes a mess in my mouth, pecans and smooth chocolate and buttered crumbs. Eden's mess stains her chin and some of the tablecloth. Cotton sighs, dabs her chin with a cloth napkin. In this moment, he looks so gentle, like a mother making herself into a whisper when the children sleep.

"The blood on your hands," I say.

"What?" he asks.

"Was that you performing?"

His laugh's full of air. "Fake blood."

"Why?"

"A photoshoot. I'll show you at some point."

The pie and too much liqueur settle in me. Cotton gives me the contract. The words swim, and my gut swims, making me want to laugh for no reason. My name: a scrawl on the dotted line.

I rise, stumble from the chair. The words seem to stick to my teeth, make a clumsy tumble into the room. "Thank you for dinner." I giggle at how ridiculous I sound. "When should I come back?"

"I'll have everything ready next Friday." He gathers the glasses and saucers and shuffles away.

"Thanks again, Eden." My heeled feet try to lead me to the staircase. They tangle. I fall and laugh on the cool floor.

Eden stumbles. She towers above me. "You walked here."

Her looming, famous face tickles me into laughter. My back feels nice on the lacquered tile. I tap my heels on the floor, and they click. I sound important; I sound like business. That makes me laugh harder. And then Eden is laughing and pulling me up by my shoulders, saying she'll drive me home. "Hurry up, before Cotton sees." We snicker and rush down the stairs—clammy grip on the railing.

Outside, I bend behind the rosebush to grab my flip-flops, tilt, land on the cushion of mulch. Eden giggles, raises a finger to her lips. She tugs me to my feet. We sway. My belly holds stifled laughter.

The hearse stinks of tobacco and pine. As we pull away, Eden hands me a Virginia Slim. We blow smoke out the window, out to the passing buildings, as we roll down Broadway.

"I can't believe Cotton left New York City for this."

"New York City, baby!" She laughs, swerves, corrects her course.

I toss the stubbed cigarette out the window. In the side mirror, the embers bounce and dim. "What do you think it's like?"

"Hell if I know."

"Why do you think he left?"

"I know why he left." She pinches the cigarette butt between her thumb and pointer, rolls it to dead. "That funeral home was his funhouse growing up, and then of course there was The Incident, back when he was just starting to grow moss in his britches, but I think he's over that now, and me and his uncle Bart was like his parents; he misses his uncle Bart. He tries to care for me like Bart did, so sweet."

The warm air from the windows feels like kisses. "What incident?"

"Pay no mind to me, I'm just gabby with the drinks, I'm just a mess, awful mess."

We turn off Broadway, clumps of trees replacing the businesses and strip malls.

"I'm tickled you're helping Cotton with his little project." A possum in the road. His last thought muffled to a thud. "And I get to doll you up. First time in a long time I've worked on the living."

"You're really good at it."

"Before my Bart died, he taught me a lot about pretty," she says. The road constricts. "We used to do each other's makeup. We wasn't in the kind of marriage you'd think. We had an agreement to please his parents. Of course, his parents didn't know about the agreement, and I didn't either until we were married for a year, and I found him laying with a florist. Craig, his name was. After that, after some broken dishes and cussing, we was only friends, Bart and me."

We turn into my driveway. Sugar Foot's car rests empty. My living room light shines.

"I practiced so much on him, I realized I could make any face I want. I run into an old friend, and they say, you got worked on, Eden? I tell them, no siree, no surgery for me, thank you."

My breathing hurts.

"No siree!"

"Could you actually drop me off at Walmart?" The one near here stays open all night. I could walk around in the fake light until sunrise. The nerve of him. But I ain't surprised. I don't think I got it in me to be surprised about anything anymore.

My voice must waver. She says, "What's the matter?"

"Nothing."

She shifts the car to reverse. "Bullshit." Her foot's still pressed on the brake. Sugar Foot might hear that colicky whine of the worn brake pads. Might see the headlights.

"I got to get tampons," I say.

She backs out of the driveway and clips the mailbox. "Why didn't you just say so?"

When she turns the hearse onto Broadway, I ease my grip on the door.

"Why'd you walk if you got a car?" she asks.

"Not mine."

"Your boyfriend?" She pinches my thigh.

"I don't got one of those." Everything I ate pushes to the top of my stomach.

"Who do you live with?" she asks.

The acid trickles up my tongue.

"Your parents?"

"That was my landlord. Can you pull over?"

"At this time of night? What was your landlord—?"

I spew chunks of that good dinner on the ribbed floormat.

She coos. "Oh no." I drown out the music in her voice with my retching. "Oh, no, your landlord—"

She offers lavender wipes. We sit in the air-conditioned dining area of a Taco Bell while I calm my stomach with ginger ale.

Eden reaches across the table and rubs my wrist. Her fingers feel chilled.

"You can stay with us," she says, "while you work for Cotton. You can stay with us."

Her smile got a pout to it. She keeps rubbing my wrist like she got all the answers in her touch. Pity in her green eyes, a stagnant lake with algae and duck shit, the kind you don't want to wade in. The kind you wouldn't even dip your toes in—unless you got a fire eating you up.

I bite the straw until I'm sure I'll shatter my teeth. "Thank you."

I look away from the lake in her eyes, pick at the dirt under my nails.

6

The room Eden put me in last night is sprawling: a walk-in closet, a queen-size bed I don't knock my ankles against when walking around the room. My own bathroom with polished porcelain, the tub made of blushed marble. I got room to stretch my legs in a bath, room to roll around, kick, and punch in my dreams. Room to breathe.

This room makes me think of my sixth birthday. The air conditioner in the trailer broke. Cherry stood sweating in the kitchen, mixing the treat I loved—strawberry cake, pink vanilla icing. I sat on the floor in the living room, hypnotized by Pippi Longstocking sponge-skating inside the box TV. Quarry came home early from work.

"Christ, it's hot. You want your present?" He took off his shirt stained with burger grease.

"Wait until after the cake," Cherry yelled.

Quarry put his finger to his lips, led me outside. In the backyard:

a plastic log cabin that I stopped playing with the year before because of bugs.

"Look inside," he said.

Inside: five yellow ducklings. I jumped and giggled. My little winged babies. That night, Mama Brown came over to give me my presents and balloons.

"Mama Brown, come look at my babies."

She said, "Hell, baby, they need more room than that. Ducks ain't meant to live in toys."

A week later, I found two of them dead in the corner covered in shit. Cherry said, "We can't afford to feed them no how." I cried and cried when she put the other three in the truck, and we drove on down to Fountain City Duck Pond. I wanted to keep them mine—until I saw them quacking and waddling up to the water.

Yes, in this room, I feel like them set-free ducks. But the painting that faces the bed freezes my insides. A black-furred beast with plate eyes and jagged teeth on a naked woman. They fuck on the grassy floor of a jungle. She got her thighs wrapped around him, moon tits perked for his hunger. But she don't seem afraid or even interested. She slicks her hair with one hand, holds a mirror in the other. She gazes at her reflection in the glass, or maybe, at her other reflection somewhere in the distance.

It don't bother me if I don't think about it, but it kept me from drifting off last night. When I scoot out of bed, I take advantage of this space and shimmy, arms out, to the bathroom. Wash my face with organic soap that leaves the skin newborn soft. Shit, this water I brush my teeth with probably filtered or straight from a deep mountain stream. Stripped naked, clean smile, my dancing starts again to the rhythm of a running bath.

I catch a glimpse of myself in the mirror and my grooving mood fades—a stopped show headlined by nipples dark as old pennies. Tits swollen. My body eager in a way I ain't—*Yes, I want to be a cocoon for this baby in me* and *Please, child, rip me apart with your life*, and *I will bear fruit and milk. Good, sweet milk.* But a heavier chest don't tell me how far along I am. Still an almost-flat stomach with unstretched love handles, no discovered sense of duty. I got time. Only a week until we start the cases.

I pump soap in the current, fill the tub with lavender bubbles.

After a long bath, after dressing and sitting at the edge of the bed until my feet numb to static, I build up the courage to go to the kitchen. Ain't too sure what they expect—do I buy groceries, is there a shared fund? The only time I moved in with someone was with Mama Brown, but I was eight, and I knew what to expect. No awkward weather talk, no farts held like terrible secrets. And of course, she fed me. Cotton told me he was old money, so I keep that in the front of my skull while I search the cabinets for a pan. Three-egg omelet with goat cheese. Dishes washed, seated at the dining room table, my first bite ain't all the way down before a fist of nausea clenches my gut and twists. *Oh, please, little one, rip me apart with your life.*

I got to distract myself. It's almost noon. Cotton and Eden still sleep—shouldn't I know more about the people dreaming where I dream? I rise, then sit. If they catch me, then what? Another hit of nausea pushes me to my feet, into wandering, away from the dining room, past the staircase, down the hall.

The first door is Eden's—her makeup clatters pass through thick wood. The door across from mine stands quiet, and my cupped ear picks up nothing muffled. I twist the knob slow, just in case it's Cotton on the other side closed-eyed in bed, just in case I wake him or catch him stroking his sunrise in somber silence. The door only creaks a little. Inside: no bed, no Cotton, only a couch, a desk, a bookshelf, and Cotton's art. On the desk, a plate of pink-dyed fingernail clippings. My hand lingers on the door. I could shut it, but shutting myself in a room I ain't invited in would just look wicked. Leave it open then, just a crack.

Right as I step in, Eden's door opens. The moaning hinges tense my muscles. Her footsteps lead away to the kitchen.

One of his paintings, still in progress, propped on an easel in the corner, a canvas with a deep violet background. A pearl-toned arched back of a woman. No limbs. The head, floating above, neckless and backward, hair swirling in the dark, beckons me with a weepy gaze. I want to say: *You lost someone, and it's bothering you.*

The hiss of frying meat, Eden's wall-swallowed morning singing. Need to creep out this room. She'd give me the same attitude she had when she found me hunkered behind the rosebush, I'm sure. A caught trespasser.

But now my attention is sucked away by the painting next to the bookshelf: a skeleton with a pink-fleshed pussy. She poses in a field of wheat, legs spread.

Heat rushes to my cheeks, and I don't want to blush. It's what the skeleton wants, for me to match the rouge of desire between her legs.

Cotton's thoughts hold hands with death. He don't run from it. He keeps it all around him like a baby blanket. Some stinking comfort. But maybe Cotton can be found in another painting, on the other side of the bookshelf—a scared boy trapped in a tarot card, banging on the window of the Hierophant.

A clanging in the kitchen (a dropped pot, maybe) brings me closer to the boy trying to escape some fate.

What if Cotton's paintings are all bright with his terrors? Or maybe he don't feel a thing about death—maybe he only paints what he's around. Maybe if he worked in a birth ward, he'd paint little gummy mouths drooling life. But if he does put himself in his work, if he's in the painting across from the tarot boy—the one with texture, a grinning man in an open casket with twine stuck on for hair, cheery as Sunday school to be buried—then, with all his wealth, what right he got to wish for rot?

The floor whines with weight, tells me to hurry up and leave, but my feet won't work. My hand disobeys, reaches up and fingers the twine. It's stiff with glue or paint, and I can smell the resin, and he's rictus smiling at me. His gap-toothed grin is aimed right at me, so ugly, God, it's so ugly, and—

"That's Uncle Bart," Cotton says. He laughs at my gasp, my jolt.

I turn to face him. "Your art is beautiful."

He shoos me away. "It's all play. But thank you for saying so."

"In your work, what do you see?"

"I haven't thought about it. Maybe a form of truth." His feet shift toward the hall, a hint that I should exit. "All art needs truth, or something like that."

"Whose truth?"

Cotton taps his hand on the wall in the hall, his body saying what his mouth won't: *Get out this room; you picking at my privacy like a fat scab.* "I'll have to chew on that."

"Thanks for letting me stay." I remain in place, tug on my thoughts—how much to say to him, how much he really got to hear. "I don't know if Eden told you what happened."

His *ha ha* is knowing, familiar with Eden's antics. "She made it clear it's between the two of you." He steps out to the hall, and I finally follow. "Actually, I think your presence here will be very good. For preparation, I mean. The cases."

Cotton and I go to the dining room, welcomed by a tray in the center with gravy and biscuits, crumbles of sausage. My now-cold omelet's cleared, probably oil-sheening in the trash. Eden sits in a purple robe, her back to us. I take my place next to her, Cotton across. She got on Dolly Parton's face.

Here, my first practice in theater: slicking my throat with no-flavor gravy, gobbling every bit of hard biscuit, ignoring my body's rocking rejection of it. A strong-stomached start of conversation. "This is delicious."

Cotton don't pretend, turns his nose up at the slop. In front of him, a ceramic cup cradling a boiled egg, a little spoon he uses to strike vein-shaped cracks in the shell. He nibbles at the white flesh.

Eden speaks with biscuit pocketed in her cheeks. "What time'll the Braxtons be here?"

At the mention of the name, Cotton pulls from his pocket a piece of twine—same shade and length as the hair of the dead man on his wall—and twiddles with it. "Within the hour."

"Is there a funeral today?" I ask.

"A memorial service," says Cotton, "and they're getting the ashes."

"They settled the bill, then?" Eden asks.

Cotton rolls his eyes and nods, a silent: *Yes, finally.* When Mama Brown got the diagnosis, first thing she did was sell her car so she could afford to die.

"So you ain't using the family car?"

Cotton swallows the last of his egg. "Please, don't be ostentatious." A hollow ring, sad like an organ, bellows through the house. Cotton tugs on the twine one, two, three times, then slips it in his pocket and stands. When he nears the stairs, he turns, and with a ghost of a smile, says, "Magnolia, don't let her be ostentatious."

When Cotton's footsteps fade, Eden turns to me with a big banana smile, like she been caught digging in the candy dish. "You got a busy day? Say no."

My shift at the gas station starts at 6:00 P.M., ends at 1:30 A.M. "No, not really."

A squeal of laughter. "Let's get dressed, then meet me out front."

Outside, only three cars take up space. A rusted minivan, two Oldsmobiles—one gray, one white. Eden ain't in any of them. A glint of light to my left, a shriek of brakes. Eden pulls around the driveway, into the parking lot, in a black limousine. The passenger window slides down. "Come on, girlie."

First thing I do when I sit down is touch the shadowed partition. Division between the driver and the carted. Faint strawberry perfume blows cool out the vents.

"Where we going?" I ask.

She lights a Virginia Slim and hands it to me, lights another, then presses on the gas, onto Broadway. Through a cloud of smoke, she says, "Shopping."

Before I can think of which lie to pick—*I lost my wallet, oops; I got a headache coming on real strong*—Eden adds: "My treat."

We take the interstate, past UTK's campus, out west where

the cars get nicer, and the teeth shine bleached. My nails find their way to my thumb skin and claw.

She senses my nerves, reaches across the steering wheel, and pats my knee. "This'll be good for you, gettin' something new. Lord knows what Cotton'll want you in."

"I've never been in a limo." I pretend my cigarette is a skinny French smoke, and: *Driver, where are my gloves, the silk ones with the pearl dotted hem?*

"Ain't we fancy." She snorts. "I swear you moving in lifted Cotton's spirits. He ain't prone to letting me drive the family car. Don't even like it when I drive the hearse."

"Why you call it that?"

"The close family members ride in the back when we do the funeral processions."

How many tissues been wet in that back seat? How many memories been repeated between brothers and sisters to make sure they still true: *Yes, it really all happened but can't happen again.* I toss my cigarette out the window.

We park near the end of the lot at West Town Mall across a few empty spaces. I only ever go to East Town—smaller, comfortable, known. Cherry and Quarry only took me there during income tax season, and they'd buy movies at FYE; I'd get dolls each time until I wasn't allowed. Mama Brown took me almost every weekend to look at the puppies, share sweet-and-sour chicken in the sun-washed food court, my eyes going back and forth between my plastic fork and the skylight where the rock pigeons wanted to enter but couldn't.

We leave the chill of the limo, that throat-scratching fruit smell, and walk into the heat, across the lot. Inside where salon-styled women walk in high heels. Eden whisks me to Versona and loads pretty things in my hands to take to the fitting room: a black dress with a plunging neckline, a snakeskin peplum top, a red pencil skirt, black leather bellbottoms, and a dancing dress with too much tulle, and it all fits like it was made for me. At the register, the woman gasps at Eden, then says, "Sorry, I thought you were Dolly Parton."

Eden pays, and her voice shifts into a high-pitched melody. "I get it all the time."

I wonder how she chooses her face each day.

We walk into a boutique, our shopping bags bumping into each other, giving us music. Maybe it all depends on whichever mood she's got; maybe, today, she's feeling as generous as Dolly and wants the world to know it. Eden picks out for me again—a leopard dress; a white, billowing blouse meant for standing on beaches and breathing in mist; high-waisted jeans—one pair, two pair, three. Swipe of a card. And again, another boutique, and then Forever 21, and Yankee Candle because Eden wants to sniff, and then Bath & Body Works because I want to sniff.

Eden takes that as a hint and says, "No, not here, I'll show you."

She tugs me into Sephora and chooses a glass bottle of Chanel for me so I can smell like a drowsy bouquet whenever I please. And then there's the makeup.

"For the cases," she says.

My feet and spine throb with ache, and hers must, too, because sweat beads at her temples and threatens to melt the wax of her foundation. "You hungry?"

"Yes," I say.

She slides the bags off her arms and adds them to my load, puts the key in a Sephora bag. "Take these to the car. I'll come back with food."

We part ways. My arms, weighed down with bags of beauty, make me want to pout and slump and drag my walk. But, for now, I blend in here with these SUV-driving families. I am a shopping-spree girl. My steps gain speed, chin rising, an easy smile to passing strangers, all the way to the limo. It's a wrestle, getting my arms and hands free from all the pounds of spending. Doors unlocked, I place everything in the back seat gentle as just baked pies, then settle in the front seat. And then I catch the time on my phone. 5:32 P.M. In the rearview mirror, Eden ain't making her way back. I'm tired anyway. A quick phone call to People's in a choked voice—"I think it's strep. Yes, thank you. I'll feel better."

Twenty minutes later, Eden comes back with Cheesecake Factory, fishes a fifth of Jim Beam from the glove compartment, and ushers me to the back seat. She sits facing the partition; I face the trunk. We eat alfredo until we bloat. Swig whiskey until our words thaw runny.

"You ever been to Kentucky?"

"I never been outside Tennessee," I say.

"Shit, I barely have, either." She lights a Virginia Slim, churns out a smothering fog. "But you should come with me to Kentucky some time."

"Shouldn't we crack a window?"

Eden tilts her head like I asked her how much she weigh.

"It don't bother me. Just worried about stinking it up."

She points her cigarette at me, her eyes full of surprise. "You're a smart little chicken." She opens the door. Her left ankle swings out, dangles above the pavement. The air clears. "Just like my Cotton."

My giggles come out louder than I mean. "Big-worded man."

"You wanna know when I knew he was smart? He was about nine, eight, and his mom was goin' on about the grass at Holston's golf course. It's just the right length, she kept sayin'. Cotton said, 'That lawn is full of shit, just like you.'" She laughs, wipes away the bourbon from her lips. "I never liked her myself. WASPy bitch, didn't do nothin' but bitch bitch bitch bitch." She gives me a smoke. "He moved in with us around twelve."

I aim my smoke outside, take the bottle, and toss some sweet burn back. Eden's hand reaches for the glass neck. I eye her to make sure she takes another sip before asking, "Why?"

"They disowned him."

"Oh, The Incident," I say.

Her eyes bulge big; she clutches the bottle to her chest like I might steal it. Precious crystal. "How'd you know?"

I lie. "You told me some of it last night." I pretend to be interested in the direction of my smoke, out and up toward the blue. "For the life of me, I can't remember."

Her fist lowers the bottle to her lap, a surrender. What she says next come out fast, words blurred into a mixed paint. "Might as well tell you it all so you don't get bad ideas about Cotton. He was going through puberty is what it was. Every weekend before, he loved to come over and help me or Bart in the morgue. Never thought it was odd. Little boys do stuff like poke roadkill with sticks all the time. But one day, I left him alone to fix us a quick lunch. He'd been reading the bottles, asking me what stuff meant all day, was driving me wild. Bart was at the desk schedulin'. There was a woman on the slab. She'd been dead about five days.

Missing for a while. When I came back with some cucumber sandwiches, Cotton was standin' beside her, looking right at her honkers, touching himself over the pants."

"The fuck?"

"Well, it ain't as bad as it sounds. See, all he was doing was readjusting his situation——" She waves her hand in circles above her crotch. "And his eyes had that glossed-over look, I like to call it daydreaming cataracts. He probably didn't even realize how he looked when I walked in. The rest was just me overreacting. Went straight to Bart, and we called his mama and daddy. They ain't talked since, not that it bothers Cotton 'cause they keep his bank account fat. On account of guilt probably. Hell, I don't know." She swallows the last of the bottle.

How can a man find lust in milk eyes and peeling skin? Stiff joints can't hold tight, but can't push away, either. "You don't think he—I mean, does he——?"

"Lord, no." Eden's plead for my trust, a shaking head. "No, nothing like that's happened since." She dabs her eyes. "Please don't say nothing. He'd be so embarrassed." She brings a shaking, half-lit cigarette to her mouth. "He'd hate me for it."

"I won't, Mom." Right as the word flies from my lips, searing shame seeps down through my ribs.

Eden pauses, her mouth twitching into a grin. "What'd you say?"

"I . . ." Nausea ripples in me. *Baby, please rip my cocoon, your life worth it all.* "I said . . ." Half-chewed noodles and grilled chicken rush up, up, gifting me just enough time to poke my head out the door and splatter my supper on the yellow line. Eden's laughing punctuates each gag until I'm just a drooling thing, heaving for air.

I'm back in the limo, vomit on my sleeves, and Eden hands me a napkin. "Neither of us can handle our drink," she says, "and I'm a begatting bitch!" That brings her to thigh-slapping cackling, the kind that dies down in whimpers: *Ooh, ooh.*

I keep my eyes cast to the clean floor, hope she sobers up soon so I can bury myself beneath blankets, a needed hiding.

"Don't you worry about it; can't tell you how many grade-school teachers was my mommy at some point." She hands me the too-much-tulle dress. "You stink."

Giggles bubble out me; I feel settled. But I stare at her before I change, wait for her to exit.

"We're both women." She urges me with a flapping hand. "If you got something I don't got, I'll shoot it off you."

I'm in my new dress, and I want to dance. We clear the back seat of trash, then sit up front and watch the sunset flash, wait a bit for our heads to clear before we drive home. The vents pump out that strawberry scent, clearing the stench of pasta and liquor and puke. New air for the next widow.

At the funeral parlor, the nausea knocks, won't let me sleep. It's near midnight. Fresh air will help, but my feet don't stay in the parking lot, just keep walking down Broadway to the bus stop.

Inside the gas station, a man I don't know works my shift. I pick up Cigarette Sammy's Pabst, apple juice, MoonPie, and sandwich stuff. He might want a good meal.

The time on my phone: 11:30 P.M. I sit on the sidewalk and wait for Cigarette Sammy. He hobbles up to the trash cans.

"How you doing, Cigarette Sammy?" I ask.

He reaches for the bag swinging behind my back.

"You got a bed to sleep in tonight?"

He shuffles his feet and makes a pebble skip across the parking lot. He grunts. It sounds like, "My, my, my."

"I'll give you this, but you got to come with me first, hear?" We lock arms and take the bus toward Mama Brown's house. The both of us, unloaded at the stop. He's at peace with the walk until we get to the patch of woods. No moonlight bleeds through the branches. A low groan rumbles in his chest. Fine, he can have his Pabst. He chugs and keeps a strong grip on my arm until we get to the driveway. His body trembles.

Sugar Foot ain't here. And besides, he won't mess with Cigarette Sammy. Cigarette Sammy don't have nothing between his legs that Sugar Foot wants.

We walk on in. The light switch clicks, floods the living room yellow.

"Sit anywhere." In the kitchen, I make two sandwiches, put them on a paper towel.

Cigarette Sammy chooses Mama Brown's recliner. My eyes keep away from the scattered puzzle pieces when I place his food and the bag on the coffee table.

"Bathroom's down the hall. You can sleep in my bed, right next to my bathroom. It's got a white sheet tacked over the window. You'll know it when you walk in."

Cigarette Sammy gobbles up his first sandwich. He smiles and lets out a high-pitched hum. He nods his head: *Yes, yes.*

"Now, I'll be staying somewhere else for a while, but I'll come by to feed you. Only thing I ask is mind your messes."

Cigarette Sammy rips the plastic seal from his apple juice, happy-rocks back and forth and back while he drinks. Huh, ain't ever seen him do that before. I go to the bathroom. By the time I come out with a towel and a rag, he's swallowed the last bite of his second sandwich and tears at the MoonPie wrapper.

"If you want to shower later." I drape the towel and rag over the couch. "I'm going to head out. You want anything before I go?"

He bites the cushion of the pastry. Right now, his mind only worries about chewing.

The twenty-dollar bill comes out my bra wrinkled. "In case you need food before I come back." It wilts on the coffee table.

He clasps his hands, shakes them high.

7

I quit my job. Well, I guess I didn't really quit. Just never showed up for my last shift and ignored their calls. I been sleeping above the funeral parlor for a week.

I crawl out my bed, throw up as quietly as I can. It won't be long until Cotton figures out my secret. Every morning for the past week has started with me kneeling at the feet of the toilet, my gut's rapid clenching urging whatever I ate the night before to shoot out me. These walls as dense as pound cake, so I don't know if he's heard. If he don't hear me, he'll see the slight rounding of my belly, whenever that happens. He'll notice my ballooning ankles and wonder why I'm asking for weird food. When I went through puberty, Mama Brown would say: *Magnolia, your face bumpy as a pickle. That's 'cause Cherry drank so much pickle juice when she carried you. Should call you Dill.* I had a lot of almost-nicknames. They never stuck.

When I step out the bathroom with my raw throat, there's a

knocking on the bedroom door. Cotton going to say: *You full of life, ain't you?* He going to say: *You full of life and sick. Go on and get.*

I open the door. Cotton stands in a tweed suit, slapping his pockets. His eyes meet mine, but he only half there. His other half's somewhere thinking up paintings.

"Have you seen a small piece of twine anywhere?" He holds up his pointer and thumb with an inch of air between.

I shake my head.

"You wouldn't happen to have . . ." He walks away. I follow him and hover in the hall while he dips into his study. Furniture scrapes against the floor, something falls. He steps out with a pink face, disturbed hair. The piece of twine's pinched between his fingers. He slips it in his pocket. "There's a funeral today." He trots to the stairs, pauses. "Oh. The case is by the fire." His steps thump down to the foyer.

By the fireplace, on the coffee table, there's a fat manila envelope with blocky letters printed in marker. "First case. Study by 5:00 P.M."

The woman in the pictures had a simple beauty. She was white with long, straight hair that dipped into an inky widow's peak. Acorn eyes. She wore a lot of striped shirts and lip gloss. A pointed nose and thin lips. Her cheekbones sloped strong when she smiled. Her smile said: *I known you all my life.* Her smile said: *I ain't never known a stranger* and *You safe with me.*

I read the letter.

Dearest Cotton Reuter, The Seer,
Our family cannot thank you enough for this opportunity. Since our sweet daughter's disappearance, a day hasn't

passed without us leaving the door unlocked. We hope for an entrance, a knock. How joyous, with your hard work, we will see her again. How generous of you to provide us with the means to commune with our beautiful Aria.

We will tell you a little about our daughter, although it is difficult for us as she was so secretive. Aria loved honey-bees. She had a tattoo of one midflight below her left collarbone. She ate the crust from our sandwiches. Aria had a lovely voice, but she chose to study song rather than create. Every summer, she went on road trips with her friends at Syracuse University. Her friends said she fell in love with every man she met. Our Aria had a lot of love in her heart. She was on one of these road trips at the time of her disappearance. She was last seen on her twenty-first birthday, June 13, 1995, in Las Vegas, Nevada.

We hope we have provided enough information for you to create a gift most needed for us. We have included her grade records and the shopping receipts she kept in her drawer. Apologies for the state of the receipts. They have faded. We have also included a check for the agreed upon amount of $1,200.

> Endless thanks,
> The Conners

PS—Your sight has yet to fail. We sold the house for over asking.

I set aside the letter. If he paying me $500, then he splitting $700 with Eden. Counting the cost of clothes, face paint, and whatever else—that's got to cut into their makings. Which tells me he ain't doing this for the money. And if he ain't doing this for the money, then why?

The stapled receipts are worn smooth, the print mostly washed gray. How many times had Aria's parents touched these receipts to see if they could feel her steady breathing? When I hold them up to the chandelier, I can only make out three items: sunflower seeds, nail file, bronzing lotion.

At noon, there's a light knocking on my door. Eden leans against the frame, eyes shut, fingers pressed to her temples. To-day, she looks like Michelle Pfeiffer.

"Cotton's going to kill me dead. I should've woke up earlier." She was late to dinner last night. She came up hankering for whiskey after doing makeup on the dead man downstairs. I al-most asked her if I could see the final results. But she got to filling her glass again and again, so I held my tongue. Can't say I blame her, wanting to drink as much as she does, when she's got to touch corpses all the time.

I follow her to her room. Folded on her bed: a striped crop-top with short sleeves and black cargo pants.

"Change, and we'll get started." Eden drops a clump of ber-ries and a white tablet in a glass of water. She drinks the fizz.

The berries floating in her glass makes me wonder if Eden knows about nature. Mama Brown knew how to work roots. If I was struck with a cold or coughing sickness, she'd give me boneset tea. Before her dates, she'd soak in a hot bath with tufts of moss and rinse her hair with mistletoe. She'd say: *Mother Earth got all I need to hook 'em.* Rarely, but sometimes, church women would come, and after making small talk in the living room, they would hurry away with Mama Brown to the garden and whisper.

They always left with horse nettle and black pepper to bring their men to bed.

The second I'm naked, Cotton strolls in the room. My scream bottled in my throat, my arms around my tits.

He don't seem to notice. He holds his hand out to Eden, asking, "Do you mind?"

Panic takes hold of my body while I dress: a lunge for the crop top, a stumble getting into pants.

Eden opens a drawer and hands over thick, black hair.

He lifts a strand to the light. "Huh." He grips the fake scalp, wiggles it above his head, makes the hair ripple. "Don't you think it's too . . . ?" Hair bunches between his fingers. "Rheumatic?"

"That's the only wig I bought," Eden says.

"Do you own one of those hair flattening . . . ?" Cotton mimes flat ironing his hair.

Eden nods.

"Could you use that instead and stencil in the widow's peak?" He makes a face like he just remembered something, scurries away, whistling. I finally stop fumbling with the button.

Eden shuts the door behind him.

A relief settles over me, flicks away thoughts of Cotton's bad intentions. Didn't even glance at my chest, not an ounce of hunger in him. But then again, I got two lives in me, two more than that woman on the slab of all those years past.

"Why does he keep twine in his pocket?"

Eden plugs in the flat iron. "He likes it on him during funerals; says it keeps him grounded." She combs out my tangles. "My Bart used to do the same thing." She spritzes heat protectant. "If you ask me, it's 'cause he likes to feel close to his uncle."

The stench of the flat iron singeing my hair is a familiar

friend. When I lived with Cherry, she used a straightener on me before I went to school. It always made my hair into frizzy tufts, but I thought I looked pretty. The heat near my scalp, the hair spray mist, the lengthening of my bunched-up coils. When Mama Brown picked me and all my belongings up for good, as the ambulance sped away, my hair was wet and sudsy from a half-finished shower. Quarry called 911, then ran away to hide in the woods when Cherry overdosed. I was in the tub not knowing what was going on. I kept saying: *Mommy, I need a towel. Where you at? Mommy, I got shampoo in my eye.* But even with him leaving us like that during an emergency, she took him back. She always did.

That night, Mama Brown twisted my hair in plaits. I said: *Stop, you pulling too hard.* I said: *Straighten it.* She said: *Magnolia, as long as you in my house, you ain't frying your pretty head.* Maybe I was mad at her, maybe I was mad at Cherry and Quarry and the police and God. I said: *You ain't mine.* I said: *I hate you.*

If I could take those words, eat them, push them down in me and never let them back out, I would.

Eden presses the last bit of hair between the ceramic plates, pins it out my face. She wipes away the sheen and oil smeared on my forehead.

"My canvas." She massages a sterile-smelling cream into my skin, humming "Are You Washed in the Blood?"

"You Christian?" I ask.

"Can't stand them." She shifts her weight. "Like their music."

My eyes shut. The smoothness of the foundation, Eden's berry breath, and her humming lull me. I've almost slipped into a light nap when she swivels the spine of the chair, taps my shoulder. My eyes open to the white light of the vanity. I don't recognize the body I'm in: pale-skinned, pointed nose, widow's peak. Even my bone structure looks brand new.

"Goddamn, I'm good." She takes a compact case out the drawer and gets close enough that I see her pores, the parts of her foundation not-quite blended. On her finger, the first lens balances, the dome nearing my face. I back away. She holds my head still. Her finger presses into my right eyeball, and I wonder how fragile the meat is—like a peeled grape, I think. Her touch blocks my sight, frenzies my blinks. Again with my left eye.

A temporary tattoo of a honeybee wet, pressed below my collarbone. It don't match the pictures, but the top covers most of it. The foundation tints and contours my stomach, arms, hands. My nails're glossy: a glow stick shade of green. While that dries, she spritzes my body with some cold liquid.

"To set the tone," she says.

We make our way to the dining room. I want to scrub off the hugging stickiness. The camera sits on a tripod. "Oh My Darling, Clementine" toots out Cotton's lips while he toys with different angles. On the table: the laptop positioned right in front of a plate of crust piled high, some with globs of jelly.

He cranes his neck at the sound of our footsteps. When he looks at me, he sucks in a big gulp of air, sprints to Eden, and smacks a wet kiss on her forehead.

"You goddamned cosmetic savant." He jabs his finger in the air. "Giving me Proteus in the fucking flesh."

Eden scoffs, but I see the corners of her mouth twitch, like she got a smile trying to break out.

Cotton forms a square with his fingers, pretends to frame my face. "Lady Palimpsest!"

That makes me giggle. Even though Eden wants to hide it, we

all know there's a ticklish energy in this room. Maybe I'm thinking this because I can almost feel the weight of those hundreds on
my palm or because I'm in a dead woman's body, but we doing
something good here.

I take my seat and scoot the plate of crust closer. Eden sits
across from me, out of the lens' view. Behind the camera, Cotton
tilts his head and eyes me like he's waiting for me to pose. "Just a
quick picture for the portfolio. We'll send to interested clients."

My penciled smile tells the camera: *I love other people's pickings.*

"No posing. Maybe chew the bread, pick it apart. You don't
see the camera. You gotta let Aria possess you."

Crumbs litter the tablecloth. The shutter clicks.

And suddenly, I ain't here. I ain't in this cushioned chair.
That white ain't the flash of the camera, but the twirling of
a wifebeater in a man's fist, a crowded dance pit, this Las
Vegas dive. I am Aria Conner. It's 1995. Shadows eat the
bar, and fake vines eat up the walls, and a man leans against
them. His outfit's pied and pretty, too bright for the way he
broods. He looks at me as I pass, asks: *Do you like this music?*
I nod. A glint in his hand——he bounces a harmonica. *Does
the child in you?* His kiss would taste just like amaretto, I bet.
Out the exit, I follow his tie-dye and his rhythm. He quick-
jumps and makes his shoes clap, carries on, and the child
in me giggles. At our feet, rats skitter; they lead the way.
The music man turns first, and I step in sync, down an alley
dark as forget.

"This is beautiful." Cotton claps.

I remain on the chair; Cotton stands out the webcam's view

and calls the Conners, mutes the microphone so they won't hear how my breathing don't match Aria's old pitch, won't hear the makeup lady clear her throat or the funeral director's nail-bitten pacing.

The call connects.

"Ohh." The Conners react like they seeing a grandchild for the first time. "Oh, Aria, beautiful baby." Both the husband and wife got smooth hair that's either bleached platinum or aged white. Their faces creased with time and loss or loss of time.

When their gushing tapers down, I drop my smile to match their serious mood.

The wife speaks first. "Goodness, there's so much to tell you, I don't know . . ." She trails off, eyes flit to her husband, eager for help. "I just don't know where to begin."

The husband nods. "You look healthy. I hope school is going well for you."

The wife's face bunches up quick, like she expecting a punch. "We moved to Westchester back in March. A big pool in the back."

I nod with a smile that say: *Please, let me come, we can dip and dive and have a cookout after. Let's eat by the water with swim-hungry bellies.*

"You can swim in it anytime you'd like," the husband says.

"We have no more pets," the wife says, her voice heavy with something like anger.

"Your mother had cataract surgery." He pats her suntanned shoulder, relaxes her body.

I tilt my head, try to make curiosity shine through my eyes, keep them on the subject before the mother's grief can boil over.

"Oh, she's fine now. I wish you could have seen her after. That eye shield. She looked like a science-fiction creature."

I force a chuckle, leave a lingering smile, notice how much I look like the mom when she looks down with a slight grin.

"A science-fiction creature. Yes, I suppose I did." The mother's smile's got a touch of sadness to it. "Aunt Linda passed five years ago, and I still make those cheeseballs you like at Christmas, the ones with the dried cranberries."

I give a look of wanting.

The husband jumps on that with a grin. "Oh, you would have adored Christmas last year. The decorations! Tinsel everywhere. Your cousins flew in from Chicago. We understand you were busy."

"We have no more pets," the wife says again. Her words rattling and wavering.

I ain't sure what face to make, so I chew the softness of my cheek and hope the husband will speak.

An answered prayer: "We're thinking about getting a parrot."

My laughter cut in two by the mother: "Buddy died two years after you."

The husband flustered, says, "After you started graduate school."

Aria been missing decades; that's years and years of lying to his self.

"You know we jested so often that the dog would outlive us all, I began to believe it." Her eyes full, her cup runneth over.

Tears won't squeeze out my eyes, so I settle on a pout.

"But we'll have a parrot the next time you're around."

The mother whips her head to the father. "I don't want to do this anymore."

Surprise, hurt. "Honey—"

Each word spit through clenched teeth. "Richard. I have had enough."

The mother stands, computer chair swiveling in her absence, and races away. Richard stays on the call. Only fifteen minutes have passed with each awkward pause, forty-five minutes left.

My face changes to disappointed: *Why would Mom just leave like that, Dad? I been missing her.*

"Pay no mind," he says, "sometimes, she misses you so much, she can't handle it. Know that she loves you."

The father spends the rest of the call spilling updates and jokes and invitations. He got an ulcer, and someone named William married someone named Veronica, and what do you call a nose with no body? Nobody knows, and, Aria, when your schedule clears, you should visit, stay as long as you like, we could even go to an orchard this fall, remember how I lifted you? Nodding, smiling, laughing, and gasping when the father needs. Whole time, his eyes catching the passing minutes in the corner of his screen, and he auctioneers decades of unspoken things like he might get struck down if he don't get it all out. The goodbye he cuts short because sobbing takes over. But "I love you" comes out.

When the time is up, Cotton ends the call.

Exhaustion eats at my bones; I'd collapse if I wasn't sitting. The parents' grief sucked out whatever energy I had earlier, and my ass is numb.

"Fuck me." Cotton shows his teeth. "You're a natural."

Eden hovers near and lets out yips of approval. "I thought it was surely over once the wife left."

"Yes, but she kept him there with her emotion," Cotton says.

He slaps the stack of big bills in my hand, says in a Transatlantic voice, "I'd smooch you if you weren't so filthy."

The cash feels right between my fingers.

In the shower, the makeup runs off my body in a creamed flow. Blue soap lathers my skin. Cotton said he still ain't got the other case, but maybe it'll deliver tomorrow. It's past sunset, and tomorrow might be busy. Friday, I'll walk on down to Planned Parenthood and see if they can help me with my problem. Maybe they got a payment plan. Maybe I can work something out quick and get it fixed that day. Maybe if things keep moving smooth, I can buy Mama Brown's house from Sugar Foot and get it fixed up. I can make more rooms. I can live there with strong locks on the doors and windows. I can live there and swallow my own brie cheese and rosemary crackers and Italian drinks.

I skip supper and hope that my sickness tomorrow runs light and easy. I'm tired, but when my head hits the silk-lined pillow, sleep won't come. Playing pretend, like I been slaughtered, already starting to get to me. I scramble for my phone and send the address to a new match, along with my phone number.

The Boy texts. "My maps says it's a funeral home."

I send a picture of my ass.

"I'll be there in fifteen."

When he says he's here, I scurry downstairs, out into the parking lot. A light-skinned man on a motorcycle parks behind the hearse. "Carolina Nettle?"

I nod.

"You live here or something?"

"Just visiting a cousin. I hoped you had a car."

He shrugs. We hunker down behind the rosebush. I hover over

him, slide my boy-shorts to the side, and poke the tip in. When I slide down to his base, he groans.

Bounce up and down, up and down.

"Carolina, Carolina."

Slap his face. He grins, wraps his calloused hands around my throat. My nails pinch him, drag down the side of his neck.

"Oh, you crazy, ain't you?"

"Yes, Boy, yes."

He slaps my face, open handed, and it hurts. I try to press his arms down, but he too strong. "I don't like that shit," I say, keeping my grinding going, wobbling him further in. This time, I press into his reaching arms, his feed-me hands grasping, with all my weight. We end up rolling. Him on top of me, me on top of him. Wrestling with mulch chips, making dents in my elbows with all the struggle. This is what that hunger breeds. This is all power is. And it can kill a woman. I fight my way on top, thighs clenching. It ain't until I pull what little hair he got that I see the fear in his eyes. My body shakes and folds. Tits pressed against his chest. I catch my breath.

When I try to stand, he squeezes my wrists. He pumps into me. I spit in his mouth. That shocked look brings me to the edge, but he cums before I can again.

His motorcycle sputters as he drives away. I don't want to go back to my empty room. If I had friends, I'd whisper all my secrets into my phone. *And then I spit in his mouth; you should've seen his face.* We'd snicker until we had to work to keep our eyes open. I decide to see Cigarette Sammy.

Down Broadway, through the forest, up my empty driveway. From outside, I hear a clatter tornadoing through the wood.

Sugar Foot got to Cigarette Sammy; he must have. But when I open the door, Cigarette Sammy thrashes alone. He throws an always-dusty vase—pink, meant for keeping trinkets forgotten. It shatters. He hog squealing, another warning in his throat to get back, watch my fists, before more things slam to the floor—a wooden woman balancing a bucket meant for quenching, another vase stuffed with fake flowers, a candle jar with mostly vanished wax. I got to dance around shards and flying things because he headed for Mama Brown's gray-smudged ashtray, ready to make a mess of a burnt past, and I can't let him. I hug his flailing body. His groaning hurts my ears: *Get off me, bad woman; can't you see this pain?* I rock him back and forth and back; his shuffling don't stop. I start humming: *You are my sunshine*—stupid, stupid, only tune that comes to me—but it works, brings stillness to his feet.

I keep him snug in my arms. Ask, "What you got eating at you?"

His fingertips pulse on my elbows. He pushes me away but grips my hand. Squeezes my thumb, then pointer finger.

"What is it?"

Then his shuffling starts up again, so I tug him gentle to the couch. We sink in the cushions.

"You ain't feeling safe," I say.

He lowers himself to the floor, squeezes my big toe. I go to kick him away, but he oinks. Then the next toe, and the next, down to the pinky. His hand crawls up my leg—oink, oink, oink.

I grab his hand; yes, I get it. "You're home."

He shakes his head: *No, no, you getting it all wrong, bad baby.* He oinks some more, his eyes needing me to hear his message, and that pleading stare makes me snap.

"I don't understand you."

He hits his face again and again, each grunt louder, an open-palmed beating, and I'm afraid he might break something within himself.

"Stop that." I grab his wrists. "Stop it." His hands fling out to the sides, done jerking. My fingers hug his thumb. Two squeezes. *You know where this little piggy went, Cigarette Sammy, on to the market to eat out the garbage.* Each finger up to the pinky, then a hand-crawl up his arm, a point to the floorboards that never dropped my growing body. His temper tugged down to fidgets, again: light pinching, a tickling squeal. *This little piggy got shelter.*

His breathing slows.

In the seeping quiet, I ask, "Anybody been by here?"

He don't answer—back on that plane that separates us. Wading in his thoughts. He rubs his stomach.

"You hungry?"

He answers by keeping his frantic hand circling. To the kitchen we go. He tilts side-to-side while I build bologna sandwiches. His tantrum's probably just from getting used to having a home. When I moved in with Mama Brown, I had my own tantrums—ripped flowers from the garden and turned my nose up at her good cooking, even though I hadn't ever felt safer.

I feel like I'm keeping him hostage. Before I can say: *You know you can leave if you want; you ain't got to stay here to please me,* he lurches for the sandwich and eats. Sucks down every bite, and I know he got a fine feeling in his gut.

When I get back to Cotton and Eden's place, I got a couple more hours of darkness to sleep through. I turn the doorknob. It's locked. Last time I left this late, it was fine. Should have told somebody I was heading out. I knock once, twice. On the third try, Eden swings open the door. A patch of her Michelle Pfeiffer face melts a little under the heat of alcohol, flushed and Irish.

"Pretty girl," she says. "Mule?" She hands me a tall glass and leads me to her room. We sit in plush chairs by her vanity and sip together. I kick off my shoes, put my feet up on her king bed, wiggle my toes against the canopy. I hope Cigarette Sammy feels as comfortable as I do. I can keep him in the house with a full belly for as long as I can keep my pregnancy from Cotton. Eden probably won't remember me sitting in her room when the morning comes. Her eyes, cloudy as marbles.

"Eden," I whisper, "if I tell you a secret, you won't say anything to Cotton?"

She leans forward, and I think she might tip herself onto the carpet, but she catches her chin with her fist, propped up on her elbow.

"I'm pregnant. I don't want to keep it," I say. "Could you, maybe, help me figure something out?" I drink the last of the mule, press my lips to the rim.

"Tomorrow," she says.

"Oh, thank you, Eden. I—"

She sings, "The sun'll come out tomorrow."

This drunk bitch. Her wavering, off-key belting follows me to my room. "Bet your bottom dollar, that tomorrow . . ."

8

Whatever gentleness I saw in Cotton ain't here now. It's Friday. The second case arrived in the mail. Eden ain't here to do the makeup.

"She thinks she's a risk fiend with these little casino excursions," Cotton says. He paces in the dining room, tugging his twine tight. "I tell you, Magnolia. She goes to the mountains with her makeup-selling friends. They play craps, nurse watered down mai tais, and she thinks she's in a Bond movie."

I pick at my eggs with a fork, watch his angry show. His Southern accent floats up when he's mad.

He wraps the twine around his finger until the skin glows red. "She can't even fathom how cliché her behavior is." He stops, mutters something, and shakes his head. "She might as well go on a goddamned cruise."

The way Cotton's acting reminds me of Cherry's old anger. One night when I was seven, Quarry didn't come home from work. I was happy he wasn't in the trailer, stomping and going on. The night before, he wrestled me. He pinned my arms down and dangled a loogie over my face. I ain't ever been as afraid as I was then, waiting for that fat ball of snot and spit to hit my face. But Cherry? Cherry was mad.

She said: *Just watch him come home stinking of pussy. Men ain't shit. I tell you. I hate him.* She rushed to their bedroom and ripped up his bandanas. He beat her later for that.

Ain't any beating going on in this house.

I raise my hand in the old Italian pinch. "For Christ's sake, we got a business to run here."

"It's more of an art than a business." He don't see the humor. "And art requires dedication. A little sobriety would be nice, too."

A wave of sick rocks my stomach. "I'm going to go for a walk." The words come out all chopped by acid.

He gives me a distracted wave. "Yes." As I walk away, he says, "Keep your phone on, will you? There's no likelihood she'll return before we're sleeping. As a precaution, please."

In my room, I get my phone and some cash, pass Cotton and his pacing by the fire, his nerves softened. His twine ain't in sight. He grins, and it halts my exit.

"Just finished a call," he says.

"Eden?"

He gives a chesty laugh, dimples dipping. "We've got another case! Express shipping." He squeezes my skull, plants a dry kiss on my forehead. "Soon we'll be busy, busy."

My nausea disappears when I step into the morning's growing fever. The high's supposed to be a hundred degrees today. I walk on Broadway with a careful step. Guilt weighs me down.

Guilt for my happiness, my hope. I'm on my way to Planned Parenthood. Maybe I shouldn't be too thrilled about coming into money when I'm using it to fix a mistake. But that bulb of life would grow dim the moment I'd touch it. Thoughts of cradling something so fragile, with new breath and trusting eyes, fly at me, add speed to my steps.

I see the people before I see the Planned Parenthood sign: men in clearance button-ups, bottom lips bulging with chewing tobacco. Women with rhinestone-studded blouses, dirty nails gripping Bibles. They talk to each other with early quietness. Some sit in camping chairs. A woman rocks a baby in one arm, raises a poster with the other: DEFEND LIFE. The other posters, held high as a prayer: WE MUST END ABORTION, DEFUND PLANNED PARENTHOOD, WHAT IF JESUS HAD BEEN ABORTED? There's little traffic. They look like they waiting for someone to pounce. I give them a smile as I pass, don't even look at the building.

I'll come back later today. They got to go home sometime.

A swollen heat in my face, I turn the corner and keep going until I'm sure the protesters don't see me, can't hear my shoes on concrete, and my vomit splatters on the surrounding ditch garbage: hamburger and a dried loogie. My stomach won't stop. It cramps and cramps until I'm emptied. Ain't nothing in me but dry air.

I buy a pack of menthols and a ginger ale at a gas station at the end of the block. My first pack of cigarettes—Mama Brown would pinch me good. But I can put them down, easy. It doesn't cool my core enough. I need something stronger to calm my nerves, to feel less alone, so I head down Broadway, phone in hand, searching for the next man. When I push through the trees, Mama Brown's driveway yawns empty. A rush to the garden.

Straight to spires of peppermint to pluck a fistful of leaves and chew away my vomit and tobacco spit. My breath puffs in the dome of my palm, fresh and ready to be shared.

A white pickup truck pulls in. He steps out, and I catch his eye by flag-waving the skirt of my dress. His muscles, swollen as a flooded river. His skin dark. His smile moonlight in the middle of the day.

I smile and beckon him with my finger to the garden.

We stand naked in the heat. He towers over me, leans in with puckered lips, and I meet him with a flit of tongue, and it feels right to touch. To be touched. With the meanness I saw today, I just know I can be tender and good. I can, I can; my cans and wills buckle my knees into a meant kneel. Twirling tongue, caved-in cheeks. He grows in my mouth. I pretend it's love.

On my back. He hunkers over me but don't blot out the sun. Too much light in my eyes. And when I squint, all I see is the beauty on his face, a nice blue sky, flowers at the edges. My vision's wedding veiled; it's easy to pretend. We been together since high school, and neither of us know what it means to be lonely. We just bought a house. We are in our garden, one we're still tending to. A shared knowing of how to make things bloom. And when we get off work—me and him both working in an office—we do silly things meant for little ones. Like tickle fights and eating cookie batter. Ain't a secret between us, and that's how he can touch my body so good, like he made me himself, knows just where to apply his pressure. And that rhythm he fucking me with is the one we stay in. These tunes follow us everywhere, like when we say what the other is thinking, fall into the same steps at the fair. Yes, we the kind of couple who go to the fair with liquor snuck in and all those neon lights, Tilt-A-Whirl, sugar, and grease.

"Yes, yes," I say in a downy voice.

"You like that, bitch?"

His question ain't a question, but a statement oat-dry, just a fact. *You know you like it, bitch. I pretty much made you, I know you like it.* And then I'm pissed, mostly at myself for making up a honeymoon just for it to turn brutal.

"All fours," he says.

And I do, a dog in the dirt.

He slides in and out, in and out.

I let him get away with it for a little while. Then I start pushing into him.

"Hold still, Carolina," he says.

I bounce back, back. *Yes, Boy, you want me to be limp as a doll. How you feel being a doll, Boy? How you feel being plastic, something to play with?* I lunge forward, take him out of me. He must see what I want in my eyes because he lies down, lets me straddle. He tries pushing into me, but I slap him. Another slap brings that shock on his face, and another, and another. That pushes me into screaming convulsions. His moans join mine. We ain't nothing but birds filling the air with song.

We stand. He wipes the streams of sweat from his face with my dress. "You on the pill, right?"

I snatch my shirt from him and dress. "You don't got to worry about that."

Once inside the house, the first thing I notice: Cigarette Sammy hunkered over the puzzle on the coffee table. He's half-finished.

I don't mean to shout, but I do. "What the hell you doing?"

He looks up at me and groans, sounds like sorrow. He jabs his finger at the puzzle pieces.

"I'm sorry." I kneel beside him and watch. His eyes got a fierce focus on the pieces. He pushes in a piece and connects a poppy flower at the bottom. "Can I put this together with you?"

He looks at me and gives a high-pitched hum, nods: *Yes. yes.*

We go back and forth between plucking pieces and fitting them in the wrong places. When Cigarette Sammy places the last piece in, he claps and rocks back and forth. The complete donkey in a flowered pasture, neat and grazing.

"You hungry?" I ask.

He mutters to the ceiling.

I pop pizza rolls in the oven.

The timer dings, the pizza rolls just starting to burn on the edges. Cigarette Sammy sits in the recliner and eats. Cigarette smoke loops and rises from my seat on the couch. The crunch of gravel shatters the silence. I place my smoke in the ashtray and peek out the blinds.

Sugar Foot puts his car in park.

My cigarette burns, forgotten on the glass, as I take Cigarette Sammy's hand and run to my room. We hide in the closet.

Cigarette Sammy grunts, shuffles his feet. He tugs at a hanging shirt. It falls to the floor, and the hanger clangs on the shut closet door. I whisper, "We have to be very quiet. It's hide-and-seek."

He reaches for the closet, moans under his breath.

"No—"

His feet shuffle against the clutter.

"We have to win the game," I whisper, "Please."

I place my hand over my mouth.

The front door clangs shut.

Cigarette Sammy places his hand over his mouth.

"Miss Magnolia, you home?" Sugar Foot's footsteps carry

throughout the house. "Miss Magnolia? You here?" I know he seen the lit cigarette on the ashtray. I got to keep my shaking under control. I got to keep quiet.

The wood groans under his weight, up the hallway. He pushes open my bedroom door, and I got to keep myself from gripping Cigarette Sammy's hand out of fear because that will only make him yelp.

"Miss Magnolia?" My creaking bed. I peek through the slit.

Sugar Foot sitting there smelling my pillow. He closes his eyes; behind his lids a fantasy must play. In his mind, I live, solely his and scented. He rubs the crotch of his pants, then places the pillow back. And his face has the soft look of daydream, longing.

He rises, walks to the bathroom. The stream of piss hitting the water, the flushing of the toilet. More moaning wood from the bathroom to the living room. The front door opens, closes. We stay in the closet until I hear his tires roll away.

I drop my hand from my mouth. Cigarette Sammy does the same. "We won," I say.

He opens the closet door, pushes himself up off the floor.

"If that man ever comes by when you around, you hide, okay? You don't let him find you. Not ever."

By the time I get to Cotton's, I got a punching heart, and I'm drenched with sweat. Eden still ain't back. My phone dings, a text from Sugar Foot: *Miss Magnolia, u around?* I block his number. I'll deal with him when the rent is due.

I walk in and catch my breath in the lobby, where Cotton is speaking in a hushed voice to a moping woman at the desk. He notices me, gives me a smiling nod. In my room, the mattress eats up my spread weight. That lit cigarette told Sugar Foot I was inside. I just know it. I ain't ever run so fast and so long in my life. Ran, and ran, and ran until I knew he couldn't get to me. When the black spots in my vision clear, I stand and strip my muggy clothes.

That's when I notice the figurine on the chest of drawers: a bronze cheetah midstride. A card propped against the frozen haunches: *Where would the dancing Black Pearl be without her Chiquita? —Cotton.* He sketched bananas around the borders of the card. The odd man got his sweet moments. I move Chiquita to the nightstand. A few minutes later, Cotton knocks on my door.

"You like it?" he asks.

"I love its little paws."

He sits on my bed, bringing a breeze of cologne with him. Black pepper and cinnamon. "You don't think it's too . . .?"

"Exotic?"

He laughs out his words. "I was going to say conservative." The old-lawnmower stammering starts. "But if it seems, well, I didn't mean . . ." He rubs his chin with silent panic.

I let him flounder a little. "It's perfect."

He relaxes, a relieved eye roll.

"This why you scouted me?" I rub my nails over the grooves of the cheetah's spots. "Eden did get me clothes fit for a stage."

"Oh, good. I thought that's just how you dressed."

That makes me snort. "You really think I look like Miss Josephine?" My eyelashes fan.

"No, but she seemed vivacious, and so do you." His lips move to the side, riddle faced. "But your eyes are sad."

"And you like that." That comes out too quick. All the details mix up in my head: Was he next to the dead woman or on top of her? Probably on top, pretending the reek was fire-cured tobacco, convinced himself it wasn't decay stinging his nostrils, only too much perfume and a nicotine habit, and he gave her slobbering unreturned kisses and it was the first time he came.

We sit in a stretched pause.

"Eden's been talking," he says.

"Oh, is she back?" A bad attempt at distraction, a crashing swerve.

"I figured this would come up. It's just . . ." He runs his fingers through his curls, gets casket serious. "My parents were nauseatingly wealthy, okay? All they'd talk about: charities, restaurants—but only the kind with a waitlist—and real estate. Their network was so small, and all the gossip. If they hadn't been so terrified of anatomy, I probably would have grown up informed each time an Ingram wiped their ass. But there was never any of that talk because everything was always so nice." *Nice*, spit-out like it's gone too sour to chew.

"You like shit talk?"

He fans me away: *No, no, if you're joking, I simply can't cackle right now.* "It comes down to a moralistic way of relating to the world, and they are always above others. Even Eden. With this gossip. Don't get me wrong, she has middle-class tendencies, but when she married into the family, she had no issues adjusting to new ethics, which, by the way, really only consist of passive aggression and elbows truant at the dinner table." He takes a half breath before finishing. "It wouldn't have taken much to designate me a pariah."

"It ain't my business," I say.

"Uncle Bart never bought it."

"You miss him."

"Just please believe I'm no licentious fuck."

"You're no licentious fuck."

He chuckles. "I like how agreeable you are."

When he leaves, I nestle my head in the plush pillows. Maybe I'm a muse. Maybe he likes all my grit, thinks I'm some walking disaster to study. Some part in me craves that attention. I'm tired. I'll go back to Planned Parenthood when I wake up. Protesters or not, I'll squeeze through their righteous anger, march inside, and tell everyone who will listen I need help. Right now, though, I drift off with thoughts of jazz, clunky diamonds, and banana hems.

Cotton's muffled yelling yanks me out my dreamless nap. It's one in the morning. My clothes scratch against me while I dress, tangy and stiff with old sweat. His voice leads me down the hallway, to the kitchen. I listen out of view.

"You're bleeding money, aren't you? And your little friends," he says.

"My little friends changed your diapers," she says.

"They aren't even interesting. If anything, they're perfumed and loquacious."

"You sure are grumpy."

A blender begins to scream. Cotton raises his voice over the blades: "You are a frigid bitch."

This must be their deal, Cotton needing Eden in more of a mothering way than she can stand. Eden loving him but not at the right angle. I poke my head in. Looking like Meryl again, Eden stares at Cotton, presses her finger to the button. Her smoothie pulses, already smooth. Her finger lingers. She releases.

Cotton says, "A goddamned tundra—"

Eden presses her finger on the button.

I enter the kitchen and open the fridge, half pretend to look for something filling. Eden stops the blender and splits the frothy orange drink between two glasses.

Cotton ends the silence. "Sorry for the awakening."

"I'm only hungry." I take a slice of provolone, shut the fridge, nibble at the circle.

Cotton plucks the twine from his pocket and rolls it between his fingers.

"Care to wet your whistle?" Eden wiggles the glasses.

The veins in Cotton's neck snake up. He mutters, "Sure, get her drunk. That's great, really great."

Eden rushes out the kitchen. As I follow her, I trash the half-eaten slice and thank Cotton again for the cheetah. Before I can catch up, she scurries out her room with the straps of a canvas bag clinging to her arm. She ducks into my room. Her bag thuds on the floor; the smoothie glasses clink against Chiquita.

I sit on the edge of my bed. "How'd the gambling go?"

She combines the smoothie into one glass and hands it to me. Her face all frantic: twisted mouth, tablespoon eyes. "Ain't every day a gamble?" Half of that question comes from the hallway, peppered with fading footsteps. She must be going to give Cotton one more piece of her mind.

The smoothie tastes of sugared ginger, goes down my throat like cool silk. Spying in her bag won't hurt. Hurried footsteps thump. I leap back to where I was sitting. Eden holds a smoking teacup, thin as eggshell; lets out a long sigh when she shuts the door with her hip. Plants the teacup on the farthest end of the dresser. Her movements got a wilderness to them: snatching two towels from the bathroom, tossing them on the bed. From the canvas bag, she takes a small, metal washtub and floods it with hot water. The steam from the tub rises from the floor in front of my feet. That baby tub with the dewed sides reminds me of Mama Brown's sink. Eden grabs my ankle. I kick back. Her grip tightens, and that fierce focus in her look makes me give in to her pull. My feet dunk in the water. My toes clench at the scorch.

"My mommy used to take me and my brother to Harlan when we were little." She tugs the bag to her side and takes out a block of something wrapped in cheesecloth, unwraps a bar of fat-colored soap. "Mommy had a Melungeon friend, Violet. Violet used to make stuff out of nature. Perfumes and makeup and lye soap like this." With a soft touch, her fingers cleanse my soles, knob of ankle, between my toes; knead the suds into my skin. Water pours over my feet from her cupped palms. Lathers again. "Violet was a real granny woman. Knew how to work magic."

"They sell homemade soap at the casino?" I ask.

"They make it at the casino, but they don't sell what nature makes for free." The smile she gives ain't aimed at me, but at some memory. "My mommy's passed on, and so has Violet. But her daughter, Louise. Me and Louise are stuck together like snake spit on grass."

"You saw Louise today."

"At her boyfriend's casino." One last waterfall rinse of my feet, and she lets them float in the warmth. "Good, ain't it? Give me that." The empty glass returns to the nightstand. "It'll help with the nausea." My gut clenches. She must remember our conversation from last night. Cotton was so sour in the kitchen; what if she told him I'm carrying? That I'm carrying, and ain't no model that can work and be pregnant. All this seems sick, Eden washing my feet and giving me a sweet drink before sending me packing. I jerk my feet out the water.

"Let them soak," she says.

"You kicking me out."

She pats my knee with her palm, and I dip my feet in the water.

"I spent all day in Louise's nursery, on the mountain. Pickin' and pluckin' and diggin' up what's rooted and what ain't." She reaches for one of the towels on my bed and squeezes my feet dry. "Undress."

"No," I say. "I won't."

"You want your problem fixed or not?"

She ain't a doctor. Only if you count the dead and their stained faces.

"Go ahead. I seen all your bits and giblets before."

My clothes drop to the floor. She gives me the teacup. I bring it to my lips.

"Not yet." She spreads the towel on the bed and sits next to it, taps the mattress. My body curls on the towel—careful not to spill the tea.

A white pill from her pocket. "This is for the pain."

"I don't want that."

She drops it in my hand. "You'll change your mind."

I rise, go to the bathroom, and flush the pill. That's all it took for Cherry to get hooked—one swallow. "I don't do that." I lay beside Eden. "What's in this cup, and why my feet got to be clean?"

"Ground black pepper, honey, oil of pennyroyal, a splash of cream. The feet, well, there's some secrets tradition keeps."

"Ain't no drugs in this?"

"Only what you can get from the earth. I want you to know what you're gettin' into." She strokes my curls, and I feel allowed to be little, even if I ain't. "I used just a tiny bit of oil instead of the dried leaves 'cause I heard you throwing up, which means you're further along than I'd like. On account of that, makes it awful strong. It'll be painful. If you bleed more than you should, it'll be the hospital for you."

"That casino you go to ain't like what Cotton described."

She smiles, shoos my words away with her hand. "How would Cotton know when he ain't been?" She slaps her thighs, sighs. "All-righty. You drink, then lay back. I'll be here the whole way unless you want me to leave."

"Stay," I say. I try to ignore the texture and taste: spiced mint lard sticking and sliding down my throat. A wet cough follows the last swallow. That ginger smoothie must be working on me because I don't feel the medicine fighting its way out my guts. The painting of the woman and the beast holds my gaze. My naked thighs spread on the starched towel, my head nestled against Eden's shoulder. We wait.

Eden coos, "Breathe easy. Breathe easy."

9

I am straw. I am sunbaked straw in Germany, locked in
a quiet room. I fill up the floor—you got to step on me
to walk. A little man dotted with warts works a spinning wheel and spindle, turns me to gold. He pulls and
stretches me, hardens me until I shine. But it's okay. It
don't hurt. It don't hurt because I am straw and I am
gold. A pretty woman in a deep blue velvet dress sobs.
She say to the little man: *You can't have my first born.* The
little man don't speak. He keeps ripping at me to make
me gold. The pretty woman say: *You ain't got no name I
can guess.* She say: *You a nameless goblin. My baby is all mine.*
The little man giggles as he stretches and pushes the last
of me into riches. He leaps out the window. The woman
cries and cries and cries at the bad deal she's made. She

don't seem to notice me and my new shape. But that don't matter. The pain got to make me brand new. I am shining. I am a heap of gold. I don't feel nothing but the glimmer.

10

My steady bleeding reminds me that loss lasts forever. My third tampon of the morning. I sit on my bed, my door locked. Since drinking the tea, little plots of rash pock my arms, legs, thighs. Fierce itching. I slide out the letter jutting from beneath the cheetah, sit cross-legged on the bed, and balance it on the web between my fingers. Hearing the last of what Mama Brown got to say ain't something I'll ever be ready for. But I need her. I need her now more than ever. The lip of the envelope splits jagged—I'm careful not to rip her handwriting. Two twenties hide behind the letter. Those bills go in the drawer of my nightstand, between my stack of hundreds. The paper smells of peppermint lotion, cigar smoke, the staleness of her humidifier. My eyes close, and I see her sitting behind me, plaiting my hair, flicking ashes to the stone tray sitting at my knee. I blink away the haze of sadness and read.

Magnolia,

I got real sad news from the doctors today. Say my memory going to go bad. I got so much I ain't taught you yet. So much I hoped I wouldn't have to teach you. I guess I got my wish. This letter will have to do. Matter of fact, since I'm seeing how watery memory can be, this might just be better. You got my knowing on the page forever. I been wanting to tell you these things for a while, but it ain't ever felt like the right time. Last night, I dreamt you was dead. The casket was closed, but in my heart I knew it was you laid up in there. Now, you know I taught you death in dreams means a baby's coming. And since my old ass ain't been getting none lately, that leaves you. I ain't sure if it's happened yet, and since I ain't sure, that means it ain't. If you get nothing from what I'm about to tell you, know this. Men ain't nothing but trouble. I hope you stay away from them long as you can. But I know what loneliness breeds. And your birth mama ain't shit. I don't know who you got besides me, tell you the truth. My mistake of keeping you so close going to leave you with a boatload of hurt. And speaking of a boatload of hurt, I got to come clean about something. I want to tell you this before you hear it from the holier than thous up at Mountain Bend. Back in my day, I was up to no good. See, back in my day I was fresh as ripe pawpaw. But I didn't know I was that fresh until one Saturday. I was at the farmer's market with mommy and daddy. They was looking at pumpkins. I ain't too sure why. We never ate them or carved them. They was saying pumpkins was the worst. Kept prodding at them and turning them over. It was so hot, I was so bored. I let my eyes wander. They landed right on a man leaning against a crate of potatoes. Thinking about it right now gives me all the feelings I felt right then. He had been watching me and gave me a wink. Baby, I felt so girlish. In that moment, all I thought about was love. So the next day was Sunday, and we had to go on to church. I said, mommy, I can't go. I got cramps real bad. When they left, I went on down to the river because that's where the young people used to go and cut up. I didn't see that farmer boy nowhere. But I did see Sugar Foot. He was just sitting on the bank and scowling at some ladies having a picnic nearby. I said, Sugar Foot, what you got on your mind? He said, look at them women. Look at the meat they got. You know how they afford that? I said, no, I surely don't. And he said, look at they shirt pockets. And I did look, and they had soda caps pinned right on the chest. And, Magnolia, would you believe he started crying? You wouldn't think it now, but he was a real sensitive boy back then. I can't nearly remember now why. It was some-thing about a horse. Yes, his daddy was going to make him put down a horse because they couldn't sell it and didn't have no money to feed it. I felt so sorry for him, I kissed him. That nasty man was my first kiss. I didn't think him nasty then. I just thought he was a little off, a little sad. He said, maybe you could help me. Maybe you could help me take care of that horse. Now, I didn't have no job then, but I wanted to eat the meat like those women was. I said, how can I do that, Sugar Foot? And then every Sunday after that, when mommy and daddy would go to church, I'd tell lies. I'd say I was going to work, I was going down to help a white lady sew. But really, I was walking the streets all day and night, soda cap pinned to my chest. Now, baby, my wrist is hurting so I'll make this short. I barely made a cent for all my hooking. Sugar Foot took most of it. And he got even more bitter when I wouldn't marry him. He sweet to you now, but I know anger like that don't just die. You got to watch out for him, but I want you to remember that's our house. Used to be my mommy's and daddy's until he bought it up when they died. You fight for that place. You don't let nobody, especially no man, take it from you. I'm only saying this because I know you got fighting in you, coming from what you did. And when my dream comes true, when you get pregnant, you best make sure it's by somebody you love and trust. Don't be like Cherry. Don't you get yourself stuck on a Quarry. You young, and men talk slick. You just be careful. I can't say I'm worried about you getting along. You got a job and a garden. I guess that's all I got to say on that. Since this brain sick going to get me soon, soon they say, I got to tell you. Magnolia, I love you more than a well is deep. I'll be on that pearl looking down on you. And Magnolia, I want you to love that child more than you ever loved anything. You got blessings coming. Just like you was my best blessing. You got them coming, alright.

Yours Forever,
Mama

PS I put you in all the cash I got on me right now. It ain't much, but it'll feed you for a week.

11

I feel the dead move through me. In the two days since reading Mama Brown's letter, she ain't left me. I ain't seen her, but she sits by me. Unseen but real as humidity. And she sits pissed. Her dread seeps in my chest, dark as wet oak. When my head settles in the pillows and I got the blankets tucked under my chin, I whisper in the dark: *What you want to tell me? What you got wrong with you?* And the room stays silent, but the answer always the same. *You in the wrong, Magnolia, and you going further into wrong, and you know it.*

Cotton oversees a funeral downstairs. In the dining room, I hear aged voices singing gospel music, the kind you read from red, cracked hymn books. Eden sits by me, her face painted to look like Sigourney Weaver, and urges me to eat the breakfast she's made: soup beans with chunks of ham hock and onion, another ginger smoothie.

"Protein," she says. "It'll fix you right up."

I want to say these beans can't fill up the cave in me. Geodes and sleeping bats in my chest. A smoothie can't calm the pain of separation. Every time I think of softening a toddler's curls with coconut oil, walking around the hot zoo with blistered feet, pushing a stroller I can't afford, I miss the rolling nausea. I try to pour all my attention on the scrawled letter.

Mr. Reuter,

My sincerest apologies for the postponed delivery of the informational packet. In all honesty, my finances are not as impressive as they were when we last met. Lawyer fees and other protective measures have consumed my savings. Perhaps I should have heeded your advice and invested at the specified time. Nevertheless, I am now prepared to receive your services. This transaction requires the utmost discretion. As I pen this, a detective has just left my apartment. The police believe me to be a suspect in a brutal murder. I fondly remember our sessions, Mr. Reuter, when you allowed the spirits to assist you with your guidance, the advice you gave me as I considered how to approach Bianca. They found her body in the Adirondacks. I deeply loved that woman. Of course, she never articulated as much; I think my assumption of her feelings being reciprocal is far from dubious. I must say, the obese detective who routinely visits me seems incapable of considering this to be the case. Sure, I'm older with a frequent case of foot fungus. In fact, Bianca was below my income bracket and someone for whom I wouldn't have typically pined, either. Our connection was ephemeral, transcendent, and inexplicable in ways that, in the view of others, warps my role in her life as villainous. I frequented Bianca's nail salon for pedicures. She had a thick accent, Long Island, I believe. Of Italian descent; hair teased high; long, gaudy nails. My noticing of her was inevitable. Yes, she owned the establishment and was the only technician who was trained for the severity of my condition, so I suppose in that way, we met. But who can say it was not fate? I regret I can only tell you what I know from overhearing conversations in the nail salon, as she was often busy when I proposed to schedule trysts. She was a gossiper by inclination. She had a son, Scotty, who played baseball. Her family members insisted against my attendance at the funeral. Can you imagine how Bianca would feel knowing they implemented security at the entrances? A true carnival! They had grotesque claims that Bianca issued a restraining order against me during her final days. Legal jargon and lies aside, I cannot find the proper words to express my gratitude. Your brilliance has inspired me to continue my adamant defense. In my forced, dim solitude, I eagerly await the finished product. Attached are images I was able to capture.

Yours truly,
V. Edwards.

The pictures of Bianca were all snapped from a distance, all in her busy salon. She filed nails, swept the floor, polished toes, talked with a limp wrist while laughing. Her smile was full of bright teeth big as peppermint puffs. She wore neon colors, leopard print, costume jewelry. Her body, burnt orange from spending too much time in tanning beds.

Cherry used to buy plastic nails and glue them on me. She

painted them clear with pink sparkles. I liked them long because they made me think I could reach for whatever I wanted. One day, Cherry was in the middle of doing my nails—two fingers pressed to my thumbnail, like her touch could make the glue dry quicker. My other hand already finished and polished. Quarry burst in my room with a rag over his nose.

"What the hell's that smell?"

Cherry didn't look up. She wiggled the nail polish bottle.

Quarry said, "Put that shit away."

Cherry didn't say nothing. Just kept pressing on my nail, hurting my thumb.

"You don't need to be doing that anyway. It makes her look older than she is."

I was only seven. Anybody could look at me and tell I wasn't grown. I just liked nails was all. Maybe Bianca practiced doing nails on her son. There ain't much in this letter that lets me know who she was. I can almost hear her cackle and wonder if her son sounded the same when she tickled him.

"When the bleeding gonna stop?" I ask.

"Could be a couple of weeks," Eden says. "You hurting?"

I trace light circles around my belly button, nod.

"I reckon you changed your mind about wantin' a pill."

"I don't do that. Can I bum a smoke?" I stand and look at the seat of the chair: inkblots of my blood.

"To hell with it," Eden says, "it's the ugliest piece of furniture in this house."

The unfinished food sits forgotten while I wash and change. Eden hides the ruined chair in her room. She walks in as I'm getting dressed. Her watching how weak I move makes me wince.

"You go as slow as Christmas if you need," she says.

We sit on pillows on the floor and ash our shared Virginia Slim in Eden's house slipper.

"How are you feelin', darlin'?" she asks.

"Sore."

"No." Her finger taps against my skull.

"Like I done murdered." The words come out cloaked in smoke.

Some unseen weight makes her head tilt. "Cotton would've lost interest, and you would've lost a job." She spits on the cherry, flushes the filter down the toilet. "Let's get you ready."

In her vanity, I see the cave ain't in me. It's on my face. My eye sockets hollowed, the skin of my nose rubbed raw and jagged.

Eden paints me. I squeeze into a tight, pink dress, pull out the neckline and see the inside stained orange with fake tan, my stomach full of bloat.

"You want one more smoke before I put the teeth in?" she asks.

I draw heat from the thin cigarette with my left hand while Eden shapes pointed acrylic on my right. I shake. She says, "Hold still." Whenever I get winter sick, colds and viruses and coughs, there's that fever-brought weakness that helps me sleep away hours until I'm healed. What my body feels ain't like that. This frailness don't let me rest, and every movement made is a heavy decision. I switch my smoking hand so she can start the other. She takes the cigarette with its pointing finger of ash and sets it on the vanity.

"You going to burn your room," I say.

"Shit, fire should be scared of me." She shoves the glue-smeared dentures in my mouth. I want to give Bianca's reflection the living she had in her pictures. I look just like her: hair stiff and teased to heaven, eyelids foggy with dark gray eyeshadow, big teeth peeking out my purple lips. But my smile in the mirror can only say: *I took a new life* and *I gave that new life to the sewer.*

"Curtains up," Cotton calls.

We follow his voice to the dining room.

He drags his green eyes up and down the dress. He holds both ends of his twine, moves it left and right and left, stares at my body for too long. "Something is off."

My anger pushes through the bulky dentures: "What?"

"Your energy feels . . ." He returns the twine to his pocket, chews the end of a Twizzler. "Pendulous?"

"She's just peachy," Eden says.

"At the risk of sounding like an ass, are you on your menstrual cycle?" His eyes dart to my swollen belly.

Eden, always eager to prod him tense, says, "You sure know how to talk to a woman, you toad fuck."

"Excuse me." I slip out the dining room, unheard, while they bounce shouting insults off each other. As I close my bedroom door, I hear Cotton yell, "Beans?"

Mama Brown ain't gone away. I feel her trailing me to the bathroom. My body aches. Stiff joints, swollen gums, pounding skull. Every bit of my body begs for a deep sleep. On the toilet, I change my leaking tampon with the tips of my nails, sure not to get the bronzer inside me.

With the flushing of the toilet, the shower drain bubbles and gurgles like it's got to clear its throat. In all my grog, maybe I flushed a tampon in the middle of the night and fucked up the plumbing. But no, the used ones bloat in the wastebasket. The pipes sound like they trying to twist free. I scoop the Drano from beneath the sink.

The shower curtain tugs open—the plastic rings scrape metal. Soggy and dripping, Mama Brown stands.

The bottle of Drano thumps to the floor.

Back against the sink, I press my eyes shut. The past can't come for me. Not right now. Not like this. I want Mama Brown back, breathing. Not full of rot. Cherry always told me growing up that haints were real, but she said they haunted mountains. She said they'd stay in cabins. She never said they could reach places they never been. In all the childhood stories, haints seemed stuck, lonely.

"Child, open your eyes."

Mama Brown sits on the edge of the tub. One eye wanders. The other: gone. Her socket filled black with dirt. Her silver curls still fresh and tight from foam rollers. She sucks in air. A pebbled breath, words pushing through her teeth in the buzzing tune of a honeybee. "Why you here?" Another struggled gasp. "You acting out." A roly-poly crawls from her scalp, across her unblinking eye, over the hill of her nose, burrows in the soiled socket. Dark crumbs sprinkle from her face. "You gon' end up just like Cherry."

"I know better," I say.

"You ain't got a penchant for knowing."

"You left me."

"You ain't got a penchant for remembering." Her wandering eye focuses on my face. "You can't let an old woman rest. You know I'm raising that baby same way I raised you?"

"What baby?" I ask.

"Your child. You want to see?"

"You a wicked haint." But she ain't, not really. I got to be hallucinating. Lost enough blood to make my mind trip. More than trip, free-fall into a wish-turned-curse. In front of the mirror, I grin until my face hurts. That smile say: *Five-hundred dollars to play pretend*. It say: *You been playing pretend your whole life for free.*

"Wait, baby, I got to talk to you about something," Mama says.

I slap my face and leave Mama Brown sitting in the bathroom.

In the study, Eden sits, arms and legs crossed, wagging her foot. Cotton looks up from the camera, grins, slips into his practiced Transatlantic accent. "There's the vibrancy."

How a man can mistake fear for vibrancy, I don't get. I strut to the camera and suck in my gut.

Eden says, "Don't you do that. Cotton is sorry for not realizing Vincent won't see your tummy, ain't you, Cotton?"

Cotton says, "Yes, we'll just lift the camera. And for the portfolio, as unnatural as I feel editing the body—"

Eden clears her throat.

"I'll clean the distension," he says. He hunkers until his eye meets the camera.

And at the bright flash, I ain't here. I am in my New York salon. I am Bianca, mommy of Scotty. Just as I'm ready to sweep the powder of filed nails into a dustpan and kill the lights, in steps a quiet man, ushered by the tinkling of a bell. I remember him. He's the bald one with rotten feet, the one who wears too-big shoes, the one who cries when I clip his yellow nails. In his hand is a gift bag stuffed with crinkled paper, tangled and green as ivy, creeping over the edge. He reaches inside the bag, shows me the gift: a pair of high heels, sharp and red. *These were made to dance. Try them.* I tell him: *We're closing.* He swings the heels back and forth like a hypnotist's watch. I take them. They fit.

You can't take them off, he says. *Would be improper.* His hand reaches for mine, and maybe it's because this feels like Christmases I never had, but I take it, and we start a slow waltz in haunted light. And my steps have never been this deep, this red; my steps ache because they move endless.

At the dining table, the chair holds my burden, and I'm full of thanks to be off my feet. Microphone muted, Cotton makes the call, rushes behind the laptop to sit near Eden.

An answer. The screen shows Vincent: a horseshoe of tawny hair, crown bald and liver spotted, crumpled white dress shirt. In the background, his apartment's cloaked in shadows, drawn curtains. I expect him to growl when he speaks, but instead his voice is hospice-visit ready, whispered and careful. "Hello, Bianca."

I wave with a closed-lipped smile.

Soft spoken, mouth squelching with puddles of spit, "You look lovely." He chooses his words slow and shy—almost afraid—like each one's a flower that might be riddled with clover mites. "Scotty and I miss you." He stammers in a way that seems familiar. "Well, no, I haven't spoken with Scotty, but I imagine he does."

This mask I wear: pitiful, wishing.

His volume rises a bit, and a new tone, nasally, pushes through. "Your parents refuse to let me see him. Why would they do that?" He looks to the side with spite; he got to let me know it ain't directed at me.

I give a toothy grin, limp wrist flinging back a casual response: *Oh, you know how parents can be. Besides, who knows why people do foolish things?*

"Baby, you know what that smile does to me." A voice meant to attract, forced deeper, but still whiny.

On the outskirts of my vision, Cotton hides his face with secondhand embarrassment, and Eden snickers.

I switch from jolly to curious, and that brings him back to sadness.

"You could have been safe, if you would have just said yes." He rifles through a drawer and pulls out a red tie. His voice is sweet. "We would have matched well. And not a church wedding." A hush. "Well, you know."

I make my face understanding, but that don't come through, or maybe it does, and he just don't care because he hammers his fist on the desk.

"I wish you would dance for me."

I look at the camera—eye contact to let him know: *Yes, wouldn't that be nice, if only.*

"Don't leave me any emptier than you already have."

Now it's Vincent looking at the camera, and I swear it ain't Bianca he sees, but it's me. *Yes, Vincent, I hurt people. Yes, Vincent, I take people from comfort and bring them my chaos.*

Now he gets to sobbing, a stumbled backtrack, eyes wide like he surprised himself. "I'm sorry. I'm only frustrated." His fingers glide across his bald spot, meant to smooth hair—an old habit of comfort turned phantom. "They lie about me."

His emotions, too unpredictable, so I stick to a polite nod.

"Please cheer up," he says, "smile for me."

And when I do, he moans.

"I want to lick those teeth."

I try to drop the smile, make him mourn harder, but Eden's squirming in a chair, fighting back laugher, and now I'm smiling at him, not with him, and that only makes him lean into the camera.

His wrist, hidden beneath the table, bobs up and down. "I want to see your biddy, please."

I hide my mouth with my hand, a performance of innocent wonder, while I speak in a steady tone. "The fuck is a biddy?"

"I think he means your chest?" Cotton says.

Eden answers, voice wavering, withholding giggles, "He means your ass."

"Show me. Do it, do it," Vincent mutters.

I stand, sure to suck in my belly, and wait for someone to say: *Hell no, sit, don't obey this hard man,* but they don't. A stolen glance at Cotton—his eyes clouded with fantasy—then turn. No lifting of fabrics, just show my covered self. Vincent moans, louder, louder. I look back at Cotton. Whatever brief spell held him broke; he look pissed.

"Sit down," he says.

"Are you sure—?"

Vincent's sputtering gasps let the room know he finished. His ugly face is dappled with sweat. Everyone, even Vincent, look disgusted, the truth of what just happened heavy in the silence.

"I'm afraid I must go," Vincent says. He ends the call.

"What a creep," Cotton says.

I try to laugh, but my lips won't lift. Shooting stars flicker across my sight. My body sways.

"You look like a ghost," Eden says.

The room blurs into a curtain of blackness.

Cotton and Eden hover over me, cooling my face with church fans. I try to rise, but Eden pats me to the floor.

"I've read literature on this," Cotton says.

"Hush," Eden says. They flap the cardboard fans, both printed with crosses in a lightly clouded sky.

"Incredible. You are incredible." Cotton places the fan by my head. "Similar to cases of possession. You allowed this woman entrance to your psyche. It's taxing, very taxing, on the body."

"Let's get you to your room," Eden says.

I rise, thankful I didn't grease the hardwood with my blood. Eden wraps her arm in mine. We shuffle.

Eden shuts my door. Fear takes over my face. "I got to go to the hospital, don't I?"

"You runnin' a fever?" she asks.

I shake my head, but I want to say: *I'm seeing things, and by things I mean my Mama Brown. My mind conjuring up a tuft of nightmare. What about that?*

"You need rest and protein. I'll call Louise."

In bed, I close my eyes, not for sleep but for rest. An hour later, Cotton brings cabbage soup. The bowl clinks on my nightstand.

"How are you feeling? I'd never really considered how this would affect your mental."

"I'll be ready for the next case," I say.

He pauses by the door, says, "You look beautiful." He shuts me in.

During the Skype call, when I started to put on a lazy show for that killer, Cotton felt something. I could see it in the nothingness of his eyes. And maybe calling me beautiful was only meant to make me feel better, but I think he gets off on me looking withered.

I go to the bathroom. Eden creeps in with a tied shopping bag, looking at me like I'm a child with a scraped knee. The maybe-love in her eyes disgusts me. I press my legs shut, wipe my eyes. "You ain't got nothing to hide no more." She places the bag on the sink.

"I called Louise, and she said this is normal, but you really need to be resting. Before you go to bed, mix that." She pokes the bag. "And put it up in you. Louise said that'll help a whole lot. I said, Louise, shoving cobwebs and soot in a woman is just praying for a big ol' yeast infection. But she knows her stuff." By the door, a pause, then, "But just in case, I'll buy monistat tomorrow."

"Thank you," I say.

She leaves me alone with my hurt.

My fingers dip in the bag, knead the cobwebs and soot. I plug myself with the dirty wad, push it just past the opening. Blood drips from my fingertips, dyes the water.

12

A little bit of strength spreads in me like moss. My body still
leaks. A week's melted away since that horny man said I
leave people empty, and he must have been right because I ain't
checked on Cigarette Sammy in a minute. Last I saw him was
when we hid from Sugar Foot.

The whole walk to Mama Brown's house, my stomach is full
of nerves. I been so caught up in the hurting from the flushed-
down life. But it's been too long. Now I'm starting to think I
abandoned him, and Sugar Foot scared him away. Maybe he came
by one day, and Cigarette Sammy didn't hide. Or maybe he did
hide, but he giggled or moved the wrong way and made noise.
Maybe Sugar Foot sniffed him out and said: *This ain't your place.*
Get, go on now. I can't work up the courage to reach out to Sugar
Foot.

When I step inside Mama Brown's house, the recliner sits
empty. Maybe I just missed him, came while he was walking the

city, and something about going all over and wearing his shoes thin must please him. I thought he'd stop that walking when he got a home to go to.

I cook his lunch, boiled rice and spicy bean mash, plated and wrapped in aluminum foil—only thing left in the house worth eating. The food still on the shelves are already marked blue with mold.

When I bring his food to the coffee table, I notice something I didn't before, and it weighs my stomach with a bad feeling: the table pushed a little, the floor scuffed raw from pressure. The wooden woman with the basket on her head stands at a different place on the entertainment center, like it fell but was put back again. Cigarette Sammy probably had another tantrum and decided he had enough, it was time to leave, oink, oink, oink, all the way to the street.

Before I leave, I order a pizza for his supper. That way he got two options. Hot water fills the sink. When I first moved in with Mama Brown, I remember being excited because she didn't make me do the dishes. Before Cherry's accident, Quarry made me do the dishes: plates crusted with old potato salad, cups and bowls sticky with chocolate syrup. I ain't ever been able to stand chores since then, but washing them for Cigarette Sammy don't feel like labor. It almost makes my insides flutter. And if he scared because of Sugar Foot, it's my taking care of him that makes up for it. Just got to show him he's always welcome, ease him back into staying, maybe even forever.

Wood creaks. I follow the sound to my room. "Cigarette Sammy?"

I push open the door and find Mama Brown sitting on my bed. The white sheet tacked to the window pushed aside. Sunlight shows me neglect, dust. She holds a black flannel pouch. I know what's inside: purple petals, lemongrass, sweetgrass, tobacco, dried wine, a puff of my breath. We made it the morning after I moved in.

Mama Brown shakes the pouch. "This was meant for your protection."

I sit next to her. She places the pouch in my hand. "I know."

"No, you knew." She shakes her head. "Little ones always know more than grown folk. Ain't that something?" A beetle pushes out her nose. She plucks it out, tosses it to the floor. "I'm sorry for being hateful yesterday."

"Mama, I ain't seen you in a week." I touch her wrist—no drumroll of a pulse, no warmth. "I thought I dreamt you."

She huffs an ain't-that-something laugh. "Time ain't nothing but a pinwheel." She scratches a patch of psoriasis on her elbow, a habit of the body, probably can't even feel that itch. "I was just confused is all, and you not being home worried me."

"I been working there and letting my friend stay here."

"What?"

"Why you here?" I ask.

She looks up to the ceiling, and I see she ain't here, but in some memory. "When I was growing up in this house, there was this white man who went around our neighborhood selling Bibles. Wanted to save us sinning nigras." She chuckles. "And oh—the sight of him scared me away from God. His eyes real sunk in, looked just like two pebbles stuck in bleached clay. He was starving skinny. Mommy used to call him Cricket. This was about a year or two before I put that soda cap on me, mind you, so I was still in church every Sunday, ruffle socks and all. Shit, what was I saying." Her hand taps her knee, a light spanking to bring forth the memory that's jerking away. "One Sunday, Cricket came to church. He'd never been to ours before, which even now seems strange since he had a bad concern for our souls. But I figured he went to services with the white folk. He sat real quiet in the back until they did altar call. He normally walked all slow, like one heavy step would shatter him, but that day, he was running and jumping in circles. Then he just stopped and shouted like he was preaching, 'Lord, you take my sheaves!' and then he fell dead. You can imagine how many Sunday suppers we sat and tried to decode but later decided it was just the way old folk talked when they didn't have family or friends." She shakes her head, beauty parlor curls still in place. "I was old enough to know better, but I still thought he'd haunt me. That I'd open my eyes and he'd be standing at the foot of my bed. Now, I only talked to him once or twice, just hellos and good mornings, but I was also old enough to think everything was about me." She chuckles. "So he was going to haunt me and me alone. That never did happen, but the day he died, I tried to bring it up to Mommy. She said, 'Alette, a haint only bother people for three reasons: a baby's on the way, somebody about to die, or you got something going on inside. Seeing as you ain't fast, everybody's healthy, and you too young to have something going on inside, no haint is concerned with you.'" Mama Brown looks at me, tethered to the now, pity in her eyes. "My guess is you got something going on inside. You got to see your baby so I can get my peace."

Her words make me feel whittled down. Even by being around her spirit self, I got a cool stillness. Any loneliness I nestled into before don't matter. This Mama Brown can remember. What peace better than us sitting close enough to whisper questions and knowing they can be answered?

"Why you can't stay?"

"You know I love you, but your baby cries and cries. Before you conjured me up, I was . . ." She acting shy, like she spouting crazy talk, as if we ain't talking in my room while her grave is filled. "You know the way sunlight looks when you're underwater, those veiny patterns it makes on the bottom of pools? Well, I was in something like that. Not underwater, I mean, and I never felt like drowning. I mean, I was moving through something pretty like that. It didn't hurt, it felt . . . Well, I can't describe it. I want to go back."

"You hate me," I say.

"Never told you I had one, too."

"Before or after Daddy?"

"It was after your daddy. He was about two, and I couldn't take another."

"Can you see him?"

"He got peace a long time ago." A little silence to show thanks. "This man you been letting stay in my house. Tell me why."

"He don't got anybody but me."

"And how you know that? You ain't his mama."

"I'm nobody's mama."

"Child." She chuckles, bobs her head up and down. "I got a baby on the other side saying otherwise."

I pretend she won't ever leave, pretend she's here for days—talking before she goes to work, and I lay down. She finger-rubs my scalp, and I pretend I don't smell the rot. Her humming is rocky with snot, but in my head, it's sweet. While I drift into a light nap, she says in a lullaby voice, "You got to swallow that truth, Magnolia."

The doorbell rings. I open my eyes to this empty cavity of a room. I got a temptation to grab the pouch, but something in me says whatever protection it held is long dead.

In the living room, a shoeless slide across the floor in socks, a squint into the peephole. It's only the pizza man. He takes my money. I kill the lights in the house and on my way out, take a slice of pepperoni heavy with banana peppers.

A quick peek in the garden—the honeysuckle is spreading, reaching fingers, hungry for the nourishment of what grows. I'll need to rip them from the roots.

The way back is a humid trudge with a belly full of buttered crust.

Upstairs in the funeral home, voices of strangers blare through Cotton's closed study. Eden ain't here. She's gambling and drinking on the top of a mountain. I bounce my knuckle on his door. When he answers, I'll ask if there's any new cases and pretend I ain't curious about who he's hosting. He opens the door in his Calvin Kleins. Puffy eyes. His hair as wild as hummingbird wings. Blue paint dries on his hands, flecks next to his eyebrow. He holds a paintbrush, sulks into a glass of Campari.

On the canvas, a party gone wrong—in a fenced-in yard, a clown covers his face with gloved hands. The family and their pet dog, back turned, look to the periwinkle sky where two detached eyes float, the nerves bundled, tied like string. Cotton returns to the scene and begins detailing an iris.

"Any new cases?" I ask.

The paintbrush clatters to the floor. He plops on the sofa. A movie projects onto the only wall not blocked by bookshelves and art. The only people he hosts in this room move in black and white. In the flickering light, a woman stands in the street, whines to a mud-splattered man about a toothache. He pauses their meeting with a remote.

"We have to let the grapevine do its thing," he says. He's drunk. "And by the way, grapevine? It should be kudzu. People should be saying, I heard it through the kudzu."

I sit next to him. "You okay? It's the business, ain't it?"

Cotton shakes his head in slow motion, raised eyebrows, puckered lips. "We're good; everything's good."

"What's wrong?"

"Could you hand me—?" He points to the bookshelf.

I hand him the piece of twine.

"It's my birthday," he says.

"You don't like aging?"

Snot threatens to drop into his laugh. He coils the twine slow, winding down his thoughts. "No, in fact, it's one of the best parts of life." He wipes his nose; it glosses the dried paint on his wrist.

Eden hadn't mentioned a birthday coming up. She's gone for the day. His uncle probably spent the most time with him, carving out traditions with each passing year. On my birthday, Mama Brown and me would go for Italian ice and walk around World's Fair Park, dote on strangers' dogs. "What do you usually do for your birthday?"

"We never had a set thing." He chuckles when he realizes he lying. "I've spent every birthday here, even when I lived in New York. Cocktails with Aunt Eden, Uncle Bart, dinner, and always charades."

I ain't even considered what holidays will feel like without Mama Brown—none of her Valentine's Day fudge, no staying up against the wishes of our drooping eyes on Christmas Eve painting our nails and watching bad love stories.

"We can do that," I say, "You already got the drink part down."

"I'm sure you have other—"

"No."

"Want to go to Urban?"

"I'm nineteen," I say.

He rubs his neck: *Damn, I ain't think of that.* But when he speaks, he sounds excited. "I want to show you something." Seeing my stillness, my energy not matching his, he says, "Oh, here," and hands me the bottle of Campari.

I guzzle the last bit in the bottle, make the bitter pass through me quick while Cotton leads me to the kitchen. Through the walk-in pantry, past organic tortilla chips, packs of Twizzlers, cases of Evian, to the very back wall clear of shelves. He leans with his words, his tipsy breath tickles my nose. "Have you ever noticed this?" His finger circles a notch in the red wood.

Since Eden makes most meals, my poking around only includes the fridge. Only time I been in the pantry was to sneak one of Eden's Ecuadorian chocolate bars to my room. The chipped away space he points to meets his waist. Another a few inches down, one more below that.

"This your growth chart?"

"What a charming thought." Humor in his voice. He places his finger in the top notch. "Eden says this is the only pressure point that matters." Pushes. The wall ain't a wall but a door; it opens to a small room with black velvet walls and silver crown molding, a bar in the center stocked with stools and all, a pool table, three beanbag chairs.

Cotton jogs to the bar. "Gin and tonic?"

And I nod because I've never had most things and wouldn't mind trying. We pour the crystal glasses into us, then bring our amaretto sours to the beanbag chairs. Our drinks splash as we sink our awkward wiggles into the cushions.

"Happy birthday." This drink laced with sugar. I swirl it around my mouth like a thought. Close to drunk, close to schoolgirl giggling for no reason. "What will we do for supper?"

His words spill into his half-tilted glass. "You're so fucking rustic." A chomped ice cube. "I love it."

"I'll order Chinese."

He lets out an "ehh," which really means: *That food is meant for heavy guts. Give me cucumbers and kale and a nice duck liver mousse.*

"Those Twizzlers you eat really vines plucked straight from the garden, huh?"

His hands fling up: *Fine.* "But I can't take part in this flagellation. Surprise me."

I send the order, and Cotton fights his way out the chair's dimple and staggers to the bar. Clinking things.

I kick off my shoes.

Cotton smirks at my socks. "Uncle Bart always insisted we dress up."

I roll off the chair, make my off-balance walk to him. "We got to."

Two thrown back shots of tequila, then we race, barefoot and snickering, out this hidden lounge to the hall. I stop him by my door. "My dancing dress with too much tulle is dirty."

He cups his voice against my ear, laughter vibrating my drum, like me and him are kids sneaking out of Sunday school. "You can borrow from Eden."

"What if she comes back?"

His playing eyes nudge me into her room; he goes on to

his. The fanciest thing I find hangs in the back of the closet, sheathed in plastic. Chiffon dress, color of noon sky. A little big at my chest, stops just above my ankles. From her shoe rack, I pick pearl-colored stilettos. My retreat is a wobble, a baby-deer walk to the living room. Cotton stops at the mouth of the hall in a shining burgundy suit, studies me, and folds himself with laughter.

I feel stupid and ugly and drunk. Ain't sure if I want to slap him or kiss him or shut myself in my room, but my first step in his direction is strong. The second, a stumble—the third a crash to the hardwood, bent joints and scattered curls.

That stops his laughing, but he don't move. Only stands with those daydreaming eyes. Is it me he sees or a body made for crumpling? Now he moves toward me, scoops me up in his arms, and maybe it is a little hypnotizing, his cologne, and how he get such a close shave. Soft, I bet he's soft. He carries me through the pantry, into the lounge. I kiss his cheek, ready to make a joke of it. I don't need to. He lowers me to the beanbag, sits beside me. A flicker of motion, he slips it out. Hard, he's hard. If we do this, and it makes sharing a roof feel wrong, then what? But part of me wants to see if it feels wrong, so I reach for him. He swats me away: *Don't move; you just stay there and watch real close.* Spit wiped from his palm to his shaft. And now he's stroking fast, and he starts choking me. I close my eyes.

"No." He sounds polite, like he asking for directions. I leave my eyes open, and he keeps going, taking my breath with his squeeze until he comes.

A quiet cleanup with cocktail napkins. He sighs, clearheaded, pours us glasses of water. "Magnolia—"

"The food should be here soon."

"Thank you." He don't break eye contact in this silence, and I wonder what words his closed lips hold. *I was in a sad place,* or maybe, *I am a bad, wicked man,* or something lighter, like, *Either way, today is a day for wet tissue.* "Really, thanks."

When the hospital called me and told me Mama Brown died, I left my register and laid flat on the parking lot. I didn't sob or beat my chest to bruises, only evened out my weight on a cracked surface. Numbed to roadkill. Grief makes people slapstick, so I say, "No problem," like what just happened was only borrowed honey.

A clatter in the pantry, something knocked over. Eden barrels through in a green, sequined ballgown with a Jessica Lange smirk. She holds the dropped-off Chinese and a coconut cake. She ain't come back this early from the casino whole time I've lived here. I glance at Cotton to see if he shares my panic—how long she been here, how much did she hear—but he only shows a confused grin.

"I thought y'all would be in here." Her voice's champagne-bubbly, but she keeps eyeing the bottles. She ain't drunk yet but is itching to be. "Magnolia, that's my wedding dress." The food plunked on the bar. "You look darlin'."

We split the food with Eden, all of us washing down each bite with neon cosmopolitans, then whiskey sours. I worry with the hurried eating and no tries at conversation that Eden is tilling over and over in her brain, *Magnolia and Cotton had not-sex.* But then she speaks after the last bite; she was only hungry. "Shit far, I forgot the candles." She lights a cigarette behind the bar and passes one to me.

We tap our ashes into a martini glass. The cake's cut with no singing; the only candles is mine and Eden's juggling embers.

Rum and Diet Coke with the sweet. Cotton's gloom been pumped out. He eats his slice with a smile, without muttering: *There's gluttony and then there's suicide.* And now the three of us give up on mixing drinks, bring a handle of Jack Daniels to the beanbags.

Eden claps like a kindergarten teacher. "Charades!"

While she makes the slips of paper, she starts hee-hawing to herself.

"What's funny?" Cotton asks,

"Oh, nothing," Eden says.

Both Cotton and Eden got blushing skin, sunburnt from the inside, all the drunken heat.

"I was just thinking about how Uncle Bart used to tell that story."

"God, don't embarrass me."

"I want to know," I say.

Eden jabs Cotton with her elbow until he submits. I'm betting he only agrees because he knows Eden will tell me anyway after the party; this way, he can keep control of the story.

Eden keeps writing, folding paper, when she speaks. "This took place about twenty-seven years ago. Cotton was eight. This was before he moved in with us, but he spent a lot of weekends here. One Sunday morning, I couldn't find my lipstick. I spent more than an hour looking under pillows and behind the toilet. All over. I nearly missed brunch." She sips from the bottle. "So, I start headin' for Cotton's room because he was already drawing at that age, and I figured maybe he stole it for some paint. He saw me coming, and he put up a fight. Cotton was always a little peculiar, even that young, so I didn't think nothin' of it. Well, I tore his room apart looking. I didn't find my lipstick. But when I pushed Cotton's bed from the wall—do you want to guess what I found?"

"It wasn't the lipstick," I say.

"I pushed his bed, and right on the wall, 'bout thirty, forty dried boogers." Eden's words come out shaky from held-in laughter. "Cotton said, 'Aunt Eden, that's my collection.'" She laughs until veins pop in her neck. "He had names for every dang one of them."

Cotton rolling with her story easy, laughing it off, but his smile don't meet his eyes. "That's an overexaggeration." He reaches for the bottle. "It was maybe ten boogers, and I wasn't eight, I was five."

"Call you boogeyman," I say. We all cackle.

The birthday boy takes the first slip from Eden's lap. Four words. Category: quote or phrase. Eden and me watch, slump bodied and buzzed while he jumps. We shout flea and kangaroo and pogo stick. No, we are wrong. And then I notice Cotton threw the paper to the ground, right by my ankle. It takes three glances to focus: *Jumping on the trampoline*. Ain't a graceful bounce, ain't a springing float. He can't pretend he's on the moon. He's losing against gravity. His play is thudding hardwood. His play is rattling glass on shelves.

13

Another week has passed; my flow is down to light spotting the color of river clay. The wastebasket in the bathroom's smeared by last night's toss—my final tampon.

In the bright burn of noon, a panty liner, tucked inside my shorts, catches the last of it. The sidewalk stretches on down Broadway to the playground. We got a new case today. I tried reading in the dining room while I broke the skulls of my boiled eggs. Cotton has a funeral going on, and something about the muffled, rackety praise reminded me of Mountain Bend Baptist. Made me think of Pastor Wooly's cane dropping, of Mama Brown's plump rocking in lilac and lavender dresses, massaging peppermint lotion into her knuckles in between claps. Lately, I been keeping all my sadness locked in a pantry somewhere inside. My grief and my self-hatred placed on shelves like canned tomatoes. But hearing those people downstairs shout their mourning and worshipping unlocked that pantry door, pulled the beaded light string, told me I need to dust.

At the park, white women walk purebreds, and skinned-knee kids play tag on hot pebbles. I sit in the shade and read. Some blog made a post about Cotton's business, and last night, he slipped the express-delivered letter beneath my door:

Cotton and Eden,

The Conners told me about what you did for them. I'm not sure of the scope of your business since I can't find a website with reviews, but I appreciate your kind cadence on the phone. The man you see in the pictures was my boyfriend, Jeremiah. We dated in college. They're old pictures. '98–'02. They are the only copies I have, so please return them with the new pictures. He disappeared in Oregon. It was only meant to be a short trip. We're from the city; I tried urging him to do a little more research before going. There was always a disturbance just beneath the surface with him; he thought there might be peace within the forest. But something bad happened, I suppose. He never made it back. Help me remember the before.

Good wishes,
Mary

In the pictures, Jeremiah holds a bottle of gin in one hand, and in the other, a bottle of tonic. His big eyes and shaggy hair, both licorice-dark. Bags under his eyes the color of lizard belly. He was taller than everyone around him, even barefoot. A beer gut. He wore a lot of band shirts and had a shaded tattoo of a crow wearing a monocle under his forearm hair.

The alarm on my phone rings: time for Eden to dress me up.
I walk back up Broadway, life of a dead man crammed under my
arm, to the fading tinkle of the laughing kids. I want to laugh
like that and mean it. When I was around seven, me and Cherry
and Quarry were sitting in the living room watching a DVD set
of *Three's Company*. My legs across Cherry's lap, Quarry next to
Cherry. He reached over and tickled my feet. It made me giggle
at first, then he got rough with his fingers. I kicked, but he tickled
harder. He tickled deep—made every little bone hurt. I hope
those kids never know what it feels like to have their laughter
turned into pain.

Then I look at their mommies and know that won't happen
to them.

Cars of the mourners push down the slope of the parking lot.
Cotton's voice inches closer to the lobby when I enter and head
for the stairs.

"Magnolia?"

Pastor Wooly bends on his cane next to Cotton. His breath
rattling. His face and neck sweat-soaked. He's still recovering
from giving that sermon. "You here for the funeral?"

"Working," I say. "You know Cotton?"

"No, I'm standing in for Pastor Fellows. He nearing the end,
bless him. We been missing you at church."

Cotton nods, allows us privacy to continue our conversation
while he goes to turn the lights off in the receiving room, the
crematory.

"I been busy." I lean my foot on the first step. The wood creaks.
The wood say: *All right, now, bye-bye.*

"I see you got someplace to be." He got condemnation in his
voice. "I just want to say I'm awful sorry for what happened.

Sugar Foot told me." He got a lake of pity in his eyes. "A woman ain't even safe in her own home. It's a terrible world we live in. Terrible!" He shakes his head, sending globes of his sweat crashing to the hardwood. "You should reach out to Sugar Foot. He say he can't get ahold of you. I think he got an apology for you."

That lights a rage deep in my belly. My face heats up with thoughts of running away and burrowing behind one of these thick velvet curtains or slapping him across his serious face. "I got to go. Nice seeing you, Pastor Wooly." The booming of my fast footsteps eat up his response. Ain't it just like church men to think the raping of a woman can be fixed by saying sorry. Ain't it just like church men to not understand how many bars of soap I done whittled by water and my skin to get the feeling of grit to go away, how it ain't worked yet. Sugar Foot can take that apology, go straight to hell, and give it to the Devil.

I lock my door behind me. The tears I feel should come don't. My hurting bundles in me and melts to a shadowed, seeping dread. Pushed against the wall, the chest of drawers rattles—brief, then with the rocking rhythm of natural disaster. Tennessee don't get many earthquakes.

"Come on out," I say.

The bottom drawer slides open. Mama Brown cackles, folded nice and neat: her left arm twisted around her neck, her right hidden beneath her back. Legs accordion pressed into her belly. She unfurls with popping joints and sits next to me.

"You ain't like my trick?"

"You getting too fancy."

"Tuh." Her sigh got a hit-possum stench. "You the one keep conjuring me up."

Her breath brings me to my feet, forces me to inch away from her decaying perfume.

That wandering eye looks past me, the empty socket aimed straight at my nose. "Did I ever make you feel like crying and screaming wasn't for you?" She claps like we at church. "You got a right to feeling mad. Just like you got a right to feeling soft and a right to feeling strong."

"What if I can't feel nothing? What about that?"

"Shit, there's a difference between can't and won't. What's bugging you, huh?"

"It ain't important," I say.

"I got to show you something. It's worrying me."

"What is it, Mama?"

Her hand fanned out—two missing fingernails. "This old body can't last much longer."

"Can you— Do you feel it?"

"I don't feel nothing." She holds her hand like she waiting for fresh pain to strike. "Not yet anyway. Can you just think about seeing your baby for me, please? I ain't even sure that's what's bothering you, but we won't know without trying."

"I'll think about it," I say. I'm the reason she got to die another death. All she wants is to float in that underwater light, now she mothering from the beyond. But every time she's back, I feel right and good and warm.

She studies me in her pause. "I think you want me to stay."

She got a sadness in her voice, a tone that says: *I got to go, baby; you already had more of me than you should.*

I point at her, all my accusation perched on my fingertip. "I can't have you in my head before work."

Her eyebrow arches with the sharpness of a scythe. "Your baby got a hunger. Just seeing you would fill her right up."

My skipping heart: a flickering light in the cave. "It's a girl?"

Three knocks on the door. I wipe my face, answer.

"You talkin' on the phone?" Eden asks. She got on Anjelica Huston's face.

I look at my bed: only the strewn case files. "I been practicing."

We walk to her room. She takes up a dark wig between her hands, bounces it, studies the limp movement of the curls. "Cotton won't like this."

"He got to. Them curls looser than mine." I grab the wig, hold it up to the vanity's glow. "And shorter, too." Since moving in, every shampoo rinse leaves a bigger nest of snapped off curls in the drain. My hair getting brittle. Dry. I thought it was the abortion at first, how sucked-out I felt. But it's this heat they keep putting on me. I'm sure of it.

"We'll do your body first, then worry about all that." She drags the costume store bag from under her vanity. "You need help gettin' into this?" From the bag, a black box. In pink letters: Baby Bump. The plastic display window shows a smooth, round belly.

A groan, accidental as a hiccup, jumps out me.

Eden rubs my shoulder. "What's a matter?" Her hand flings off me, slaps her thigh. "Oh shit, oh damn, oh honey." She hugs me. "I sure wasn't thinkin'. The beer belly . . ."

I do an earthworm wiggle to get out her tight embrace. "It's okay," I say, "it's all right."

The Guns N' Roses shirt wraps around the big gut, makes my body look like a bad gift. The black jeans and steel-toed boots ain't much better. Eden paints my arms, the creases of my elbows, then stencils the marking of the monocle-wearing crow. The sponge-blended blues and grays beneath my eyes, a fog around the almost-black contact lenses.

"I'll be back, sweetie." The wig's wrapped around her fingers, wisps trail behind her, down the hallway. By the way she handles it, she ain't got plans of putting it on me. We only used one wig out of the four they got, but they got money to blow on wigs, and fake bellies, and good food.

Eden comes back with an annoyed look. "It ain't going to work." She shoves the wig in a drawer of the vanity. "Straighten, cut, curl. Deal?"

"That wig is just fine. I ain't cutting my hair."

Eden places her hand on her hip, tilts her head, looks at me like she talking to a kid who decorated the bathroom with crayons. "You've got real coarse hair. It'll grow faster after a cut." She say *coarse* like my hair is covered in fish guts.

Mama Brown used to tell me white women thought of our locks like black mambas, something with a dangerous beauty. Something that can't be tamed. Instead of saying: *You want to take my venom, Eden, you want to take my fangs,* my mouth is plugged by thoughts of my dwindling wad of cash. I need to save better. "How short?"

She pulls my longest piece of hair until it's straight, traces her finger down my spine, stops halfway down my back at the end. "Only a few inches." Her finger brushes the bottom of my shoulder blade.

"Fine," I say.

The sound of the shears clipping and cutting away at my hair make me think of a butcher. Eden got to marble me just right. The searing wand heats what's left on my head, my shoulders kissed by the frayed ends of wide curls. She teases and picks my hair, makes it frizzy, then greases it down with blue globs of gel.

The squeaking of the swiveling chair, the hateful truth of the mirror. I should have known like the other cases, I'd turn out just like the pictures. "Shorter than you said."

"It's only the curls," she says, "and I've got roots you can grind up and eat to make it grow faster."

Meanness drives me to the dining room. Eden's the one who feels the need to carve new bone structure in her face each day, all the Meryls and Sigourneys, and what if I took her makeup? And said: *It's only your identity.* And she got the gall to offer me roots. The last time she gave me something from the earth, it made me awful sick and dizzy and empty. I guess I wanted it, just like I want this job. Maybe I'm ungrateful. But some people got a magic way with what grows. Eden don't.

Already sweat starts to dew beneath this fake gut. Cotton nods, like he's being convinced of something. He stands behind the camera, floats his finger above the button. "Go to the twilight," he says.

I ain't here. This fake baby bump ain't making me itch. I am Jeremiah, standing in the cocoon of Oregon forest. I don't know what it's like to be almost-mama. The only thing my stomach know is the berries I shouldn't have consumed. Which is probably why I feel sick. And probably why ahead, a bridge that hadn't been before stretches over a vast expanse of nothing. On the other side, summer blooms, tended-to pastures. And to my left, three goats with too-wise beards graze on moss. I am lost. The bridge, rickety and wooden, sways with no wind, the rope handles choked by star jasmine, and maybe it won't hold me. At the edge, I get my answer: a man in the center who looks made of mountain, dirtied and blemished with lichen. *I am hungry,* he says. I look behind me, hope for someone bigger, tastier. The goats have gone. Through drool, the man says: *You cannot cross.* The bridge cradle-rocks, and if I could just sleep on the damp wood—but no, the mountain man's bones creak closer. *Are you all alone?* he asks. I get a chill. He looks back at all the green. *You can't have it,* he says. And the bridge carries him just fine, weightless over all that absence, straight to me.

On the table, in front of the laptop, a gin and tonic with a slice of lime floating. Cotton reaches over me to start the call, mutes the microphone, and that cologne makes me tingle, makes me wonder if he feeling a fever being so close to me. Then I'm reminded of my reflection in the camera and try not to laugh when Mary answers. A thin woman in a pink shirtdress with little cows and ducks printed all over. Her hair sits in a high bun, black with strands of gray. In the background, a window open, a breeze flapping the white lace curtains. Beyond the window, a field.

Mary's smile wavers. She taps her finger on her desk. No ring with fat diamonds clicks against the wood, bare knuckle, and I wonder if the loss of him left her loveless.

"Do you know I talk to you every day? Do you hear me?"

I nod. *Yes, woman, I listen.* But she doesn't sound like a woman; she sounds like a toddler, stunted and cartoon.

"I see you in stars and in numbers and in every animal I meet." Her hands rub together like she putting on lotion. "But I don't want to hurt your feelings." She say this like she half-believes it, but a bigger part of her wants to see me wounded. "Truth is . . . you know, we don't have to get into that right now."

A twisting mouth like I just got to know, but I can wait.

"The land is doing good," she says, "you'd tell me land can't be anything but, isn't that so?"

I nod, yes, that is something I would say, and sip the gin and tonic.

"I cheated on you."

Bringing my hand to my face, the empty space where my hair hung pushes me into my act, sad and asking why.

"Just the other night." She scratches her finger on that patch of skin where a ring might sit. "We met for dinner."

I try making my eyes understanding.

Mary looks around like she's embarrassed even though nobody else is in her room. "Am I selfish?"

Am I? Me, holding Mama Brown prisoner in some in-between. Two missing fingernails could be an accident. Next time I see her, they'll probably be right back. She'll even have soft cuticles, probably in need of a manicure. Maybe it's something about the way I don't mean to conjure her—if I could bring her here when I'm feeling light and got it in me to giggle, I bet she'd look like a picture of her past self, in the spent days. I can't tell Eden about this—maybe Cotton, but probably not. Cigarette Sammy would listen.

"I just had to let you know."

Just as Cotton reaches across me to end the call, Mary weeps. Her time is up.

"That was good. You looked totally despondent." Cotton wiggles his twine and slips it in his pocket. "So good."

"Eden," I say, "can you give me a quick ride?"

"Sure, sweetie. Where?"

"I just need to get a few things."

Fifteen minutes later, we pull into Mama Brown's driveway. The windows dark. Not a sign of life or anything beyond.

"Can you wait here and honk if anyone pulls up?" I ask.

She nods.

I walk up to the door, creep into the empty darkness, flick on a light. "Cigarette Sammy? It's me. It's Magnolia." The pizza boxes I been sending here sit on the coffee table, open and empty. At least he been eating. I check the rooms, the closets, the tub. He ain't here. He really left me. I lock myself in the bathroom and sob. Mama Brown said I got a right to feel, but crying don't feel right, don't feel like some baptism.

Once I'm back in the hearse, Eden says, "You didn't get anything."

I don't say anything.

"You been cryin'?"

"I couldn't find what I was looking for."

"That's got to be hard, you goin' in there where your landlord . . ." She pulls out the driveway. "It's better to forget."

"One more place," I say.

The hearse rolls into the parking lot of People's Gas Station. No one at the pumps. No one searching the trash cans for treasures.

"We can go now. I just wanted to see something."

"You sure?" she asks.

When we get back, I go to my bathroom and stay in the shower long after I got the white and gray washed off me. The water runs cool enough to invite goose bumps, but I don't want to step out. The cold drops slide down the small hills of my tits, down the popped balloon of my stomach. My bloating and bleeding all gone.

14

At breakfast, I still got nerves ticking my heart over Cigarette Sammy. Only thing I can think to do is call Sugar Foot. Rent is due next week anyway. Call and play nice. I don't want to hear that grime in his voice, that rusted saxophone talk he think is so smooth. And him, making some confession to Pastor Wooly, talking about sorrys.

Eden and I share two pieces of burnt toast scraped with grape jelly, oatmeal dusted with cinnamon sugar.

"I'm off to the mountains," Eden-as-Diane-Keaton says.

But, first, I got to go to Mama Brown's one more time just to see, and Cigarette Sammy will probably be there, and I'll fill his belly and know he's okay. "I'm going for a walk," I say.

My feet hit the sidewalk; Mama Brown choir steps behind me. She belts in a voice louder than the passing traffic. Gritty, sweet: "Goin' down the road feelin' bad. Honey, babe, Lord. Goin' down the road feelin' bad."

My feet match her rhythm.

"You remember that song?" she asks. I don't turn to face her—keep my eyes on the long stretch of sidewalk ahead. "We used to sing that when we'd go on our little walks. You remember?"

I put my phone to my ear so the passing cars won't think I'm crazy. "I remember."

"You good at tapping into memory when you want to." She coughs, sounds like she been smoking a cigar.

"When'd you get that cough, Mama?" My pace's down to a trickle, let her catch up.

"It could be last Christmas or two seconds ago, shit. It all feels the same."

We pass a plaza with a smoke shop, a Big Lots, a beauty supply. "Eden's been frying my hair."

"I didn't want to say nothing, but you looking a little crispy."

I keep my phone pressed to my ear and laugh with her. "Let me see your nails."

Mama shoves her hands behind her back like I told her I can palm read and her future is littered with broken things.

"Please."

Her right hand is fine, her left hand: fingernails gone, pinky dislocated, curved into a shepherd's crook. "You said you'd think about it," she says.

"What happened to your pinky?"

"I saw Cricket." She tries to pop her pinky back in place—it falls to the sidewalk, rolls light as an empty coin wrapper to the gutter.

"Creepy Bible dude?" That stops my legs. "No, you imagining things."

"Says you to the ghost." She scratches her arm with the no-fingernail hand, don't seem to remember they ain't there to take away her itch. "He wasn't nothing but a flash, like when you close your eyes after looking at the sun and can still see the shape just floating behind your eyelids."

"That's just old fears coming back," I say. When I was little, if I was acting up, she'd wait until my back was turned and knock on the wall with her knuckle. She'd say: *Magnolia, that woodpecker coming for you.* And that always made me stop. Here she is now, trying to scare me into behaving, into seeing that unformed child.

"You know the first time you talked was to the crows?" she says.

That makes me giggle. "What?"

"You was around eight months, crawling around the garden while I was pulling weeds. There was a murder of them on the edge of the tree line gobbling up some acorns. Once you caught sight of them, you cawed, and they cawed right back. That's when I knew you was smart." Another cough, sounds like pneumonia. "Since you so smart, tell me what happens when the already-perished got to perish again."

"Just give me a little longer." I pick up speed.

"You making more problems for yourself the longer you put off seeing your child. I'm trying to help you."

The distance between us grows. "It don't even got lungs."

She stops, discarded, with a twisted mouth by the curb.

No one's in Mama Brown's living room aside from a couple flies, perched with praying hands on the stack of empty pizza boxes. He got to be too scared to stay for long. He must hate me for putting him in Sugar Foot's path.

The phone glows watery through my eyes. My hands shake—takes me three times to retype the address and send the message to another stranger who can only offer a fleeting warmth.

Twenty minutes later, a purple hybrid pulls into my driveway. A guy with shaggy hair, big brown eyes, pale skin marked with stick-and-poke tattoos, meets me by the garden. I lead him in, and our feet are cushioned by a carpet of honeysuckle. It has claimed the space. We go to a shaded spot next to budding White Nancy. He kisses me with salted lips and a popcorn-tasting tongue. I stroke him until he bloats in my fingers, but the heaviness in my chest don't go away.

First, he gets on top, and I try to play pretend, lying memories—our first kiss was by the Tennessee River, dripping in moonlight, and we eat at the same wing spot every Saturday for date night, and we just adopted a puppy named Cookie. But he don't touch me like he knows me, not enough sense in him to feel my body and mean it. Ain't a beat of good rhythm in his thrusting.

"Say you love me."

He pretends he don't hear me. Why can't he match my groove, why can't he shove his tongue in my ear and taste my thoughts and know?

I straddle him and grind. He thinks I want more of his off-key humping, and I quit my moving with a look of *you finished now?* until he stops. He twirls his thumb on my nipple. I slap his hand away. "Boy, you couldn't touch me if you wanted." It goes like this for too long—me trying to cum, him reaching for my body, me swatting.

"Carolina, what is your problem?"

That brings me there. The feel-good shaking brief as a breath.

My sadness don't go away; feels heavier with each layer of clothes I slip back into.

On his back, sweat-free, dirt-caked. "Where are you going?"

I wave bye-bye.

He grunts like he's annoyed he paused Wes Anderson for this.

I leave the garden, middle finger raised high, into the forest threaded lush by kudzu.

At eleven, I open the Domino's app on my phone, send a large cheese pizza and a bottle of apple juice to Mama Brown's address. The sight of another pizza box at the doorstep might make Cigarette Sammy spray vomit all over the yard. It's all I been feeding him lately. Maybe I could start cooking for him again. Maybe if I came more often, I'd catch him. He'd see me frying something salty and forgive me. But then there's that thunderstorm boiling green on the horizon: Sugar Foot could always stop by while I'm there. To hell with Sugar Foot. I got to call him and say: *Have you seen my friend?* and *Why you talking about me to Pastor Wooly?* and *Please, where is my friend?* and *I hope each time you speak my name it feel like swallowed tacks.*

After lunch, I join Cotton in his study. He sits on the sofa, nose tucked in *The Breast* by Philip Roth.

"Can we watch a movie?" I ask.

"Of course," he says.

I'll only watch one. Just one movie, and then I'll handle this Sugar Foot business. We watch *Purple Noon*. I want to go to Italy. I want to go in the summer and drink up the blue and bright white of the days, strut on cobblestones in nothing but a bikini and coconut sunscreen. I could write poetry on hot sand and then cool off in that yawning mouth of sea. The drama of the ending fades to black. He asks, "Want to watch another?"

Sugar Foot can wait. I go to the kitchen and make popcorn with Hershey Kisses while he searches the internet for *Taxi Driver*. We watch. With every mouthful, I suck the salted puffs and chocolate, shrink them with my warm spit. Near the end, when the guns shoot and blood sprays, my gut pokes out with the pressure of too much butter and sugar. Cotton leans into the projection, hypnotized by the gore. "This is a feeling," he says.

"Is that how you paint," I ask, "with those feelings?"

"I can show you." He leaves the study with a quickness, like he knows an unwatched pot's about to froth over, and returns with two blank canvases. Props both on easels. "I guess painting is intuitive."

"What's your intuition got to say?"

"You're in a rush," he says. "Let's see where it guides us."

We face each other and paint, both canvases hidden from each other. Our background's lit up by another movie, *Eyes Wide Shut,* and I am the lingerie dangling over a hooker's tub. Our eyes play tag between the two of us, the canvas, and the rich orgies with fancy masks. When the credits roll, we show our creations. Mine: blues and purples swirling and swimming in black. His: a man with a clock face, walking down a flight of stone stairs.

He don't comment on my painting, only gives it a smirk. "What did you think of the movie?"

"I don't know. Maybe it's telling America the rich get to be naked and shameless."

"It's obviously commenting on how embarrassing it is to be middle class."

"I don't see that."

"Oh, so you're right and I'm wrong?"

"Is that what your intuition telling you?"

"No, in fact—" In a bowl, he mixes crimson oil paint and linseed syrup with his finger. "It's telling me you should take off your shirt."

I finger the edges of my leopard print and give him a playful smile. We ain't talked about his birthday. Most we've acknowledged it is by trading glances heavy with mystery. My shirt raised just above my belly button, I make my voice sultry as candle smoke, ask, "What do you think of my hair?"

Mixing the paint, his eyes fix on the fabric that flirts with my finger pads. "Like a blackberry bush."

"Stop burning it," I say.

"No office talk." The paint and oil got a ruby gleam.

I slide my top off the rest of the way, let it fall to the floor in a whisper.

He stalks over, wrist still vulture-circling in the bowl. "Do you want to see *Basic Instinct?*" He grips my chin with his red-slick hand, don't seem to notice it weeping on our shoes, the floor. His palm slithers down my throat. Another dip in the paint before he lowers the bowl; his hand rises with a gruesome handful. Uses both hands to massage it into my tits, brushes circles on my nipples. "Let me know if I hurt you." But the truth in his eyes don't match any tiptoed care. Looking at me with a distance so thick it could slough off at any moment. He squeezes my face, leaves the mark of clenching fingers on my cheeks, my lips, temples. "Does this feel truthful?"

"Yes," I say, "yes."

He kisses my forehead, and I think it's in that fairy-tale way, but then he sucks. He leeching his way from the edge of my eyebrow, down the bridge of my nose, right on my mouth, along my neck. Teeth burrow in my collarbones. And that nibble turns into a gnaw. Searing pain, throbbing muscle.

I push him away. "Good night, Cotton."

He stands unmoving in my exit, panting and rose mouthed in heat.

I go to my room with a bottle of Campari. Chug it in the shower. Poke my head from behind the curtain with each pump of soap until I'm sure I ain't still a bloodied-looking doll. In the aftermath, the scrubbed-away hue leaves me stained pink. Cotton's hunger is something I got to pick apart before I feed him. Because what if he swallows all of me he can get, leaves me nothing but bone?

Out the shower, only moonlight filters through the windows; it's past eleven. I search: Is it bad to eat pizza for a week? The internet say: *Did you mean, is it bad to eat pizza once a week?* I know Cigarette Sammy's stomach must be full of bloat and hurt. I just got to save up and build a good picket fence around the house.

I unblock Sugar Foot and dial his number. He picks up on the first ring.

"Miss Magnolia," Sugar Foot says. "Where you been?"

"I got rent money to give you," I say.

"Now you know you ain't got to worry about that. I thought you was calling 'cause of my texts." His voice sound like sorrow, like he been falling asleep remembering how he got warmth from all my flailing. "Come to think of it, you ain't answered any of my texts. You block my number, Miss Magnolia?"

"My phone been cut off," I say.

"Oh, you mean you ain't seen nothing I said? I been real worried about you. I got something real hard to say."

I stand and pace in the sound of his breathing. I know he licking his lips thinking of the right words.

"Awhile back, I stopped by to see how you was doing. And wouldn't you know I saw a lit cigarette on the coffee table. And I thought to myself, now Miss Magnolia don't smoke nothing."

"I smoke sometimes."

"I got a bad feeling in my bones when I seen that. I thought to myself, now who been up in here? 'Cause that ain't Miss Magnolia's smoke. Later that night, I parked my car up the mountain and walked down to your yard. I hid in that little thicket of trees and I waited and waited and waited. And right before midnight, wouldn't you know it!" His giggling telling me he's too full of excitement. "Some dirty man stumbling through your front door. Like he owned the place. I ran on up, and I told him to get. But he wasn't listening to me. He just moved his feet, and I knew he was on some kind of drug."

"He ain't—"

"It take more than some crazy man to scare Old Sugar Foot. Don't you worry your pretty little head, Miss Magnolia. I got him locked up right away." More of his little kid giggling. "I know how to protect me and mine; if I ain't got but one talent, it's knowing how to protect."

"What you mean?" I feel like I got a cherry pit lodged in my throat blocking the: *Oh, you motherfucker.*

"I called the cops. And then I told that bad man to call on the Good Lord above if they ever let him out. I tell you something, he better thank God I ain't have my pistol."

I can't steady my breathing.

"Miss Magnolia. I want to apologize."

"For?" I ain't ever known Sugar Foot to turn to the law like that. Shit, he helped Mama Brown make money back then.

"For that man coming in unannounced. Look like he cleaned your dishes though. That bastard ate the food you been leaving out for me. You a good woman, feeding your man like that. I just pulled up to your place, Miss Magnolia. I see a pizza waiting. You around?"

My finger ends the call. Cigarette Sammy locked up. I just know he in his cell bent in a corner, muddy and bruised, tears and snot leaking out his confused face. I dart out my room with Campari in my grip, shut my door on the way to mute the chirping of my ringtone. Into Cotton's study, alcohol burn sitting in my throat, and try to tell him what happened with calmness.

"What? Slow down," he says. He looking on edge, half-mad at me for leaving him to stroke alone, half-worried he put too much fear in me, and the twine in his palm is bunched up from his stress tugs. His mouth and teeth tinted a faded rouge. With his lips shut, he only looks healthy, a good, pumping heart.

"I need a ride to the jail," I say.

"What's going on?"

"My friend." I flood my mouth with drink and push it down, over the lump in my throat, then explain everything from gas station cigars, to Cigarette Sammy's shuffling feet, to Sugar Foot and his awful talk, making sure to leave out the litter: Mama Brown's funeral, the flushed-out life.

Cotton rolls his wristwatch to his concerned face. "Aunt Eden will be back within the hour. I'll take you."

Watching YouTube videos, painting my nails can't distract me. I got to move, got to walk out this bad energy until I don't feel like a struck tuning fork. Outside with a pack of my smokes, I pace barefoot on the still-warm asphalt of the parking lot.

All that money and time I spent thinking it was going to Cigarette Sammy. Thinking I was giving him peace. Thinking I was bringing dawn to that cave in me. Whole time I was nurturing a briar-prowling coyote, the reflection of my naked body glinting off his drool-shined teeth. Cigarette Sammy probably done shuffled his shoes down until they thin as wet tissue. When he see me, he going to spit right in my eye. I will say: *I'm the sorriest I ever been.* And he will bunch up all the spit in his mouth and aim it right at my pupil. He going to say: *Don't look at me with that lake in your eye.* He going to say: *You swamp-face bitch.*

The hearse scrapes and bumps up the parking lot. I fumble my cigarette, almost fall over trying to pick it up. Eden got the window rolled down with the fog of tobacco curling out her singing lips: "You are my sunshine, my only sunshine."

I holler at her.

She shuts her eyes, lifts her head to the roof of the hearse, the cords in her neck bulging and wiggling. "You make me happy when skies are gray."

I pull open her door, but she don't look, just keeps the song, the smoke, the punching scent of whiskey spouting from her mouth. "You'll never know, dear, how much I love you."

"You drunk bitch," I say.

She cackles, yells as I rush inside the parlor. "Please don't take my sunshine away."

I leave her wasted ballad and gather all the cash I got out my room, find Cotton in the kitchen smearing soft cheese on rosemary crackers. "She won't get out from behind the wheel."

Cotton crams a cracker in his mouth, follows.

It takes both of us to pull her limp body off the seat. She spills onto the parking lot, scrapes her knee, pebbles denting her flesh. A clumsy giggle. "Humpty Dumpty had big balls."

I slide into the passenger seat and tap my feet. Cotton stands in front of a headlight's beam with clenched fists resting on his hips, angry and holy in that baptism of light. Eden makes snow angels on the asphalt. He lifts her and guides her to the door, and she leans against the frame, arms dangling. I can barely hear them over the noise of the air conditioner.

"Home," she sings, "home on the range."

"You scraped the hearse. What did you hit?" he asks.

"Where the deer and the antelope play."

"No one wants to cart dead—"

"Where seldom is heard—"

"—bodies around—"

"—a discouraging word."

"—in a goddamned hooptie." Cotton ushers her inside. One minute melts. Two, four, six.

The smell of rotting meat pushes out the vents. I look in the mirror. Mama Brown sits in the back seat. "That white bitch is a whole mess."

"Mama . . ." I bring the flame to a new cigarette, poke my hand out the window to scatter the ash. Can't bring myself to say: *I see you falling apart, and I might just lose Cigarette Sammy, and Cotton's a grabby man with a morbid tongue.*

"It don't hurt, really, it don't."

"She is a mess," I say.

Her laughter forces out more stench. "Somebody need to D.A.R.E. program her ass."

A small laugh presses through my lips.

"About Cricket——"

"Mama, this ain't the time. Please."

"Your baby's crying, anyway." She turns to shadows.

Cotton steps into the night, his face red as a garden tomato. Grunts when he plops behind the wheel. "Tomorrow is intervention day." We pull onto Broadway. "That does it. We have to intervene." Cotton presses his foot easy on the gas.

"Can you speed up a little?" I ask.

"Magnolia, about earlier——"

"It was fun," I say.

"I'm sorry about your friend." He stops at the light, turns his head to face me in the glow of the street. "Jail is the most anachronistic institution." The light changes to green. "Aside from religion and marriage."

We go on shadowed backroads, over flattened bodies of raccoons, possums, skunks. Outside Knox County Jail, cloned rows of waxed police cruisers. My whole body tightens. Cotton clicks his tongue. "A parade of fascists."

I'm out the hearse and running to the tall glass door of the jailhouse before Cotton shifts the gear to park. Inside, an old woman sits behind a desk, cracks sunflower seeds with her teeth. Her hair: cropped short and dyed the color of cattails. Two cops walk by and glance at me over the rim of their paper cups of coffee. I walk with a gentle step across the floor flecked with vinyl chips.

"I need to bail somebody out," I say.

"Name? Date of birth?" The earth and salt in the woman's breath hit my nose. She got suspicion on her face, looking at the color on my skin.

"Sammy," I say, "Samuel."

"Last?" She crunches a shell, spits it onto a dirty paper towel. "I ain't sure."

She looks away, shoves her short fingers in the bag of seeds, pockets a handful in her cheek. Her words're blocked by the wet cluster in her mouth: "Can't help you, darlin'."

"You got to help me."

"You want to bail out every Samuel in here?"

An arm wraps tight around my waist. I got to stop myself from swatting and clawing. Cotton speaks in his laminated drawl. "What's goin' on here?"

The woman's mouth opens just a little, revealing flesh-colored mush in between her teeth and on her tongue. "You're with her?"

"Yes, Shirley. Yes ma'am," Cotton says.

I look at her name tag. Shirley Jones. I wonder if she's related to Quarry.

Shirley's bunched-up face relaxes with his response, but she lifts her slim nose to the cork ceiling tiles. "What'd he do?"

"Breaking and entering. Or maybe trespassing," he says.

The keyboard clicks. "That don't narrow it down much. When was the arrest?"

Cotton still got me belted in his arm. "Within the past couple of weeks," he says.

Shirley rotates the monitor to show me a grained mugshot. Cigarette Sammy boxed in the screen: eyes lost in a murk, body in a sweet potato jumpsuit. "That's him." I poke the screen with my finger as if I got to convince myself the computer ain't something my head made up. "That's him. How much is bail?"

Shirley scratches a phone number onto a card damp with her stray spit. "You ain't going to want to pay the whole thing I imagine. Call Jimmy for bail bond arrangement, all right now."

I don't feel my legs take me to the two folding chairs next to
a watercooler. Don't want to sit on metal and call a man I don't
know and get a lesson on how the law runs on extension cords
and bony fluorescent tubes. In the year after I moved in with
Mama Brown, Quarry left Cherry three times. Every time he
left her, she got herself into some kind of trouble: possession,
disorderly conduct, assault. And every time Mama Brown would
get that call at one, two, three in the morning, she'd bundle me
up, and we'd drive on down to this jail. But she'd never let me
get out the car. She'd say: *You just wait here, baby, where you safe.*
She'd leave the car running, the heat or air conditioner on, the
doors locked. I'd always see her walk out with Cherry. Mama
Brown would leave her on the sidewalk and join me in the car.
As we drove away, she'd say, *If I let her in the car, she'd stink up your
mind with bad thoughts. She a grown woman. She'll find her way.* The
third time Mama Brown got her, she got in the car with a huff.
*No more of this. She draining my account and she want to come at me
with bad attitude? Tuh!* She never let me go in with her, into this
place.

This place blinding and sleepy all at once, like I'm in a hospital. Instead of rubbing alcohol and latex, I smell boiled eggs and
burnt coffee. But I guess both places got the grim reaper lurking
in their walls.

"Great, thanks so much." Cotton ends a call and slides his
phone in his pocket, looks up at me from the chair. I ain't realize
Cotton plucked the card from my hand, or that I been standing
this whole time, hypnotized by the cool stasis of the watercooler.
Cotton skates his palms back and forth and back across his thighs.
"Jimmy speaks like a mechanic."

"What'd he say?"

Cotton's voice comes out wrapped in gauze, as if our being here is a secret we got to keep.

"What?" I ask.

"He's checking the system to see if Sammy Cigarette has prior history with failure to appear. He'll call if we get the green light."

I ain't expect there would be a possibility of not getting him out tonight. Mama Brown would always pick up Cherry the same night. But like Mama Brown said, memory is a watery thing.

"I'm going to find a bathroom," I say. Down, down a hallway with the hum of fluorescent. I'm in the ribs of a great breathing beast. At the end of the hall stands a door with a cartoon woman in a triangle dress. Door locked behind me, I avoid the mirror, drip my attention to the porcelain bowl of the sink. The lips of the drain, crusted pink with soap. The faucet runs cool over the softest part of my wrist. Then, a muffled whine, the pipes singing when I shut off the flow. The sound gets louder, but I can't make it out. I pull the paper towels, rough as pavement, and dry my skin. My foot pressing the trash can pedal, the lid pops up: two broken eggshells, caulked lumps of boiled yolks, on a hill of soggy paper. That's when I hear the colicky cry of a newborn and scramble for the door, almost knocking into a woman pocked with acne scars. She wears pajamas, rocks a baby.

"Sorry," I say. I jog until I'm under the stable glow of tight, twisted bulbs. Cotton ain't at the seat. I don't see him anywhere.

Shirley clicks a paperclip on her desk. "He went to Jimmy's. Just down the road."

I go through the glass doors smudged with swirled fingerprints of cops and janitors and freed men and women, stand next to a trimmed bush. The sharp leaves shine plastic in the moonlight. Halfway burned through my second cigarette, I hear the slamming of a car door. Cotton saunters to the front of the building.

"Any updates?"

He jumps at my nicotine-choked voice, then shifts his direction to me, the tips of our shoes kissing.

"I paid the man. He's going to call Shirley, and then we can get him."

I stretch my neck to a window. Shirley grips the macaroni handset to her ear, bobs her head. "How much I owe you?"

"Don't worry about it."

I drop my ember to the sidewalk. "You sure?"

Cotton plunges his wrists in his pockets, nods at the window. Shirley leans across the desk, mouth pressed flat, beckons us with fluttering fingers. I hug him quick. His body as stiff as stalk. By the time we get to Shirley's desk, Cigarette Sammy shuffles out through a big black door. He don't see me, only shuffles on to the vending machine and stands in the space between the wall and the keypad. Cotton moves antsy with sadness in his eyes. He squeezes my elbow.

I trudge to Cigarette Sammy's turned head. He kicking little tufts of dust.

He leaps and faces me when I call his name, makes a tornado-siren sound in his chest and wraps his arms around me. I hug his plump body, smelling like rust and onions. The thorns of his stubble poke me. We rock back and forth in our embrace, both a little crumpled by relief of touch. When we let go, I smooth a couple dollar bills and buy a MoonPie and a bottle of apple juice. He gobbles up the sweet as we guide him to the hearse.

Sandwiched between the two men, I sit, waiting for Cotton to start the engine. "I am so sorry." I turn to Cigarette Sammy, searching for his eyes, but they look past me, through the windshield, at the dozing cop car in front of us. "I am so, so sorry. It won't ever happen again."

He tilts the bottle of juice to his frown, stares down the dead headlights.

"Where to?" Cotton asks.

I type in directions to Mama Brown's place. We ride, windows down, to the free jazz of crickets and bullfrogs. The night air got a living warmth.

Cigarette Sammy lifts a strand of my hair and grunts.

"Short, ain't it?" I say.

Cigarette Sammy drifts off, the first time I seen him deep in rest.

"Laconic man," Cotton says.

The tires chomping the gravel driveway jolts Cigarette Sammy from his dreams, makes him twitch like fresh-hit roadkill and drop his juice on the floor. I got to stop myself from saying: *If we can get puke out them fibers, we can clean your drink.* Cotton don't know about all that.

I reach across him and open the door, and we scoot out, struggle to get on our feet. The gravel kneads my soles through the thin flip-flops. "Come on in," I say. "You hungry?"

He look at the house, and I think I see what he sees: dark, curtain-draped eyes, an unlocked mouth hiding jagged teeth.

"It ain't a monster," I say, "it don't even bite." I hook my arm in his and try to walk, but he rooted to the loose rocks. "It won't ever happen again." Another step, my body snapping into his. "Come on now. I know you tired."

Cotton kills the engine and steps out. "What's going on?" He slips out his drawl, talks with his practiced, natural voice.

"He don't want to move," I say.

Cotton approaches with a careful step, as if Cigarette Sammy a rabid hog. He reaches out, massages Cigarette Sammy's shoulder. Cigarette Sammy swings his knuckles; they thud against Cotton's jaw. Cotton staggers back. Now everybody got shuffling feet.

"Get him under control," Cotton says.

"Leave him be," I say. I tug on Cigarette Sammy's arm. He yanks his weight out my clasped fingers and runs, emptied bottle of juice and plastic wrapper tumbling to the dirt behind him. I chase after.

"Leave him be," Cotton says.

Cigarette Sammy goes into the trees. He calls back, "You ain't my-my."

I stop at the edge of the forest, beg the milk stars to shine on the twigs and acorn shells and gnarled roots so I can follow his footprints. He makes the leaves gossip when he pushes past—my eyes catch his shape. He look back, beating his feet into the night, and on his face, in that branch heavy darkness, is hell-inspired terror. He afraid of me and all the bad news I bring. I don't feel my body crumple or the rocks scrape my knees, don't feel my hot tears. I don't even feel Cotton's touch carrying my folded self to the hearse.

Because I ain't here. I am a pretty hairbrush. I am a pretty hairbrush with a handle of bronze, teeth made of boar bristle. I am studded with eye-size emeralds. I am in Germany. A woman uses me to smooth her long butter hair. She sits me on the dresser and unspools her locks out the window of the tower. The sun heats the ground and sends up the smell of wild strawberries. She look to see the ripe fruit, and there's a man standing instead. *Get me out this gloom,* she say. *I want to touch.* He climbs up her locks, not a tangle to be found, all the way to her roots. The man say: *Let's eat like the bees do.* The long-haired woman say: *Let's nibble like butter-flies.* They leave me in the small room at the tip of the tower. But it's okay. I am a hairbrush made for working knots. I am a hairbrush. I don't mind being by my lonesome.

15

It's been two weeks since Cotton said we'd give Eden an intervention. The blood dripping from her Susan Sarandon nose bounces on the edge of her saucer, splatters finger shaped onto her poached eggs. "Aw, hell," she says. She scurries to the kitchen, returns with a blue dish towel and wipes the chipped china, smears red from the peppered egg. "This weather's breakin' me down." Her teeth tear into the white rubber, nostril plugged with a damp rag. "Heat drier than a nun's cunt."

Across the stretch of table, Cotton grins at his phone screen. He don't see the blood or listen to her lie, don't see the edges of her jaw flex, hear the hard scrape of her molars. He keeps telling himself and me, no more of this. But every time Eden pushes past her limit, he scoops up vomit into a dustpan, scratches away the hardened candlewax she smears on the walls. When she strips in the parking lot, he races to cloak her cantaloupe tits with a quilt.

Cotton don't look up from his phone, speaks, "Oh, Magnolia, I was able to get the charges dropped against Sa—"

"Cigarette Sammy."

"Yes, yes, sorry."

"How?"

"Quick phone calls to Sugar Foot and the prosecutor." What he really mean is: *My name carries weight; can't you feel it?*

Cotton brings the phone to his ear. "Cotton speaking." He walks out the dining room.

"That's the fifth call this morning," Eden says. "Why ain't you eatin'?"

I coax my eyes away from the sangria-colored crust on the neck of Eden's fork. "I was trying to hear what he's saying."

Eden giggles, tilts her ear to Cotton's faraway voice, cushioned quiet between the walls. "A girl after my own heart." She dips her finger in the spilling yolk and sucks. "He can't keep a secret for long, you wait and see. He'll let it slip by the end of the day."

Cotton whistles some old piano song when he parades into the dining room, his wide smile deepening his dimples. "Business is going to blow up." He clicks his heels three times. "I'm talking Fourth of July in our wallets."

"How many cases we got?" I ask.

He leans on the table, pitches his hands into tents by his sparkling water. "Get this. We have—" His phone vibrates. "We'll talk later. We'll go to Chesapeake's tonight to celebrate. Need to make a website." Good shoes click, click steady across the floor. The door to his study booms shut.

Eden wiggles in her seat: a coked-up wooly worm. "We'll be eatin' good tonight."

It ain't until after I clean the dishes and wake up from a nap that Cotton comes out of the study, phone still pressed to his ear. He shuffles into the kitchen and takes a bottle of chardonnay. His laughter sounds like the caw of a crow, pushed out and loud, to let the other person know he means it. "Yes, the analytics—" He retreats to his study to discuss coins and appointments. I hold my breath for thirty seconds, then tiptoe to the door and cup my ear to the oak. All I hear is the trickling of the wine to glass and the spirit in his *mm-hmms* and *oh, yesses*. My neck aches from leaning into his secrecy.

I give up, sit by the fire. Somewhere in the house, Eden snores. I don't like the direction she's headed—she either talks like an auctioneer or walks all syrupy with sleep. Before Cherry gave me up to Mama Brown, her snores sounded like rearranging furniture, the corners of her mouth lined with cottony spit. A parched mouth can only say so much: *Get the mail* and *Buy me smokes* and *You ain't ever been, far as I can remember, you ain't ever been*.

My thigh tickles. One, two, three carpenter ants crawl across my skin. I follow the growing number with my eyes. A trail of them leads to Mama Brown, trudging up from the stairwell. She hollers when she catches my eye.

"Magnolia, you got to get out and fix this."

Her coming in here like this in the open space. Knowing I'll look crazy. I whisper, "Fix what?"

"He's going to take." She inches closer, heavy stepping.

My lips start to quiver, leaves ready to fall, but I don't let the tears come. "Mama, you looking rough." A clump of her beauty parlor curls missing, a pus-slick wound on her scalp. A wink of bone just beneath. Even when she was near the end, even when I was sure I'd be reading her to sleep any night, and she'd just never wake up again, she at least had her body. Whole. Weak and easy, but she had that.

"He came back again." She sits on the floor, squirms up to me, puts her hands on my feet. Only three fingernails left. "Didn't say nothing. Just kept clutching that Bible to his chest and grinning at the swaddle."

"What you going on about?"

Her eyes plead: *Don't make me say it, baby; if I say it, he'll come and snatch us both.* "Cricket."

She going on again about that scary salesman from her little girl days. I thought she was trying to trick me, but I can see she really believe he coming for her. A couple months ago, around the time when I realized ain't no miracle on its way to beat the dementia, she started staring above my head, saying: *Hi, Mommy, what you doing here?* I'd say: *Your mommy ain't here, I am.* But she swore her mommy was in the vents, telling her to peek inside. Now I'm starting to wonder if what plagues her body reaching out to her mind, too. And where the soul fit into all this?

She kneads my shoes. "Even saying his name . . ." Her breath smells like cooking hamburger meat. "You remember how I taught you that a popped egg yolk meant you could make a wish; and blown dandelions, two; and a shooting star you could make three?"

She really losing it. I got to fight the urge to soothe her, finger comb her hair. That'd leave me slimed and stinking. Instead, I nod: *Yes, I remember.*

"That's 'cause I really believed in wishes. In saying something will happen and it will." She struggles to grip the couch, sits upright on the floor, back against the skirt. "I should've never said his name."

"I thought you said you only saw some kind of afterimage of him. Just for a second."

"This was after I spoke on him some more."

"What he wanting from you?"

"I ain't sure." She takes a deep breath, sounds like she got flimsy pieces of plastic flapping in her lungs. "He been forgotten for so long."

I nudge her with a chuckle. "Maybe he tired of being forgotten."

"You don't listen to me serious."

"There ain't no Bloody Marys or Candymans." I tug on one of the ends of her curls, gentle. She don't break. "Only men who too happy to find a woman alone."

Her laugh sounds more like a *huh*. "Not even a heart attack stops them." She turns to me, one remaining eye holding me hostage. "He wants the baby."

"Let him," I say, "you don't want it no how."

"I want to get back to my peace, and if that child is my only way . . ."

"Send him to me. I'll cuss him back to hell."

She gets to cackling. "It sure is nice to see you." Another squeeze of my foot. "Don't think I don't miss you fierce."

"Everything'll be all right," I say.

She turns to me, slow as an old door, pauses. Listening. She whispers, "I hear him." She rises with groans, limps away with hurry down the stairwell. The ants follow.

The flushing of a toilet, footsteps weighed down with grog. For a moment, I half believe Cricket coming out the pipes to snatch me. It's only Eden——she staggers by the fire, a fan of false lashes drooping from her right eye. Her foundation's wrinkled, her Susan Sarandon face a little melty. I wonder if she letting the paint peel away.

"I had this awful nightmare." She yawns. "Where's Cotton?"

"On the phone still. How you feeling?"

"Bone tired," she says. She stretches her arms back toward the flames. "Lordy, what time is it?"

"'Bout 6:30."

"Shit," she says, "you ain't wearing that, are you?"

While Eden touches up her face, I slip into a dress toned like my flesh, laced with black roses; pat eyeshadow the color of fool's gold on my lids; and slick a soft pink gloss on my pucker. Eden shimmies into a scarlet dress with a cowl neckline. We wait in the dining room, perfumed with Chanel, and swallow merlot. We've almost drained the bottle when Cotton strolls in, wearing a black turtleneck beneath his teal suit.

"You ain't goin' to be hot in that?" Eden asks.

"Sacrifices for fashion," he says.

The restaurant stinks of boiled lobster. The hostess fingers through a black book until she finds our reservation, guides us through tables of wrist-watched men and pin-haired women, and I know if I were to lean down and sniff, they'd smell like mara-schino cherries and cut wood. They don't notice me. They don't know I don't belong here.

We sit in a booth. The hostess places glossed menus on the table. I scan the room's cozy dimness: pearly light fixtures, bub-bling aquariums. "This place is nice."

A moon-faced waitress approaches the table. Her name tag: Dinah. She got sad eyes and a pretty smile. Sparkling water, White Russians. No one cards me here. All the meals cost somewhere between twenty-five and forty dollars, a week of groceries in one night. Hell.

"This place is real nice," I say.

The waitress thumps the heavy glasses of the creamy cocktails on coasters. "Are you ready to order?" Her notepad: black leather, lined with gold.

Cotton orders seared ahi tuna salad, blue crab cocktail; Eden orders shrimp and grits and please burn the sausage; I order a cup of crab bisque, but Cotton says live a little, it's a celebration, so I get pan-blackened scallops with rice.

Dinah grins as she writes and leaves us to our dewed glasses.

Eden sips. "You ready to tell us why you've been busier than a cat covering shit on marble floor?"

Cotton spreads his arms back, rests them on top of the plush booth. "I was being interviewed, get this, by *Vice*. They're writing an article about our art. Apparently, a smaller website penned something about us, and other media outlets want to know more." He drops his arms, leans his smooth face toward us. "We have five new cases, and the article hasn't even been published yet."

"Lordy, Lordy," Eden says.

I want to chase the waitress down and tell her to add filet mignon and truffle fries and a bottle of ancient wine.

"Another thing, Magnolia, and I hope I haven't crossed a boundary. Your landlord . . ." He slips his hand in the inner pocket of his suit and brushes his thumb over the thick edge of a packet of paper. It flaps, makes a breeze in the shellfish air. "I bought the house." He slides the document into his pocket. "I was going to tell you tomorrow after I changed the locks. You can move back in if you want. But I think having you around has been . . ." He looks at the ceiling, taps the table. "Like a revival."

This smile I got makes every muscle in my face ache. That house is mine, mine with no trespassers. Sugar Foot can't come back. I don't need to build no picket fence or iron gate around the yard. I ain't even got to string up padlocks or bar the windows. Long as Cotton keeps his word—I got my own house. My own house where I can lock away all my hurts, and no one can get to them but me.

This good feeling of ownership. Cherry knew this feeling once. When I was ten, Cherry came over to Mama Brown's for supper. We had catfish. Cherry looked pretty, her face a little filled out, her lips smooth.

I was smearing too-cold butter on a roll when Cherry said, "You know, I've been doing real good here lately."

Mama Brown sipped her beer and nodded. "We see that. And we so happy for you."

Cherry gave a little smile to her hands. "I've been clean for a month now. I got a typing job. I moved into my apartment yesterday."

"That's so nice," Mama Brown said.

"Magnolia, if you want, you can come back anytime. I left Quarry. Things is different now." Cherry had a pleading in her eyes. It hurt to see.

After she left, I helped Mama Brown clean up. "Does she mean it this time?" I asked.

Mama Brown stood with a stack of plates in her hand, stared at the floor. She spoke in a soft voice. "Shit, no. But I tell you what. If she stays this way for three months, you and me, we can pay her a visit. It ain't my goal to keep you from your mommy.

But this is just something you got to ease into. But if I find out she's back with that sack of piss, if she even been talking to that sack of piss, it won't ever happen."

Two weeks after that, she was back with Quarry. Two months after that, they lost the apartment and moved in with Quarry's mom. But once, Cherry had a place, all on her own.

I wiggle out the booth and wrap my arms around Cotton's cologned neck. "Thank you. I got a million thanks for you. Thanks." I sit down and squeeze Eden tight in a side hug.

Dinah comes with two other servers, balancing full platters blowing out locks of steam. We stay rooted to the booth, eat and drink until our guts bulge. When the hostess leaves the restaurant with her hair down and a purse clinging to her shoulder, and the piano music dies, Cotton says, "Looks like it's time to scoot."

As we drive home, past red and purple and frosty lights of tattoo parlors and drive-thrus, Eden slurs a broken tune: "Someone's in the kitchen with Dinah, someone's in the kitchen I know. Someone's in the kitchen with Dinah, strummin' on the old banjo."

Turning on the dining room lights, Eden's singing is even more mashed. We sit with a bottle of wine. "Let's play Scrabble," she says.

Cotton leaves to search for the game. Eden's eyes droop. She drools, slumps. I get up from my chair and find Cotton in his study.

"Eden passed out," I say.

He pulls the red box out its snug place on the bookshelf. "Wanna play?"

"I've never. Sure."

We drop to our knees on the carpet, and he unfolds the board, explains the rules.

"You go first," I say.

He drags his eyes back and forth and back across his hidden tiles. I open and close my fist on the carpet, watch the fibers' shade turn from dark to light to dark. "I'll be back," I say. I walk to the dining room. Eden's placid. P-l-a-c-i-d. That's a good word. I'll play that. I snap in her ear until her eyes fling open and guide her to the sofa in the living room, wrap her fingers around an unopened water bottle. The fire's got a static crackle. The bottle of wine comes back with me in my grip to the study, seated in front of Cotton. His tiles on the board: s-h-o-v-e. I twist the corkscrew and sip from the bottle. He reaches for the green glass, drinks.

"Did you cheat?" I ask.

The corners of his lips twitch. "You don't trust me?"

"You did have blood on your hands the night we met." My tiles click on the board: h-a-r-d. Drink more of the wine. Bitter stains my tongue.

He stands and chuckles as he exits the room, returns with a blown-up photo framed in silver. His hands: bloody, aimed at the neon sign of People's Gas Station. A white moth perched on his thumb.

"You just let that omen sit on your nail," I say.

He lowers his chin, examines the picture. "You see an omen in this?"

"Plain as night."

He frowns. "I work in death. I guess omens are everywhere."

He don't just work in death. He's fixed on it. He got nerves about what's after life, or is it love? "What do you think about death?"

"I don't," he says. He either lying to himself or me.

"I do like the colors." I unbuckle the clasps of my heels, bury my toes in the carpet, and spread my legs so the Scrabble board sits between. "And the wings all open." My head feels like a Ferris wheel. I let my skull fall to the floor, gaze at the swirled patterns on the ceiling.

He leans the body-size frame against the wall. "Do you want to go to bed?"

"Yes. Can you help me up?" I spread one limp hand on my forehead like a damp rag and reach the other out to him. He towers above me. When he touches my fingers, I tug him to the carpet. My shaking laughter. "I got you. I got you good." I roll over to face him. "Just like I'm 'bout to get you in this game."

It was nice of him buying the house from Sugar Foot. All I been working toward, he went and did it for me. Paperwork signed and all. Even got Cigarette Sammy off the hook.

He flicks my nose, but he still got cold shock painted on his face.

I crawl and plant my knees on the board, raise the upper half of my body like I'm ready to pray, the tiles pressing into my bones. I ask, "What word am I?"

He stands in front of me, body unmoving as a tomb. The teeth of his zipper grind. "Fecund," he says. My gums, cheek, tongue wrap around his throb. "Fecund." F-e-c-u-n-d.

We skitter, half-dressed, to his bedroom. A stack of frames, facedown, in the corner. The only hanging painting is a sad woman, naked on a horse. Pretty hair drapes her curves. My words come out filtered through my dress as I slide it off. "Who is she?"

Cotton pants, watches, strokes himself. "Lady Godiva."

I throw myself onto the bed. He hovers over me, slides in, lifts his freckled nose to the ceiling with a grunt. "Warm, so warm."

I reach to move my fingertips down the ridges of his abs. He lets me, but his eyes tell me he wants me to stop. I do. From a distance, him pumping into my stillness would probably look like good Protestant sex, the scheduled kind where the man acts like he clocking in to climax. But that ain't it. His rhythm thrusts steady, hard, and I keep from singing. In his eyes, he say: *I'll admit it, I'll admit it right here. I love death and the way it shines muted; I love my dull little promise. I love a dozing lady, body slack with so much want she dreaming about it.* He lowers, still gliding in and out and in. Says in my ear, "You feel me." In and out and in. "How hard I am." Licks my neck in wandering circles. That makes me moan, and I don't like this swollen warmth I feel, on the cusp of gushing. Got to be on top, need to be.

So I make the move careful. I won't scare him, just a soft pull on his shoulder. A hint to switch places with me, pretty please. Instead, he presses his chest into mine, and I am fecund. I am fecund and shaking with heat. Finally, I roll on top of him and give his chest pillowed kisses, a playing gnaw. I grind, bounce: *Is this pussy a house to you? What is it you want, Boy? You want to fuck death in the face, don't you?* His chin in my grip, eyes focused on mine, I search his face. Looking for any truth. Only shock on his face. "You looking at her," I say.

And then I come, and he must like the spirit in my body because he say, "Whoa. Whoa, whoa, whoa," and fills me up. I move off him, head on his chest, legs spread. Leaking on the bed. I know when I leave this room, he'll need his twine. We sweat, knotted and breathless, in our own June drop.

16

"Magnolia?" Cotton looking at me with urgency. *Why you acting like you done went and got a lobotomy?*

Eden, with the face of Sigourney Weaver, peeks at me over the edge of her orange juice.

"This hangover," I say. Laugh a little to scrub their attention off me, to let Cotton know I'm not replaying thoughts of last night.

Cotton gives me a slow, disbelieving nod; peels his egg. "So—a case a day this week."

"But we got cases pouring in," I say.

"These people like things a certain way." In his eyes, he say: *You don't listen to me serious; I said this already.* "They especially like waiting lists." Cotton bends beneath the table, then rises holding a thick manila package. "Now, about today's case—"

"Oh, don't bring that up while she's eatin'," Eden says.

Cotton says, "She's a big girl," and I could slap him. He might as well say: *I had a sip of her*; might as well say: *My seed in her right now, what about that?* "We won't be using Skype because this person . . ." He glances at Eden: *Auntie, help me talk to the big girl*.

He slides the package across the table. The first case in a batch of five.

Eden scoots to me with fury and hands me a paper towel. "You'll want that."

Paper towel in my pinch, I use it to slide out the case. The letter's stiff and stained clear with a drenching spray of something. I lean over, sniff—smells like cum. All the times I gummed up my stomach with the same stuff.

"That's just glue," Eden says.

"That's definitely semen," Cotton says.

The letter is addressed to me.

Hi Magnolia,

Heard about what you guys do on Reddit. Totally think it's smart you guys have opted out of using the internet for advertisement. It gives me the vibe of reaching out to an apothecary or a hitman. Deep web type shit! The article said you make personal photos for "passed on loved ones" but that's not why I'm reaching out. This is embarrassing, but I don't think you're above fetish shit. I can see it in your eyes in the posted pics in the replies. I trust you, Magnolia. You can come in clutch for what I want.

My dad used to have these old-school sex tapes that he bought when he was my age. I'm talking 1980s. There was some woman on a few of the tapes who went by the name "Ambrosia Smith" but my mom made my dad trash the tapes after she caught me looking through them. I'm lucky I snapped a picture, but the quality is trash because I snapped it back in 2003 with a Nokia. I can't find her on the internet anywhere. Not on Google, not on Reddit, not on Pornhub or XVideos. But every time I want to stroke my cock, I think of her. I can't even remember her face right, she's as blurry in my mind as the picture. I don't know shit about her as a person, but I also saw in the article that you guys like to have personal facts about the person when you take the pictures. But I can tell you the personality I've built for her in my head all these years. Ambrosia has red hair and really thick red pubes and eyes that are the color of amber in the sun. She wears a lot of leather and likes to eat fistfuls of marshmallows. She doesn't drink beer, but she loves liquor. She can do a fucking split on the side of a mountain. She has a fishing license, but she doesn't need a pole. She leans down in rivers naked and catches smallmouth bass with her nipples. Oh, and she smells like cinnamon apples so I was wondering if you could spray the pictures with cinnamon perfume.

Thank you a lot,
Pr!nce$$fucker1994

PS—I left you a present, soaked into my words, it's like we're blood siblings, but with a better bond if you know what I mean. I'd really like to pay extra to see you without makeup maybe you could edit the pictures of you kissing Ambrosia but if not I get it that's not what you started the business for

When I look up, both Eden and Cotton drinking in the sight of my face.

"Just pictures for this one," Cotton says. "It'll require editing. If you're comfortable with it, of course."

The picture glides, whispers against the envelope when I dump it out. It's grainy, blurred, boxed in by the cubed bubble of an old TV. A woman with a bramble mess of strawberry blonde hair bent over a futon, getting fucked by a squat-bodied man. Every inch of her pixelated and glowing. Her arms pinned behind her back. Her face buried in the cushion of vintage furniture. The whole of her self—what she liked to do in airports, which teaspoon she favored in her kitchen drawer—handed to some secret man through VHS, through an old flip phone, then down to me to pick apart.

"How are you feelin' about this?" Eden asks.

I ain't saying disgusted, at least not in front of Cotton, because I am a big girl. I am a big girl who wears shorts and giggles high pitched and likes to have fun.

"Cool," I say.

She shakes her head like she's struck by the spirit. "I think it's just God awful." Her earrings make music. "Are you okay with this shoot knowing you'll have to be in your birthday suit?"

"I ain't realize I'd have to be naked."

"I think you'll do great," Cotton says. Too much confidence in his voice that Eden don't seem to pick up on.

When the plates are cleared, I go to my room and click the lock.

A sliding sound, fabric on the hardwood—Mama Brown crawls out from under my bed. Her shoulder pops. She wiggles it into the socket. "I felt you getting upset."

I whisper, "I ain't upset."

She grunts while rising, sits on the mattress at the opposite end. "What is it, then? You pregnant again?" She laughs before I can say don't be silly, Mama, so silly. On her hand with the missing pinky—a space where the thumb should be.

"You lost another," I say.

"No." She rubs her palm like dough, and I look away, afraid the flesh might split. "It was took."

"Not this grasshopper man again."

"It was Cricket."

I face her. "I thought you don't like to say his name."

She grins: teeth there, strong, but lost luster. "Nothing I do now going to shake him off me."

My eyes go back to her mauled hand. A flicker of hope in my belly. "He got the baby, then."

"Me and him made a deal." She stretches her legs out on the bed. A maggot pokes out a sore in her knee, burrows deeper. "He think if he get one soul, he can go on to heaven. I told him ain't no heaven like you think. He wasn't having it. So now, every time he come around, if I don't give him the baby, he take a piece of me."

That bastard eating away my time with Mama Brown. Every limb he kidnaps is less of her for me to be near. "Should ask him what part of his good book is okay with playing vulture."

"Shit, they took a rib right in Genesis."

Even in the in-between, Mama Brown got to pay a tax. When I found her back at her place in my bedroom, she held that dead mojo bag and then she held me. But now she carry an eye-watering reek with her wherever she go. Even in this big room, I'm choking.

"What if I made you some protection?" The sight of her—healthy chub melted to sag—maybe there ain't no point.

She lets out a shrill laugh. "Oh, what, you got the know-how?"

A pout forms: *That's sweet, child. I see you trying, but if you'd just give in a little, just buckle and see your baby, wouldn't be a need for all this.* "You ain't going to tell me why you conjured me up this time?"

"I guess I did something stupid."

She leans near me, and I want to leap away. But I don't. "Men, drugs, or money?"

"I did it with Cotton."

"Hell, if you ain't having sex you end up regretting, you ain't living."

I smile. "I guess. He did buy the house from Sugar Foot, so that's a plus."

"Magnolia, that's the one thing I asked you to do. Keep that land for you, and you only."

"It's still mine," I say.

She slaps the fitted sheet. "I know how tempting it is to think this man in his nice house with his nice clothes is going to save you from worries, but that's a big move for somebody you don't hardly know." She rises, shuffles toward my side of the bed. "He spoil you rotten, huh? Give you presents and tell you how the world work?"

"Whatever."

"Whatever my ass." She shakes her head on to the bathroom. "You wait and see if he ain't just like Sugar Foot."

I get up to follow her, to say: *Mama, let this be good for me;* to say, *Mama you loving too hard.* But she's gone.

Three knocks on my door.

Eden creeps in. "I didn't want to get into all this at break-fast, but you tell me if you're uncomfortable, you hear? It don't amount to a hill of beans to me if you keep on your clothes or leave them off, but you be comfortable with what you decide. To hell with what Cotton has to say."

We walk, holding hands, to her room, to the spotlight of her vanity, where she tacks the picture of Ambrosia to the bulletin board.

"How you going to do this?" I ask.

"By usin' my imagination." She smears gristle-colored foundation on my face, dusts freckles on the peak of my cheekbones. Lines my eyes with thick wings, colors my lips with a muddy brown.

She steps back and admires a face that ain't mine. "I have a surprise for you." She digs into an orange-taped box with a pocket-knife, removes a package, the plastic wrap crinkling, and cradles it like a sick baby. Keeps her voice low. "I don't have the slightest clue how you convinced Cotton to go with a wig."

"Damn," I say. She twists my hair into plaits. I wonder if my conducting his groans last night made him cave in on his rule against wigs. But that ain't the case. Truth is, I ain't got enough hair since the chop.

She finishes melting and blending the edges of the wig to my forehead, smooths and clips away the stray hairs, then holds my hand in the shell of her palms. "You made your mind up?"

"I'll do it naked," I say. "I don't mind."

I rise and shuck the clothes off my body against the chilled breath of the room, my nipples hard and light as new pennies.

Eden lightens my skin, contours a tighter gut. Clicks her tongue. "Youngins and their razors." She walks behind me with a pair of blue-handled shears. "Hold still." The thin ends of the wig float to the floor. She sweeps them into the cup of her hand. "Stay."

The choking smell of latex, the sponge bouncing against the bald slope. It burns cool. She pats the hair to my skin, fans until it dries, making it cling to my pussy in clumps: red lichen. She stands next to me in the mirror. "What do you think?" Her squeeze pulses on my shoulder. "Some men like natural."

I make my steps to Cotton's study slow so I don't crease the makeup. Find him standing behind the camera, stammering, and around his pinky, the twine is tied in a bow.

"It's got personality," Eden says.

Behind the camera, Cotton looks satisfied: *I knew she could play a good whore.* He pushes the button.

In the blinding light, I ain't here. I am in the living room of a hunter I met, next to the apples at the market. I am Ambrosia Smith. We stand naked in the sleepy light. He got a camera balanced on a bookshelf against the wall. The man say: *Let this camera see you.* He say: *If you let this camera see you, I'll give you all the fruit you can gulp.* I bend over his futon fuzzed with cat hair and tufts of lint. I say: *I will chew the rind and meat to pulp. Let me eat.* He hunkers behind me, into me, stinks of weed and bottled musk and spearmint. He pumps into me, and ain't nothing gentle about this man. I say: *Go soft, man, be easy.* He sinks his nails into my ass. He ain't easy. But it's okay. It don't hurt so it don't matter none. Because to him, I am the fruit, rind, and meat to be chewed to pulp.

The steady flashing stops. "Round two," Cotton says.

I shower, scrub the pasted shades off my tummy, legs, tits. The red curls cemented to me now circling the drain. The way Cotton looked at me back there—his eyes were too-feeling marble. I don't even need to try to squeeze out every bit of confidence for this next shoot. My body already saying: *I was born for this.* Already saying: *I am breathing glitter. Ain't I pretty?*

Swaddled in a towel, I go to Eden's room. The hugging dampness of my thighs on her leather chair makes me squirm.

She bends to my face, and before massaging a shimmering moisturizer into my skin, she says, "You got a glow."

I clench my gut. What she mean, I got a glow? Talking like I'm a host of life. Ain't no way Cotton planted something in me. Too soon to tell. For now, I'll pretend to be lust for Cotton and his camera and his cash. Tonight, I'll march on down to the pharmacy and buy Plan B.

Eden pencils in my eyebrows, brown-feathered strokes. Waves a wand's black chunks over my eyelashes. Smooths a lip-plumping coconut balm across my lips. Mists me with a cool sheen. In the mirror, I see a self that's had the ugly filtered out. No shaded hollows beneath my eyes. No ash-cracked lips or ghost lines sitting where my smile should be.

My catwalk to Cotton's study, toe-to-heel, toe-to-heel, fresh and dewed as valley dawn.

Cotton glances at me from behind the camera. His eyes flicker down, away, back to me, no distance in this moment. I feel him sinking into me. Cotton mutters something that sounds like *spunk.* He counts down from three.

And that familiar light washes over me, lets me know I ain't here. I'm in a living room with wood-paneled walls. Half-finished cigarettes scattered on the shag carpet like lost teeth. I am Carolina Nettle. Daughter of none. Ambrosia stands next to me, says: *Camera, camera on the wall.* She brings a blinking flame to the end of her cigarette, passes its glow to me. She say: *How you get in this forever place?* I suck the old tobacco, char my breathing, exhale the white out. Snowfall of ashes. I look at her pixelated face, ask: *What you mean?* She takes the cigarette from me and her hand flickers. She say: *Hostage, in video.* In her palm, an apple. Waxed, fat, a fresh promise. She bites a chunk of the apple, keeps it between her teeth, beckons me with her finger. We kiss, trade the fruit back and forth with our tongues. Our chests balloon, pop, balloon to the same fast beat. A little groan slips from her throat. She shoots the apple from her mouth to my throat. I cough, but the fruit won't budge. Together, we are static.

Cotton lifts the camera from its nest, collapses the tripod. "Really beautiful, I mean, really."

I slink into my room and lock the door. Pacing, drumming fingertips against my hip. That primal painting looming over me. A dull hunger trickles down, down. The bed creaks with my weight. Kneeling on the mattress, I pinch each pillow until I feel the firm foam I need. The satin pillow bunched into a knobby hill, my thighs wrap around, rock back and forth and back. Back and forth and back until I get to ecstasy, like I know heaven is the dip of my navel. Every muscle a frayed rope. The sun sets.

Nighttime walking ain't scary until the roads empty and everyone sleeps. I got a couple of hours of safety, but if I wait until it's late, maybe I can catch Cigarette Sammy at the gas station. I just want to say sorry, is all, and make sure he know those charges are dropped, and he don't got to worry about Sugar Foot at all if he come back. No court for Cigarette Sammy. Pictures of wooden benches, powdered wigs, fat file folders flash in my mind as I drift off.

I claw out of sleep an hour before midnight, dress and inhale a stew Eden simmered during the shoots. Lamb and rice and sweet carrots.

The dots of sage and streaks of gravy rinse from my plate. "Going for a walk," I say.

Shuffling down concrete, next to the dying traffic. Mama Brown waits by a light pole.

"What you going to do now that little Ms. Carolina Nettle died?" she asks.

A stopped walk, phone up to my ear, I say: "She ain't dead. She alive as ever."

"You think the dead don't recognize dead when they see it?" She leans against the pole; the old red cedar takes some of her burden. "There was a time I liked hooking. Got some kind of power from it. My strut was all the glamour I needed." Her voice croaking. "But one day, I was in some cheap motel off Cherry Street. It was sunny outside, but the drapes was drawn, and so much cigarette smoke in the air, it felt like it was going to storm. I kept looking at that little sliver of sunlight shining through the drapes, and I felt all that power drain out of me. What kind of power I got, being trapped in fake wedlock for an hour or two when I could be out by the lake sunbathing and cutting up?"

I nod into my phone. "I could go lay with a stranger right now if I want."

"You'll find something else to help you deal with the world." Her voice strains, like she got a tickle in her throat. "You just make sure—" She coughs; a white moth set free lands on me. I crush it with my fist. "—that you pick the right thing."

"Why would you cough up that omen on me?"

Her coughing settles. "Baby, a part of you died. That's just confirmation."

Our footsteps match each other.

"Your mommy couldn't deal with the world and look what happened to her. Pills and needles."

"You seen Cricket anymore?" I ask. Maybe from the other side she got a way of healing, body and mind. Then I notice a chunk of ear gone and know that ain't true.

"He's due soon," she says.

"This ain't going to make me agree to seeing that child, Mama. If that's what you think."

"You remember having to beg Cherry to show you something that was even close to looking like love? I ain't about to put this baby through that. Dead or alive."

I leap into a sprint, leave her mean words.

The speakers in Walgreens sing: *Show me the way to the next whiskey bar.* My flip-flops slap the tile. *Oh, don't ask why. Oh, don't ask why.* Plan B shelved, the lilac box locked in a plastic case. At checkout, I pay and tell the wrinkle-frowned cashier she can go to hell with that ugly judgment in her eyes.

Outside, I sit on a bench leaning against the brick wall and try to open the Plan B. Another layer of plastic. Pulling and twisting the corners of the casing until my fingertips ruddy. The flame from my lighter leaps, first to warm and soften, then to burn a hole. The pill goes down easy. It's near midnight. My trash sits alone on the bench. I make my way to People's Gas Station, light a cigarette in the parking lot. The last of my ash snows to the oiled asphalt. 12:05. Across the lot, through the doors, into the smell of fried potatoes and dying fruit: some woman at the register I ain't ever met.

"You seen Cigarette Sammy?" I ask.

"Who?"

"Dude who digs through the trash."

"Oh. I heard about him but ain't seen him around since I started," she says.

The roads sleep empty. Where could that man be? Maybe under the bridge down Broadway, on the hem of downtown, next to the Salvation Army. Where the people with no homes gather and sleep. I walk on the sidewalk, through crosswalks, to the funeral parlor. The thought of him out there, alone, won't leave me be. Folded, sleeping on sun-bleached Starburst wrappers. Dreaming to the mean whispers and groans of passing cars. My feet don't stop when I reach the funeral parlor; they carry me downhill, to the quick traffic, in search of my friend.

I halt under a jaundiced streetlight and bring a flame to my smoke. Sunbaked earthworms curl rigid where the last of daylight fell, at the edge of the underpass. Darkness smothers the chunk of street that runs under the bridge. I pass beneath the heartbeat of interstate cars hitting the same pothole. Thudthud. Thudthud. The concrete inky with black algae and spilled soda. Blots of tarry bubblegum flattened by hordes of traveling soles. Clusters of people around sleeping bags sharing cigarettes. I stop beside a wooden post with a sign that reads ONE WAY and scan. A woman who looks like Cherry staggers by in a tight rainbow crop top. A mad-faced man steadies her when she tilts. A semitruck rumbles above. Now a warm breeze, smelling like piss and mint mouthwash. An empty tuna can skitters down Broadway leaking gray water. Sleeping bags, tattered plastic bags, crumpled paper.

Three teenagers sit on the stoop of the closed deli across the street. One of them hiccups like a bullfrog. They laugh the only way teen boys can: loud with a little fear beneath. Out of the people I've seen so far, they look closest to my age. I wait for a street sweeper to move its slimed bristles out my way and cross. They stop their chattering and eye me as I approach.

"Hey, I'm looking for a friend," I say.

The hiccupping boy says, "Baby, I'll be your friend."

The boy next to him with the weeping willow hair smacks the back of his head. "Shut the fuck up, Bugle."

"My friend go by Cigarette Sammy."

The third boy holds a bottle of strawberry soda, guzzles the last sip. "That dude wear a coat on days that give you swamp ass?"

I nod.

The hiccupping boy says, "We ain't seen him in a while."

Weeping Willow points. "But he's usually over there when he stays."

I thank them.

As I shuffle back to the other side of the street, I hear, "Baby thick as hell" and "Shut the fuck up, Bugle." The empty bottle rattling against the sidewalk. The boy hiccups, and the laughter that follows is swallowed by the traffic overhead.

I listen for Cigarette Sammy's mutters. Beg the shadows for his pudgy shape. A man dozes in a motor scooter parked against the wrought iron fence. That's when I see all the bodies on the ground behind the fence, in the gravel lot, deep in pebbled slumber. Cigarette Sammy ain't on the sidewalks. I walk up a side road and cut through an opening in the fence, glance at the sleeping faces. Cherry must be on my mind because I see her in the face of a woman sitting against the graffiti-tattooed column of the underpass. Her skull lolls side to side. I'm near enough now to see if there's anyone behind the column and smell her perfume. A soft touch of vanilla swimming with sweat and vinegar and the dull smell of sick.

"Cherry?" I say.

Her eyelids sag, bounce open. "Who the fuck are you?"

"It's Maggie," I say.

She look like she got a song in her head but can't remember the lyrics. She ain't getting the tune right. She want to say: *I know this song.* She want to dance and belt along. She want to say: *I love this song.* Her mouth gapes. She touches her jaw and winces. "I'll be damned. My baby girl." She licks the dried spit from the corners of her mouth. "What are you doin' here?"

She got mascara and eyeliner smudged around her eyes, down her cheeks. Raisin-colored bruises bloom along her collarbones. Her shirt used to be a clean white, I'm sure. It's blotched with grime, like she been walking through exhaust.

I look at the nearby sleeping people. "Is Quarry with you?"

She scratches her head. "No, the fucker up and left me to go live near a swamp in Florida. He's got a family now. It's the shittiest people that get the good in life."

"You want to get some food?"

We walk to Waffle House in silence. As soon as we're inside, she says, "I'm going to the bathroom."

I sit by the window and wait for her.

After a few minutes, Cherry sits in front of me refreshed: a washed face and oily hair tied in a neat bun. The waiter comes to our table, lanky as a scarecrow. Cherry orders the kids' meal, and I tell her that won't fill her up, so she gets the double angus cheeseburger with bacon and mushrooms, with a side of hash browns, and I get the same.

"How are you?" I ask. As if I ain't find her rolling on the concrete under a damn bridge.

"I'm holdin' up," she says.

"Nah, don't give me no bullshit. Why you living on the street?"

"I ain't got nowhere to go," she says, "shelter's full."

Mama Brown's home could hold her in its empty warmth. I ain't going to be there as long as Cotton pays me. And I doubt Cigarette Sammy will ever want to touch his toe to a blade of grass on that property. I'll need to clear out everything Cherry could sell. Stock with food. I'm sure everything in that fridge sits in a cold rot.

After the waiter sets out plastic cups on the table, Cherry thanks him, then stabs the straw into her tea. "How's schoolin'?"

I nurse my water. "I graduated two years ago."

She slumps her shoulders, gazes out the window. "Been awhile, ain't it?" Her chewed nails drum on the table. "What have you been doin' since graduation?"

"I been working at the gas station," I say.

"People's?"

I nod. "You know a guy go by Cigarette Sammy?"

"Yes," she says, "he stays somewhere on Selma. Why?"

"Ain't important," I say.

"How's your mamaw doin'?"

"Mama Brown is doing just fine."

A small pause, Cherry chewing on what to say next. She settles on a crumb of sorry. "Maggie, I remember Quarry takin' your dolls."

"What's that got to do with anything?"

"I got regrets, is all."

We bloat ourselves on thick meat, buttered bread, fried strips of potatoes. Cherry sucks bits of mushroom out her teeth. I don't want her to go back to the street tonight, but the house ain't ready.

"I got to put you in a room."

"I ain't goin' to Peninsula," she says.

"A motel."

She relaxes. "You ain't got to do that for me. I don't mind goin' back." She chomps half-melted ice cubes. "It was nice of you to feed me."

I shoo her words away with my hand. "A motel room for a night or two, and then we going to figure something else out." I dust the crumbs off my palms. "It ain't safe."

I pay, and then we drag our legs out the door.

"Can I borrow one of your cigarettes?" she asks.

I pluck two smokes out the pack. We stand on the curb and suck down nicotine. There's a wide enough space in the trickle of traffic—we cross, billows of smoke trailing behind us. Only three cars in the parking lot of Regency Inn. It'll be easy to get a room. We balance our half-finished cigarettes on the brick ledge of a window, then enter the lobby: hardwood with a peeling finish, mint walls. The head of a wild boar hangs, tusks carved in a hateful smile, on the wall behind the oak desk.

The desk clerk looks to the ringing bell above the door as we enter. He got mud-brown hair, slicked down and crusted with gel. "How are y'all tonight?"

"Mighty fine," Cherry says.

My clasped hands rest on the desk. "I'd like to get a room for a couple of nights."

He clacks away on the keyboard. On the other end of the desk, a tabletop fountain bubbles: water falling off a tiny stone cliff into a pool. The clerk asks me booking questions; I keep my sight on the flow. How does the water return to the top from the stagnant dip?

Cherry pokes through the stream with her finger. She sings, "'Don't go chasin' waterfalls.'"

I grin. "'Please stick to the rivers and the lakes that you're used to.'"

The desk clerk sings, "'I know that you're gonna have it your way or nothing at all, but I think you're moving too fast.'"

Cherry lets out a breathing laugh. "I like you."

He bows and slides the room cards across the desk. I slip one in my pocket while Cherry jokes with the man. "Get your key," I say.

Outside, the heavy sighs of passing cars. The ends of our smokes black and cool. We revive them with my Bic and sit on the ledge of the window. Two twenties, crumpled from my pocket. "Here."

"You don't got to do that," she says.

I jab the folded cash in the air. She accepts.

"Wanna see my new place?" she asks.

Up the stairs, we creep along the concrete balcony until we reach her room: 414. Cherry waves the magnetic strip across the lock until it blinks green, then swings open the door, the stench of cigar smoke punching us in the face. I hover in the doorway. The room floods yellow with light: a full-size bed with a comforter and pillows the color of boiled oatmeal, carpet as stained and white as Cherry's skin. Same mint walls as the lobby. A painting of a freight train next to the bed. A box TV shouldered with crystal ashtrays.

"I got so much room," Cherry says.

Something searing, guilt or sadness, spreads through my belly. "I'll be back day after tomorrow and we'll find you something permanent."

"My rest is going to be so good tonight." She plops on the bed, makes a small crater in the mattress.

I wrap my fingers around the handle of the door. "See you soon."

She beams in the lamplight, and I realize there's a hole in place of her left canine. She look like a kid getting ready for bed, knowing the glittered fairy going to take that tooth hidden under her pillow. Knowing the glittered fairy going to leave her enough silver to get gumballs or a sucker at the corner store. Once upon a time, Cherry was a little girl.

"Love you, Maggie."

My fingers grip the handle. "Love you, Mom."

The door is hard to shut.

17

Before going out and clearing the house for Cherry, I go to Eden's room, looking for a foundation brush that might blend better than the one I got. She ain't in here. Probably off in the cove mixing the first margarita of the day. In the drawer of her vanity, sandwiched between the contact case and powder-caked makeup brushes, a thin stack of wrinkled paper—once wadded, now pressed smooth. A pen stroke across the writing. I peek at the open door. No approaching footsteps, no shadow limbs nearing. I keep the contacts balanced on my fingers, just in case Eden storms in with clenched teeth, hissing: *I trust you as far as I can throw you, snooping woman, after all I done for you.*

Neck craned over her drawer, I read the letter without lifting.

Dear Cotton,
I read your interview in Vice last night, and while I admit
I was initially dismissive, after closing the tab, my mind

kept returning to it. What would I say to my wife, if I could have one more conversation with her? The part of losing her that I cannot seem to cope with is reckoning with the fact that the most traumatic events happen on the most insignificant days. Two years ago, Vanessa and I were eating dinner, sushi, our typical Wednesday night. She told me she had trouble sleeping. We should get a new mattress, a new bed frame because there was something under prodding her, she said, giving her back pain. We bought a new bed and a back brace and Icy Hot. Finally, she went to the doctor. Spinal cord tumor. Inoperable. A month later, she died. She always ate right, smoked cigarettes in high school but never developed a dependence. We met in graduate school, both in the history department. She danced ballet. If she wasn't preparing for lectures or walking our dog Truffle, she was in the studio, and that woman could move in ways I've really only ever seen in nature. Vanessa was happiest when dogwood trees were in bloom. We never watched much television, but I know she had a secret affinity for soap operas. I've attached the photos of Vanessa in this envelope. I was unable to find pricing information online, so please do call me at your earliest convenience.

Take care,

Dr. Stephen Garland

Beneath his name, a circled phone number. I give in, put the lenses on the desk and shuffle through the pictures: Vanessa pirouetting on a laminated stage, box braids in a high bun. Vanessa cuddling with Truffle on a leather sectional. Over a steaming pot, she smiles, wooden ladle stained yellow and lifted toward the camera: *Here, taste this, babe.* Eden got this letter, this life tucked secret in her vanity like a pair of blood-browned panties. Pen-strike the response—not this case, not ever. The only case we got of a Black family. I got a want to ask her why. Eden might give it to me straight; Cotton will say: *You see, you're missing a key part of the analytics, and when the demand is rising and then the accruals and bookkeeping and beekeeping, we are the keeper of bees, Magnolia.*

In the kitchen, the applause of a cocktail shaker, footsteps. I shove the pictures to its hidden place and shut the drawer. She blocks my path when I reach the door.

"You got a foundation brush I can use?" I say. Eden tosses me one.

"I got a hankerin' for some pizza. I'm goin' to order. You want some?"

I'll save the question in my cheeks, and it's better if she's a few drinks in. "Sure. When I get back."

"Where you goin'?"

"I got something to take care of." I jog to the stairs, call over my shoulder. "I won't be long."

Shadows of clouds stroll across the parking lot. A breeze bites at my still-damp skin like a birch switch. The breeze say: *Fall time coming early and stillborn.* My chest rocking with shivers. The breeze say: *You getting blood leaves and pumpkin stink.* I trot down Broadway until the day feels like summer. An awful feeling settling in me. Only thing I can think of is Eden and Cotton feeling too exclusive to serve a Black family's grief.

So much flying through my head. Cherry's bruised collar-bones and missing tooth won't leave my mind, either. After I move out what little valuables Mama Brown left, after I fill the pantry, I'll cook soup beans. Cherry always did like soup beans and onion with chunks of ham hock, and slices of cornbread dense as candles. I'll bring her to Mama Brown's, and we'll talk about everything. Maybe we could pop in a DVD of something we used to watch, if I don't hide the TV. We can watch *Fried Green Tomatoes,* and she can tell me who hurt her. Her job, her rehab, her brain fixing, all that sits in the future, waiting.

I push past the tree line, into the forest, and remember Cotton changed the locks. I ain't got a key. Maybe he left one for me under the doormat. The window on my room won't stay locked, so I can always sneak in that way.

The trees thin. White eats my vision. A U-Haul truck sits parked in the driveway. A man in a sweat-soaked shirt with his arms wrapped around a green tote waddles to the open front door. A woman follows behind with two stacked boxes lined with tape. A boy and girl in pastels chase each other around the yard, weave around the seeding heads of dandelion, caw their good times to the sky.

I stumble back, fall, land on soft loam. Cotton renting out Mama Brown's house to a family who look like they believe in Neighborhood Watch. To a family who look like they think a church picnic means chicken salad sandwiches and Jell-O cups. I scoot up against a moss-blanketed boulder. I ain't ever felt anger like this: harsh tongue of a whip, lashing my insides.

Mama Brown steps out from behind a blackberry bramble. Another finger missing, somewhere unseen bouncing in Cricket's pocket. She waddles with scratched arms. Her blood congealed and dark as debt. "Damn thorns."

Pushing this want away ain't easy. To hug her stinking self. A black cloud of flies follows her. "Damn him," I say.

She towers over me, blotting out the sun. "People like him damned the moment they step into shined shoes."

I squeeze an acorn between my thumbs. "Look at that family."

Flies flock above her skull. "I ain't sure why you so surprised. I'll be damned if this ain't what white men do."

"It'll be okay." I throw the acorn against an oak trunk.

"Shit, least Sugar Foot let me stay and kept the rent low. You remember how you used to treat your dolls? How you'd break off their arms and legs and drop them when you was done?"

"I remember."

"That's what Cotton doing to you. And you can't even see it."

I rise, dust the bits of dirt and cracked bark from my shorts. "I'll fix it."

She shoots bad-breathed laughter to the sky. The flies part, then congregate again. "Baby, you ain't fixing nothing. I'd rather him rip out my veins than take my dirt." She eyes me with a look that say: *Magnolia, you done smeared banana all over the bed.* "But shit, what's done is done." She runs her fingers through her thinning curls; they break, float, held hostage by the breeze. "You see how you stressing me?"

"Mama, I said I'll fix it." I leave her standing in doubt and walk through the acorns and twigs and grape-scented flowers toward pavement, the sun baking the nape of my neck. Bad thoughts swim in my brain: those people leaving dried clumps of cool blue toothpaste on the sink, spraying the bathroom mirror with their brushed plaque, charring bits of cheese around the stove eyes. Stripping the core of mine and Mama Brown's life out the place. White weeds swallowing our garden. The walk back to Cotton's don't seem nearly as long as it usually does. By the time I step onto the burning asphalt of the parking lot, I'm sprinting with no room for air in my lungs.

I burst into the lobby. Cotton glances up at the sound of my hail-hard footsteps. He whispers behind the desk to a tall man cloaked in black. I tell him *come here* with my finger. He gives the mourning man an apology with his eyes. I can't hear Cotton's shadowed words, but I know he telling the man: *Just one moment, I'll be back, and then you can suck my fecundity and pay me, too.* He hurries to my side, props his arm on my shoulder, and I push all my rage to my toes, fold them tight, to stop from punching him in that roach of an Adam's apple.

His voice comes out hushed. "I'm with a client."

The man waiting by the lilies, his tear-soaked face the only thing plugging the holler in my throat. "I got to talk to you. I'll wait right here."

He returns to the desk. One minute passes, three, five. My feet won't stop their panic-tapping, carry me right outside. I light a cigarette and sit on the mulch, by the rosebush, and take a deep drag, blow the poison cloud to the roses. Let the flowers brown. Let the buds die. See how he likes it when something he owns wilts in the hands of an outsider. The crying man steps out. I've worked my way to the other side of the bush, filling the leaves with my fog.

He clutches a thin tissue. "What the hell are you doin'?" He clears the snot from his throat, spits on the pavement.

"Fumigating," I say.

He looks at me, moping face all twisted in surprise. His voice fading across the parking lot: "What in the blue hell?"

I go inside to find Cotton still planted behind the desk, scribbling in an event planner.

"Cotton." I rush to him, plead to him in silence.

He raises his finger to his pink lips. I scan the room for any more paying people, any more sobs. "You got a funeral going on or something?"

His pen slithers across the page. He pokes the page, ends with a faint period, then closes the notebook with a thump. "Just finishing up. What's going on?"

"Huh." I mime piano on the shining wood. "He say, 'What's going on?' This man."

"Are you okay?"

"Who the hell you got living in my Mama Brown's house?"

He builds a wall with his outspread hands against his chest. "Magnolia, calm down."

"Calm down," I say, "calm down!"

"I forgot to tell you, just with the new cases and I've been working on this painting—did you know that decaying bodies grow some sort of wax? Like a death soap—"

"Cotton," I say.

A silent moment of surrender. "Sorry. I have an envelope for you in my study. It's half of the family's security deposit, first and last month's rent—"

"Where Mama Brown's furniture at? I know you ain't got them living in there with my stuff." My pacing on the verge of skittering. "I just know you ain't."

"Everything is in storage."

"Why you ain't just talk to me about it first?"

He runs his fingers through his curls, the corners of his mouth weighed down, anger brewing. "To be fair, I did buy the place."

"You sure did. Ain't you? And an envelope. Tuh! Why you got to act like a landlord to me?"

The way he casts away his eyes, he pretends the answer got to be hiding in the tiles of the floor. "I thought you'd appreciate the opportunity—"

"Why everything got to be a goddamn profit to you?"

"I only wanted to help."

The velvet in his voice almost mutes my rumbling. "Tell me one thing since you so horny about profit." Horny about profit and death. "How much you charge these people?"

"I didn't know you were interested in the parlor, see the funerals—"

"The rent," I say.

"Seven-fifty."

"And what about that family whose case y'all threw away? What about that?"

"I'm not sure what you're talking about," he says, "you'll have to talk to Eden about that."

"You always got to hide from me." The meanness I feel caves in, and my chest sags heavy with hurt.

He pouts, slides his hand to his pocket, probably to squeeze that damn twine, then shuffles to my side of the desk. His hug smells like lemons and wood. "Have you been comfortable here?" Kneads my scalp. "The rent should help you save." Kisses my curls. "And hey, business is really picking up." His hand wanders south, near the hill of my ass.

I pull away and snort up the snot leaking from my nose. "Right. It'll be better this way." I squeeze the meat of his arm.

He gifts me a half smile. "You were right to react as such. I'm in here too much." He pokes his head. "I should have talked to you about it. And earlier." He steps away, studies me. "I have more exciting news, but I need to work out the details. Before I go do that, are we okay?"

I rub the drying streams from my cheeks. "Sure are."

We trudge up the stairs, then he snakes into his study. I scurry to my room, lock my door, sit on my bed, trying to find a way to hide my anger, calm my breathing. But everything in my chest beats rapid. I feel as grime caked as when Sugar Foot finished with me. If I were the running away type, I'd take all my money and go. Somewhere with a beach or a desert. Somewhere with enough stretching land to make me and all my troubles feel small.

I punch my pillows, throw them at the wall, to the floor, against the dresser. My fingers rip off the comforter and sheet, toss them in a tangled heap at the closet door. That don't make me feel any peace. The tears come and don't stop when I see the rust-colored bloom of dried blood on the mattress. Sitting by the stain, that dark memory of my murder, I claw at it. Claw and claw and claw until my nailbeds ache more than what I got going on inside me. My face pressed against the blood, the smell of new pennies. I whisper to the ugly gore, "You always going to be with me, ain't you? You ain't ever going anywhere." Lips against it, so my words come out all stifled. "You a forever tumor. Damn you." Screaming, mouth smashed to my could-have-been, until I work my throat raw. My wrecked body: folded in the shape of a kidney bean, breathing in the silence.

Down the hall—the polished tap, tapping of Cotton's shoes. I leap to the mess on the floor, wrap the fitted sheet around the bed, move in a sloppy rush until my bed is made, worried he'll come in and see my devastation and want a little more, sprinkled with stiff-lipped kisses.

Calmed, I got to ask Eden about that trashed case. Cotton starting to shed skin, showing a raw and smooth ugliness. Eden got that, too? Her door sits open. The light of her vanity spills into the hall. She must have heard everything.

"Eden." I knock.

She turns to face me, looking like Meryl Streep today. "Hi, sugar."

My sureness about asking her flees at the familiar sweetness of her voice, the look that say: *What is it, baby, you want some mothering, some gentle?* Instead, I ask, "Could you give me a ride?"

"I'm goin' to the mountain, sugar. You want to come?"

"Yeah, I'll go. You mind if we make a quick stop first?"

In the hearse, we crack the windows to ease the trapped bake. She lights a Virginia Slim, passes one to me, cruises down Broadway.

Eden taps the end of her cigarette on the window. "Cotton means well."

"Turn left at the next light," I say.

"I didn't think this damn dead voyeuristic gimmick idea would pan out." The turn signal clicks. "When he told me his idea, I said, boy, if brains were leather, you wouldn't have enough to saddle a June bug." She takes the turn. We pass a man in a gorilla suit spinning and flipping a sign for a cell phone repair shop. "But he proved me wrong. And whatever you're mad about, I'm sure he'll prove you wrong, too."

"I hope you right, Eden." All these incoming letters Cotton rakes in from past clients. They worship him. He must got some know-how braided under his curls. I hope they right. Because if anything happens to Mama Brown's house—one hole in the wall, one scuff on the floor, I'll rip all the curtains in the parlor.

I'll cremate Cotton's books. Pound Eden's vanity into shards so fine, they'll feel like flour. "Cotton said you need intervention."

"Did he? Me? He ain't got a clue." She lights another cigarette while steering with a steady hand. "He needs intervention himself." Smoke blows out in a punch of breath. "He used to rub his winkie in the big cemetery on Tazewell. Used to hoard funeral programs under his bed like they were fuckin' *Maxims*."

"What?"

"Intervention my ass," she says.

Eden parks in front of the motel's lobby and waits with the idle. Pushing away thoughts of Cotton's secret self, I race up the stairs to room 414. "Cherry." My knuckles fiddle on the door. "I got to have you stay here a few more nights." After this week's cases, I could get her set up in an apartment. Anywhere but the North Side. That's where she started eating her communion crackers: oxys, hydros, fentanyl. I knock again. "You sleep? You need food money?" I crane my neck over the balcony and search the lot for her, sure I'll find her next to a thought bubble of Newport smoke. I pinch the keycard out my pocket. "I'm coming in."

I swing the door open and squint into the shade-drawn dimness. The room stinks of burnt rubber. The light switch clicks. On the bare mattress, Cherry and the pomade desk clerk breathe and twitch in their naked sleep. The comforter, sheets, and pillows built in a fort in the corner of the room. On the nightstand, two packs of Newports, a drained bottle of whiskey. A spoon, sticky and caramelized. But I barely notice that mess.

I ain't here. I am a house. I am a house made of sticks. I sit on a pretty plot of land: thick grass, blushed clover. And inside me, a little pig lives. A wolf—big and bad—prowls up to my front door. He say: *Little pig, little pig, I got to come in.* The little pig say: *What you got, Mr. Wolf? Are you nice and thin?* I want to say: *Little pig, why would you bring this bad to me? Can't you see I ain't built right?* But I can't speak. I am only a house of sticks. The wolf growls. He say: *Little pig, I got something you want.* I feel the little pig creep up to the door. She say: *That's fine, Mr. Wolf, but are you good and gaunt?* The wolf presses his ear to me. He all bristle. He stink. He say: *Little pig, you best let me in, or I'll blow you down.* He say: *I'll blow your life in.* I try to say: *Don't. I am no life. Can't you see I'll break?* But the wolf sucks in all the air down his gullet and blows me to pieces. The wolf going to eat the pig. I just know it. But I can't say it matters. I can't say anything at all. I am only rubble.

I close the door, walk down the stairs, and enter the lobby. An old couple in matching Hawaiian shirts wait at the abandoned desk.

"Do you work here?" the woman asks.

I stride past them, to the corner of the desk where the ceramic waterfall flows and rip the power cord from the outlet, hold the fake cliff in my hand.

"I don't think she works here, Don," the woman says.

I smash the ceramic to the tarnished hardwood.

The seat of the hearse been cooled by my sweat and the frosted blow of the vents.

Eden pulls the gear in reverse, leaves her foot on the brake. "You get your mommy settled in?"

"Yes," I say.

We leave; Mama Brown sits in the back, clinging to the

sides. Another clump of hair gone. I watch the side mirror, eyes locked on the motel, until only a sliver of the roof peeks above a hill.

"Baby, I know you upset, but I just don't know what you expected. That woman don't care about nobody but herself."

The radio sings: *Try me, try me.* The road constricts. *Darlin' tell me: I need you.*

"And besides, you chasing after the wrong love——"

I turn up the radio before she can mention seeing the baby. Glance in the rearview mirror. She's gone.

"You ever been to a casino?" Eden asks. Sunlight filters through the matted leaves, hits the asphalt in flecks.

"I ain't ever been," I say. "Shit, am I old enough to go in? I just realized——"

Eden giggles. "You'll be just fine."

We sit in silence, and my nerves can't wait for the drive to finish, can't wait for the truth that always come when her liver working overtime. All those mixed-up meanings when speaking to Cotton, one bit of realness would feel like getting out of a chokehold. "When I was looking for a foundation brush, I saw——"

"I ain't got the skill to do hair like that. I ain't got the makeup that would match."

"Does Cotton know you got it?"

"He does, and he agrees." Her mouth twisted and ready to defend. "Besides, that man didn't send money. That's a red flag."

"You could just hire somebody with that skin tone."

"You know how picky Cotton is."

Eden's crutch when they got to explain bad behavior——*you know how that man is, it's braided in his muscles, it's painted in the color of his eyes,* and *boys will be boys.*

She glances away from the rolling lines of the interstate in my direction. "Can I ask you something?"

I nod.

"I know you've been fuckin' Cotton."

My laugh come out fake, forced. "Not at all."

"I've been around long enough to know what it looks like."

"Nothing like that," I say.

"All I'm saying is the minute pants is dropped is the minute the mind loses ability to keep clear. Keep your thinking on your own business."

I ain't nothing to them; I'm just in their house. We pass a blue sign: WELCOME TO KENTUCKY and beneath that: UNBRIDLED SPIRIT. I stay quiet.

She chuckles out a tornado of nicotine. "Oh, now don't get all riled up. I was just saying."

The ride to the casino winds uphill, strangled by dogwood, oak, juniper. Red lights and stop signs lost to the past. Squeezes down a backroad, and after a mile, crumbles over gravel. We stop at a gate with a sign, in curved and looping letters: BLACK BUSH RANCH.

"What kind of casino is this?" I ask.

She pokes her hand out the window, punches her polished nail into a keypad. "You ain't ever seen anything like it." The teeth of the gate part. "Louise will be here; you'll meet her in a bit. I told you she was Melungeon, and that Irish blood in her makes her mean as a snake."

My stomach folds into itself. Meeting the woman that helped me flush out that life. I can't pretend in this place. Can't act like it never happened when she had the knowing to juice pennyroyal and put it in a tea. "Does she know who I am?"

"Oh, don't worry about that. She knows when not to talk." She creeps past the gate. The hearse lurches down the unpaved road. "Her fiancé, Rowdy, he's a horse dentist. Owns this half of the mountain. You know, they've been engaged damn near fifteen years. I said, 'Woman, what spell did you put on him?' She gets that marriage loving but she can walk away without a lawyer whenever she pleases. The casino is their barn. It ain't fancy, but it's nicer than it sounds." The road stretches on and on, narrow as a nail. "This ain't exactly legal."

The driveway unfurls: a field-size gravel parking lot. Pickup trucks, jeeps, a four-wheeler. In the corner, a bile-yellow monster truck. Eden sandwiches the hearse between two pickups. I stretch my legs against the butt of the hearse and finish my smoke. A silver ball sack dangles from the trailer hitch of the truck to our right. A rain-faded bumper sticker sticks to the truck on our left: COWBOY BUTTS DRIVE ME NUTS. Eden joins me. She nests her sunglasses in her bangs.

"Eden, are these people—"

"Christians? Lord, no." She pats my back.

We walk toward the three-story barn strung with green and red neon lights. They strobe. Bluegrass bleeds through the walls. A rooster crows. I want to say: *Eden, are these people Republicans?*

A donkey, munching a mouthful of turnips, trots, blocks our path. A fat horsefly lands on his eyelid. He blinks, sends it into a frenzied halo of flight. Eden tries to rub his head, but he whips his neck and brays, drops the crushed purple bulbs to the dust.

"You mean ass," Eden says. He brays again, the spaces between his block teeth clogged with bent straws of hay, bits of turnip. "Oh, go on and floss." He trots on, further into dusk.

In the barn, the light burns low and orange from flickering

lanterns on the walls. The slabbed floor blanketed with hay, alfalfa, tiny balls of shit. Johnny Cash sings, hidden in speakers: *There's a silver lining behind every cloud. Just poor people, that's all we were.* Scarves of weed and cigarette smoke float. *Trying to make a living out of black land dirt.* Three bald men sit at a round table, a deck of cards split and fanned between them. *Daddy sang bass, Mama sang tenor.* A stocked bar built against a wall reaches to the rafters. A bulky man in a black Western shirt with a feather sticking out his pocket, Rowdy leans across the bar and smiles with lightbulb teeth at Miss Louise. Miss Louise is a hair-teased woman, with skin the same in-between shade as mine. Red tanktop, bleached denim, leather boots. Eden takes my wrist, leads me to the couple.

"Smells like y'all are talkin' shit," Eden says.

Miss Louise says, "You fat bitch!" She hugs Eden.

Rowdy wipes the clean bar with a stained rag. "Y'all act like you don't see each other every week."

Eden and Miss Louise sway in their perfumed embrace. I stand with limp arms and wait.

Mama Brown shuffles up, stands next to me. "So this the woman that gave you the abortion. What she use?"

"Pennyroyal and some other shit," I whisper.

"The fuck she been reading, almanacs? Everybody know you supposed to use cotton root bark." Mama Brown rubs her chin with her two-fingered hand, walks to Miss Louise. "Silly bitch, could have killed my baby."

Eden and Miss Louise untangle themselves. Mama Brown kicks Miss Louise behind her knee.

Miss Louise's leg folds. She falls. "Ooo, fuck," she says, "I got a charley horse."

Mama Brown waddles back to me. "You have your little drink, have your little fun. But promise me, you don't listen to nothing this woman say. She just like Cherry. Her and Eden." Her choice of sulking space: an empty table.

I want to say: *What, Mama Brown, all granny women got some competition in them? What she gave me worked, didn't it?* But Eden and Miss Louise too close by, they'd think I'd gone and lost it.

Eden helps Miss Louise stand. "You just a mean old curse. The minute you get around, my body acts up," Miss Louise says.

Eden shakes her head. "Woman, you'd make the Devil retire."

Miss Louise rests her thin arm on my shoulder. "You thirsty?"

"Yes, ma'am."

Rowdy climbs a ladder and scoops a mason jar of cloudy liquid, then climbs down; the spurs on his boots spinning like pinwheels. He hands the jar to Eden, who hands it to me, slices of peach and strawberry sunken in the murk.

"I'll open a tab," I say.

The three of them boomerang looks before snapping their heads to the ceiling and cackling. They carry on their conversation. I sip the moonshine, sweet burn in my mouth and throat. Two slot machines blink and flash against the opposite wall. I wander over and jam the jar in the crease of my elbow. It takes both hands to crank the lever, got to pull until my chest hurts. A little moonshine laps over the edge, splats on the floor. A fat rabbit with matted fur hops, sips away my mess. I squat to the rabbit and finger-rub its head. The bunny sips again, hops away, under the table of the bald men. The spinning ends: four cherries. In the port, my hand bounces until I feel my prize. A joint dried stiff by time, pocketed behind my ear for later. Last time I got crossfaded, I puked until constellations blotted my sight.

Cherry don't think about shit like that. I chug my moonshine, chew the soggy fruit. A tinny voice belts in the speakers: *I am a man of constant sorrow.*

Miss Louise puts a hand on my shoulder. I jump. "You walk quiet," I say.

"You don't want that." She plucks the joint from behind my ear. "Probably moldy as all get-out. We got fresh ones by the bar."

We stand side by side, staring at the flashing slot machines, listening to the blaring song. I glance at her. "Thank you for what you done."

"I been asking Eden to bring you here so I could check on you. But you was always busy, she said. I'm glad you stopped by. You look good. Quick healer."

"I don't think I know what healing means," I say.

She pats my back. "You just come on to the bar and get some drink and some smoke. If that don't help you ease your mind, I got something that will, hear?"

I look over to the empty tables. Mama Brown leans her head on her hand, scowling.

"I'll take a drink and a smoke," I say.

We walk, arms locked, to Eden and Rowdy.

Rowdy whisks away my jar, replaces it with a dewed can of beer. Miss Louise hands me a fresh joint.

"We're playin' poker after shots." Eden seesaws a knife into a lime.

"I don't know how to play." The words come out my mouth webbed.

"I can teach you," Miss Louise says.

"Y'all got horses?" I ask.

Rowdy nods his head to a door.

Beer clutched and stumbling, I twist the rusted doorknob, knock my ankle against a bin of Granny Smiths. Pinch a stem and carry the drooping apple. There's only one horse in the stable: skinny, pinto-colored, left eye milky with blindness. My hand hovers over the gate, tongue clicking like I'm calling a cat. The horse huffs hot breath but don't move. I balance the apple on top of the gate, light a cigarette, and he stretches his wet lips and accepts my present.

The dank taste of smoke—it was the joint I lit. The tickle in my chest makes me wish the horse could laugh with me. And I'm glad to be away from Eden. Couldn't stand to happy-slap cards with them, and if I lost, Eden would say: *You got the money to put down, or ain't you?* Then go on about red flags and what happens to the brain after spreading legs. Eden acting like she hold a jealousy for Cotton, like it's only room for her and him in the swaddle. I ain't got a want to be in their swaddle or anywhere near it. Maybe it ain't that—maybe she got a fear of this body I hold. Thighs thick and meant for slithering. Plump lips ready to suck souls. Like I'm some kind of Medusa. This brown skin telling her: *I am a whore, I am a hungry whore, won't you fill me up?* If I was put on this earth to strut and rock men into concussions, that ain't none of her goddamn business.

My gut swimming in that seasick way.

I bring my attention back to the horse. "Why you by your lonesome?"

The horse gazes at his cramped space.

Joint down to a splinter. "You wouldn't know lonely if it spit in your eye."

The horse huffs.

My vision, spur-spinning, trying to guide me to a heap of

hay. Drooled gags take over. Flies flock to the pool of vomit. Horse shit, musk, apple rot, and maggots. A cramping gut. I dry heave: emptied out. With my shoe, I fold fresh straw over my puke.

The horse whinnies. Here, an apple from my cupped palm. He nudges my hand away with a wet mouth. Another apple left on top of the gate, in easy reach of his brick teeth. "If you was really lonely, you'd eat it." From the bottom of his eye to his parched muzzle, my fingers stroke.

"Sorry you had to see all that." I leave it and the horse to sit in the smothering stench.

The old-sounding country and bluegrass switches to skillet-clang songs. Huddled at the bar, sharing a blunt: Miss Louise, Rowdy, Eden. "Who won?" I ask.

Looking at me with low eyes, sprayed red with vessels, they snicker.

"We ain't got to it yet," Rowdy says. His chuckle, a carried breath: burned indica, kiwi, liquor.

Much as I'm growing to hate Eden, she the only one I know enough to tell her my need. I tug her wrist. "Will you step outside with me?"

She passes the blunt to Rowdy, a globe of smoke trapped in her mouth, nods. Arm in arm, we stagger toward the door. Miss Louise catches up and locks her arm in mine. I gnaw the flesh of my inner cheek. My ears ache in the new silence of outside: a cloudy night with a warm touch of breeze. Three lighters flickering, three lit cigarettes.

"You just wanted fresh air?" Eden asks.

"Well, I—" I study Miss Louise. Eden's best friend might not

be white, but she ain't got a problem bobbing her head to Kid
Rock like he invented rhythm. "Just wanted fresh air, yeah."

Eden sways, props her slump body against the neon-flashing
wood. "What's a matter? Your eyes tell you're lyin'."

"I'm hungry."

Miss Louise smacks the meat of my arm with her knuckles,
and I resist the urge to bruise her eye. "Why didn't you say so?"
She presses her lips in the crack of the door and throws her shrill
voice above the music: "Rowdy, fire up the grill."

While Rowdy cooks, we sit at a table near the three bald men
and chain-smoke with bottomless shallow glasses. Whisky, vodka,
rum. Miss Louise talks over harsh guitar.

"But my granny and them was from Virginia. And then they
passed the Racial Integrity Act, so they moved over to Kentucky.
And my mama, Violet, she grew up learning about how to heal,
and so did I—"

A weight pulls my skull to the nook of my folded arms, and
I drift into a light sleep. A nudge on my shoulder; Eden's gone.
Miss Louise holds a basket lined with checkered paper. Next to
my nose, the boat thuds heavy. The steam of food revives my
energy. Eden's cussing drawl—she sits with Rowdy, both talking
with stuffed mouths.

"Thanks," I say.

Miss Louise rubs the nape of my neck. "You still got sadness in
your voice. The drinking and smoking didn't help none, did it?"

I shake my head.

"I got something for you. I'll be right back."

"Who are those bald men?"

Her face stiffens. "I thought you knew them." She laughs,

walks away with a limp wrist. Over her shoulder, she shouts, "Rowdy's cousins."

Mama Brown joins me at the table. "What she got for you ain't no good."

I look at her dead and knowing eyes. "I just want to try." Mama Brown got a way of picking people apart, seeing all their bad in one quick glance. I'm starting to see it, too, how Miss Louise got a longing to be just as pale as starlight. But her magic been working on me so far, took that burden of a child from me, so when she eases a chipped teacup balanced on a saucer to the table, I thank her.

"Poppy tea. This should help you relax," Miss Louise says.

Back at the bar, she fixes herself a drink. The brim of the teacup touching my lips.

Mama Brown slams a fist to the table. "Don't you sip that shit. You might as well pop a pill."

I gulp the tea, warmth sliding down my throat and into my belly. Before Mama Brown can open her mouth to scold me, to talk about the baby, to warn of Cricket and all his imagined bad, she fades away, taking any pain in my chest and head with her.

The loaded nachos: silk cheese, smoked pork shoulder, clots of sour cream, diced onion, jalapeños, black beans, and a small river of barbecue sauce. Let the food soak up the liquor. Let me have more liquor, for my salt-cured tongue. The bald men sit in their unmoving crescent, finger their cards. I stare at the soggy crumbs in my boat and try to listen. I think I hear them:

Bald Man 1: "The world's puzzle is . . ."

Bald Man 2: "My most important forget . . ."

Bald Man 3: "I don't know about . . ."

Rowdy groans, tosses up his arms to the rafters like he praising Jesus. Miss Louise leans back and laughs. She tilts too far, spills herself and her beer on the dirty floor. The rabbit sops up her brew.

Her smile almost too wide for her face, Eden rakes a pile of hundreds to her chest. "Y'all can kiss my fat ass." Bills stuffed in the mixing-bowl of her bra. "'Til next week."

Eden and I walk the long stretch of the parking lot. Our arms bump: dumb and directionless as June bugs. We toss our weight in the seats, cause the hearse to rock. A sputtering cough, then the steady growl of engine. Back down the driveway, past the gate, on the mountain road. We roll down our windows and smoke our throats raw. Downslope, she speeds, twists the dial of the radio. A man with a hum in his voice speaks: "Getting through this week's record highs with your favorite oldies station, Breezy 98.9." His voice fades to throbbing music: a creeping drumbeat, saxophone. *Summertime, and the living is easy.*

Eden swerves, misses a ravine, straightens her course. "I love this song." She boosts the volume.

Fish are jumping and the cotton is high. I stick my head and torso out the window, suck down the fast air. She don't care if her driving kills us, how she speeds, and for now, I don't, either. *Oh, your daddy's rich, and your ma is good-looking.* I close my eyes and let the wind soothe me. Good heat. Good, good heat perfumed with honeysuckle and early redbud, sumac. *So, hush, little baby, don't you cry.* We ride in cursive to the twinkling city.

18

I got to talk with Cotton about Vanessa. Her and her mourning husband won't leave my mind. I'll say: *There is a man who loved a woman with a starlet name,* then add: *She died from a pregnant spine; where is your heart?* I don't think what we do helps—but if there's even a chance it could—

—It's breakfast. He ain't sitting at the dining table, picking away at an egg. Eden shuffles out the kitchen, robe wrapped, her face shrouded with a clay mask, soles of her slippers sighing against the hardwood. She hands me a plate.

"You look like hell," she says. Disappears into the kitchen. Returns with two Bloody Marys. "Hair of the dog. Cotton wants to see you in the study after you eat."

"He say why?"

She shakes her head. Feels like I been called to the principal's office. Eden probably brought her gossip to him, that I been asking questions that don't concern me. That I been dipping into lunacy because that's what happens when a woman gets to fucking.

I thank Eden for breakfast, walk to the study a little tipsy with a full belly and heartburn. Cotton looks up from a massive book of paintings: haggard medieval sufferers, garland-hugged cherubs. He pats the cushion of the couch—no glare that say: *You a real bad girl*, no glare that say: *You did it.*

I sit.

The silence swells into a chorus of glances. And all I can think of is being kicked out, him saying: *It pains me to say this, I mean really, all doors are locked for you.*

"Cotton," I say. "A man went to a funeral and asked the widow if he could say a word. She was, like, *yeah, sure.*"

He squints. "What?"

My stammering starts. "The man gets to the front, and he says, 'Plethora.' The widow said, 'Thanks, that means a lot.'"

He chuckles. "What's your deal?"

I make sure to hold eye contact. Steady, curious. "My deal?"

"You seem . . ." He plants his finger on his cupid bow. "Brittle? Trepidatious."

"You misread."

"I don't misread."

"It's just . . . remember I found a letter you might've lost. Dr. Stephen Garland, wife Dr. Vanessa Garland."

He rubs his temple like all he got for me is a migraine.

"And when I asked Eden about it, she said that my mind must be cloudy from taking you to bed," I say.

"Eden is acting a trifle vapid," he mutters, "an expected development."

"I don't like this drama," I say.

"I'm sorry she's bothered you, Magnolia. I'll have a talk with her."

"No, that's fine." I ain't keen on the thought of Cotton scolding Eden for me, playing man of the house and setting his rules with a raised voice.

"What explanation did Eden offer when you presented the question? Her lying is habitual. I don't say that lightly, you know." He mimes tossing back alcohol. "Really, the case wouldn't work because his wife had a proper funeral."

"Why?" I ask.

"We answer to people who were denied a proper goodbye. He had his. Am I making myself clear?" He straightens his posture, scratches his chin. "I apologize if I'm being too cavalier."

"Yes, that makes sense." What he really means: some people's sorrow matters more than others. Acting like the purpose for all he does got to be pure, got to be just so to match his artistic vision. He didn't see a problem in having me answer to horny Reddit men, them swelling and thrusting to me on camera. At this point, I think all that matters to him is keeping my body limp as a swinging rope. Got to control my breathing while he stroke the meat of hisself.

"Really, I mean it—if you'd like, I can call Eden in here right now, and we can all have a proper discussion."

"No," I say, "that's fine. Why'd you want to see me?"

His face softens: *Everything's cool, fine, chill.* "I have a surprise for you." He stands with wild ginseng energy, claps. "I'll make this quick because I have to run. I'm creating two new packages. The first: you'll be in character while interacting with the families in person. Think a family reunion, or more like a cocktail mixer. The second: you'll be the stand-in during the funeral ceremonies."

"Cotton, I don't think—"

"When configuring the prices, I tried taking into account your discomfort: two grand for the family gatherings, and thirty-five hundred for the funerals. How does that sound?"

I swallow a burp. "Okay."

Cotton rushes out the room. I follow. "Wait."

He turns around and picks at his watch. His face say: *Go ahead, child, I ain't got the time for this.*

"Where's the storage unit? With my Mama Brown's things?"

He digs his phone out the pocket of his suit.

That piece of twine he keep floats to the floor unnoticed.

"I'll text you the address." He goes away, across the hall, down the stairs.

The face of my phone lights up with the address, and then another text: *Key on bookshelf in study.* Cotton, keeping the key to what's left of Mama Brown's life. A flash of anger. I pluck the piece of twine off the floor, his own private mojo, and pocket it. Whatever attachment he got is gone now. Let's see how he like it.

The place is only a mile from here. I look for the key on the top and middle shelves, find it on the bottom in front of the cracked spine of some novel: *Disgrace.* I scoop the key, but before I leave, I'm drawn to the desk with the growing pastel pile of nail clippings. It won't hurt to open a couple of drawers, just a glimpse. The top drawer: ballpoint pens, a blank legal pad. The middle: a pair of golden scissors. And in the bottom: a copy of the picture of my Nettle death, me kissing Ambrosia, tucked away for his own viewing pleasure.

I leave the room feeling like I'm covered in humid, unwanted kisses. In my hand, I finger the twine and decide to bundle up all my cash, stuff all my pockets. Bye, Eden. By the time I get to the bottom of the stairs, I got to weave through the crowd of incoming mourners.

The sun beats down on the asphalt of the parking lot. Wavering notes of the organ's welcome music bleed through the open doors. I walk a little faster, faster to escape the song. I ain't ever liked organs. Like the lonely whistle of a train. A sound that chills the hollow in me.

With all my unease, I feel a little grounded; I feel a little bold. This twine working something in me, letting me know that each step I take is deserved and meant. I see why Cotton likes it so much.

My feet don't slow when they hit the sidewalk but run me straight to the Save A Lot, to the aisle of spices. I buy a bottle of poppy seeds so I can sip peace when I choose, leave the store with the plastic bag hanging from my wrist.

On to the maze of storage units, faced with green slate. I bounce the key in my palm, flip it in search of a number. It don't say. I text Cotton: *Which unit?*

I wander through the lot. Maybe whatever the wisp of my soul knows can guide me. After Cherry started to lose weight and hair and teeth, she'd plant me in front of the TV while she ran off with Quarry. I watched *Labyrinth* over and over, until the VHS tape got tangled and torn. All the mystery, magic. Glamour and crystal balls. Like how I feel now. A two-headed creature hides behind a red shield, guards unit three. Another behind a blue shield guards unit four. One guard always tells the truth, the other always lies. One of the units leads to a gory death, the other to Mama Brown's things. I say to them beasts: *I don't like your breath, and y'all wrinkled as bath hands, and I ain't following your rules.* I stick the key in unit three. Won't turn. Damn, I died.

My phone dings: *Unit 11. Any chance you've seen my twine around?*
I say: *No sorry,* then walk uphill, watch the numbers grow and the
size of the units shrink. Twist the key in the lock. The door rolls
up, invites me to cramped shadows. The furniture crammed in.
No room to walk. My phone's flashlight wavers around the coffee
table, boxes of Goodwill plates and snow globes, until I see it.
The velveteen ballerina box packaged in bubbles and stuffed in a
corner. I stretch my arm over the nightstand, pull it close to me.
The plastic pops when I tear and finally hold its softness.

"You think we was living small," Mama Brown says.

I scream.

She sits twisted and hunched on her recliner in the darkness,
with boxes crushing her lap, laughing. "You got an apology for
me?" She shifts her weight, a box tumbles from her body to the
others hoarded. "You was acting evil in that barn."

"I'm sorry, Mama." Every fight we've had flickers through
my mind. Wasn't many *I hate yous* in the itchy rage of puberty,
wasn't many slammed doors and *leave me bes*, but there was
enough to add to my heap of regret. "I just had so much going
on yesterday."

"I wish you'd talk to me about these things, baby." Her voice
carries a sad bass; she singing our blues. "I ain't sure how much
longer I got left." She pulls her arm out from under her—her
hand no longer a hand, but an oozing, fingerless knob.

My legs jerk in her direction. I got to hug her, at least pat her
shoulder, but all these packed-away things block my moving. All
the times that same hand weaved my hair to the scalp, slammed
down cards yelling *Uno,* fed my little self rice. "Why you here?"

"I was homesick." She gives me a knowing glance, the corners
of her mouth twitching to a grin. "What you got in that bag?"

"Garlic powder." I put the ballerina box in the bag. "We was out."

Her mouth opens just for a second, and I know she was fixing to say we got fresh bulbs in the garden, but she catches herself. "I want you to think, really think—" She raises the hand that still got fingers. "Once this is gone, I imagine Cricket will move on to the toes. I ain't keen on finding out what's after that."

"Do you hurt?"

"In a way you can't know, yes."

I reach for the roll-up door. "What does she sound like? When she cries?"

Her head tilts, lips pursed in consideration. "Something like you."

The door clangs shut with my tug. Unit locked, key tucked away. My next stop a little farther. My fingers keep fumbling to my pockets, checking the padding: cash, key, twine. Yes, this twine making me walk with purpose. And Cotton's money got a weight to it. All these hundreds I been letting sit around, un-spent, been weighing me down, making me trudge.

On Selma Avenue, the sun hangs past its peak. The first house on the block has a pretty red door where a woman sits on the porch with spread legs. Bag of sunflower seeds in her grip. I walk up her yard, past a tipped-over tricycle: pink with grass-stained tires. She eyes me.

"Ricky ain't here," she says.

"You know where I can find Cigarette Sammy?" Cherry told me he stay on Selma, didn't say which end.

The woman splits a shell with her front teeth and shoots it to the lawn with glossed lips. "What you want with him?"

"I got to give him something."

"He stay on the corner." She chews. "If you get to the cross with flowers, you went too far."

The house on the corner ain't got a yard. I shuffle around an SUV sleeping on a small bit of gravel, just off the road. The porch: a tight square, carpeted green. I knock on the door. The barks of a dog echo. Heavy footsteps—the knob turns. Cigarette Sammy stands. His feet ain't still.

"Who is it, Sammy?"

He groans, rushes away, leaves me lingering in the doorway. A thin woman sits in a recliner, bonnet snug on her head. *Judge Judy* plays on the TV—the court channel. On her lap, a green comforter printed with burgundy diamonds, the same design as Mama Brown's bed set. She studies me: my head, the ballerina box, my shoes, then back up, and I know how I look in these clothes. She turns her head to the TV.

"I ain't buying nothing," she says.

"I want to help Cigarette Sammy."

She looks at me, embers in her eyes. "That ain't his name."

"When he was arrested—"

"I sit up waiting and waiting for my baby boy to come home. Come to find out, some woman took him home and got him put in jail. And I had to sit here and wait and save enough to get him out. Lucky he got out when he did 'cause it would have been weeks more on my end."

"I didn't know."

"What?"

And now telling his mama: *I didn't know he had a home* is just foolish. *I didn't know you loved him; I thought I could take your place. When he oinked at me, I thought he meant I was home, not you, not that he missed your loving but needed mine. Hello, I am an uppity woman, look at how nice my pants cling to me, look inside my pocket—can you see I done stole a string from a white man? Watch the way it make me move, and can I adopt your grown son and maybe sell you something, too?*

She pushes away the comforter, walks to the door, props her hand on the doorframe. "Please tell me you that bitch, 'cause I got words for you."

"I got the charges dropped," I say, and what I really mean is: *We from the same place. I ain't what I look like, not really.* I dig some money out my pocket: five hundred. "Here," I say.

"The fuck I need your money for?"

"I thought—"

"My Sammy don't want for nothing." She grabs the doorknob. "He sure as hell don't need saving from you." The door slams. From inside, she yells, "My Sammy just fine."

I whisper to the closed door. "Yeah? Why you let him wander so much?" I creep around the SUV, to the mailbox planted at the edge of the gravel lot, on the lip of the ditch. "Why he know people under the bridge?" I open the flap, push dollars between letters and an IGA sales paper. Five hundred, a thousand, more and more. I stop when I know I got just enough to last me, until the only thing I got in my pocket is the twine, a key, and my new thin stack of money.

I leave feeling lighter. Feel like I could float on, easy as milkweed seed. I run around the curve of street, past the memorial cross, down the hill. Pass through side streets shouldered with dense woods, by grills churning out the smoke of tender meat. Past natural-haired toddlers yipping down a dish soap lathered Slip 'N Slide, by bouncing trampolines and a dark father and light son practicing golf on trimmed Bermuda. All these empty houses and full yards tell me: *You ain't ever been as lonely as you are right now.*

A squirrel on the edge of the road stops with a rigid spine. It got the cloudy sky of a robin's egg cupped in its little hands. A twig snaps as I near. It skitters away, treat pouched in its cheek. *Even the wild don't want you.* To hell with the wild. I step off the road and follow the fat squirrel into the woods but get distracted by the black eyes of halved walnuts on the ground and lose sight of its bushy tail. I sit against the thick trunk of a shagbark hickory and peel away its soft rind.

Mama Brown crawls from behind the tree, sits next to me. Her breath hitches.

"He had a home," I say.

"You remember when you'd play witch?" she asks.

When I first moved in with Mama Brown, I spent most of my playtime in the woods. Mama would be hunkered in the garden, making cherry tomatoes and mustard greens drink. And I gathered pine needles, acorns, and rubied spicebush seeds. My cauldron was a bowl I snuck out the kitchen—clear, plastic, stained orange from microwaved spaghetti. I'd stand on an ant-covered log, raise my mountain mix above my body. I'd tilt up my head and whisper to the birds perched on branches: *I'ma fly like you.* Then it was the caterpillars I'd call on: *I crawl wherever I want, but my flashy wings coming.* I'd look down at my feet, clamp my eyes shut, dump the mess on my head.

"Yes."

She chuckles. "You remember that bug?"

Once, I ain't realize a granddaddy long legs had crept in my cauldron. My screams carried to Mama's plants; we met, mid-sprint, where jungle turned to mowed lawn. She chuckled when she plucked it from the nest it made in my coils. Later, in the tub, she chuckled some more as she kneaded coconut shampoo into my scalp. *You was just going to let that mean old spider eat you. What do we say to mean old spiders?* My eyes shut to avoid stray suds: *My mama's got a gun.* Her fingers would still in the clean clutter of my hair. *That's right, baby.* And then she would croon: *I think of you every morning. I dream of you every night. Darling, I'm never lonely whenever you are in sight.*

"I remember."

She nods, scratches her chin. A bit of her skin falls to the ground, and I'm reminded that each time she comes around, there's less and less of her. She finds it under a leaf, presses it on. It falls. "You put that role of magic worker onto yourself way back. But when you put roles on to somebody else, it's too heavy for them. You get that, don't you?"

"Maybe." I can't take this weariness in her eyes, the way each suck of air from her got a whistle to it. Hurting in ways I can't understand, a pain too far away for me to feel.

"Cigarette Sammy could've never been your friend because you wanted a son out of him."

"You ever done that? Put a role on somebody who can't have it?"

She cackles. "I had a history teacher right around the time I started bleeding. Thought I'd marry him and carry his children. Can't tell you how disappointed I was when I found out the grown man was married to a grown woman."

And suddenly there's a cold stillness in the air, the chill of a movie theater, in the middle of summer, ice on my skin.

Mama tries to smile, but her muscles too weak. Her blinks slow.

"What is it, Mama?"

"You hear that laughing?" she asks.

I listen: only forest sounds, chittering and tweeting, dropping acorns. "What?"

Before she can answer, the corner of her forehead droops, flaps over. Edge of the fallen skin meets the tip of her eyelash. And the silliness in her face is what makes my breathing stagger, her look of: *Oh, I got a hair in my eye, oh foolish.* Trying to blink away her breaking body. Like a flush of water can fix this.

"No, no, no," I say.

"What is it, child?" Her hands follow my look, touch her face, and she look embarrassed. Like she should be the one apologizing now.

I'll get in touch with Miss Louise. I bet she got answers, how to get rid of Cricket. That won't stop Mama Brown's decay. It'll at least slow it. Feeling like I solved the problem soothes me. I stand with too much air held in my lungs and rush away because I can't lose again, not right now. No parting words with her, keep running and running, hoping my last memory with her ain't steeped in melting time on a forest floor. On land that ain't ours. Mama Brown's living voice replaying in my head during the long journey back to the funeral parlor: *That's right, baby* and *Dandelions got wishes in them* and *Ain't nothing in the closet, see?*

Inside, I get Miss Louise's number from Eden. My asking seems to please Eden, seems to make her think I'm on her side. That I can behave, kick and buck to Kid Rock like one of the good ones. The ballerina box lies on my unmade bed. Calmed by a shower, I sit on the edge of the bed, hold the box, watch my footprints dry. I call her.

"I got to get rid of somebody," I say.

She don't answer, just static and silence on the other end.

"It's Magnolia," I say.

Finally, she speaks. "You got a pen and paper?"

19

Soon as I wake up, I get dressed, Miss Louise's instructions pocketed, ready to go down to my first stop, Big Lots. Cotton in his pink robe stops me right before I reach the staircase.

"Oh, good, you're up."

"Just running to the store."

"There's no time." He whisks me away, hurried footsteps to Eden's door. "We have two cases."

Mama Brown's melting face sears my thinking. "Today?"

"An in-person and a stand-in a week from today." He knocks. "We have to prepare—Eden!" More knocking.

Makeup clattering on the other side of the door, she finally answers, misting her Daryl Hannah face with setting spray. "This is why you don't have horses; you just can't hold 'em." She eyes Cotton's hand and its loose rest against my hip, ushers me into her bedroom.

"I'll be in the dining room when you're ready," Cotton says.

Eden shuts the door. "Heaven help us; he's lost his twine."

I got it tucked away in Mama Brown's ballerina box, just like they got that case cloaked in shadows.

Eden's hand gives a voilà spin. "We got a long day ahead of us."

Big Lots closes at nine. If I miss it, maybe Eden could drive me to Walmart, but I don't want to answer the questions she'll throw. On her bed: a nude waist trainer, a little black dress, and beside that, two silicone bra inserts. They look like chicken breasts. On the floor, shining black heels with red bottoms.

I undress. "Why I got to wear all this?"

She grabs the waist trainer, wraps it around my back. "Hold the bottom together." I pinch the bottom closed. Her fingers go to work—hooking the first clasp, the second. "Need to break everything in." Her knuckles dig into my gut with the fourth and fifth clasps. "And it don't hurt to practice being uncomfortable." She wrestles with the latex until it closes around me.

I can't bend to pick up the dress; got to curtsy. The party dress sticks to my body—smoothed and squeezed into an hourglass, and I can feel the time sand falling, falling. Eden hands me the bra inserts. They press against my nipples, push up and round my flesh to say: *Hello, world, I am ripe. It is time for harvest. Hello, I am sweet and would like to be plucked.*

Eden holds my hand when I slide into the heels, and we walk with careful steps to the dining room. A spread of appetizers on the table: blue tortilla chips and guacamole, syrup-glazed figs topped with slices of bacon, tiny toasts with a seafood-smelling paste, bowls of fat grapes and oranges, and a bottle of champagne.

Cotton enters holding a saucer, pink sticks of bubblegum

fanned out on the ceramic. "First thing—we need to manufac-
ture an accent." He hands me a piece, sets the rest on the table.

I chew. Sweet spit.

"Say, 'I am going to the stables. I am an equestrian.'"

I repeat.

He shakes his head. "Your vowels are too yawning, and you
dropped a *g*, and your *r* was too harsh. Try again."

I repeat.

"You could sound a little more . . ." He looks to the chandelier, searching for the right word. "Articulate." He must pick up
on my rage because he starts stammering. Pauses. Collects himself. "Picture this: you were raised reading Sir Francis Bacon and
own original copies of Encyclopedia Britannica."

I repeat, make sure my words come out clipped.

"Much better."

"Why's she got to chew gum?" Eden asks.

"It enhances cognitive performance. I'm also hoping it will
work the muscles."

I hope Eden don't pick up on the excitement in his voice at
the mention of my mouth's insides.

"Lazy Southern tongue," Eden says.

"Let's work on tone," says Cotton.

I can feel the minutes ticking with every hugged breath I
take—does Mama Brown still got legs and teeth? Where are her
eyes? Did Cricket play pretend God and abduct a rib?

Cotton cups my chin, tilts it upward like I'm trying to sniff
heaven. He runs his hands up my side; I straighten my posture.
"You'll want your voice to be an almost-whisper with an under-
belly of sarcasm."

"I am going to the stables. I am an equestrian."

"A little deeper," Cotton says.

And I make my voice sexy, dripped candlewax on skin, silk-rope sexy.

"Yes, and a little softer."

Eden hands me a glass of champagne, and my drinking is eager. The coldness hardens the bubblegum. A stream of the tang dribbles down my chin.

"I think this is a good place to discuss dining etiquette," Cotton says. "Which of these is most appealing to you?"

I point to the chips and guacamole.

Cotton nods. "Go ahead."

I place the old gum on a napkin. Scoop the dip, wiggle it to the center of the chip, and bite. A green splat in my cleavage. "I am an equestrian."

Eden grabs a chip and mops up the mess on my chest, swallows.

Cotton interrupts our giggling. "That's what you don't want to do." He points to the tiny toasts, the figs. "You should stick to one-bite foods."

One summer, Quarry quit his job, so we ate lunch for free every weekday at my elementary school. Bosco sticks and square cuts of pizza. Hamburger patties with so many fatty circles like they were growing pale colonies of nostoc. When we'd leave, Quarry would nudge Cherry into going back to the register to ask for three more trays to take home to the brothers I ain't got. The head lunch lady always snarled, but the other one would give us a church smile and pack the food for us in a plastic bag, probably knowing it was our supper.

"Do I need to know which spoon does what?" I ask.

"Only finger foods, no seated interactions."

Eden taps the tightness of my belly. "You sure can't sit in that thing."

"Show us your walk," Cotton says.

I walk, eyes cast to my inching progress: heel toe, heel toe, the snug leather biting my feet.

"Look up, honey," Eden says.

I do, and it makes me wobble, makes me wonder if Cotton's counting on me to fall, a damsel in tumble.

"Go slower," Cotton says.

"Lean back a smidge," says Eden.

I pace wide rectangles around the table, imagine I'm walking on a tightrope, and if I stumble, well, I won't be hurt because I'll land on the cushion of a trampoline. And ain't the feeling of dropping more freeing than this small-stepped march? The bra inserts cling to my tits and feel like some bad mouth, sucking out sweat. My back itches. To reach my spine and claw's only going to lead to Cotton sighing out a *Start over, you,* all while the sun keeps moving, keeps streaking the sky with past hours.

"She'll be glidin' in no time," Eden says. Hands me another glass of champagne.

I sip with a pinched mouth made for nursing.

"We'll work on that," Cotton says, "Let's try role-playing."

"How was the drive here?" Eden asks.

"It was lovely," I say, "dare I say, exquisite."

"Magnolia, please, you aren't a European butler," Cotton says.

We talk about houses and paintings and movies, my practiced voice tugging every cord in my throat, them both grinning every time I hit the right note, sling wit from my mouth.

Cotton sits and nibbles a fig. "Okay, you can change now."

I scurry to Eden's room, kick off the heels, shimmy out the dress. The waist trainer resists my fumbling knuckles—I got to slow down and pick at each hook. When it finally opens, I got new breath and a fierce itch across my stomach, beneath my bra, down the slope of my back. A bouquet of welts along my hips where the latex pinched most. Back in my walking clothes, in my flip-flops worn by miles, out Eden's room.

Before I make it to the staircase, Cotton calls my name from the study.

Trudging footsteps guide me to him. He got the projector beaming, paused on a wide field ruffled by wind. "Have a seat." A bowl of popcorn beside him.

"I thought we were done."

"With the debutante rehearsal, for now." He takes a handful from the bowl, crunches. "We have several documentaries to watch."

"Can't we scatter them throughout the week?" I ask.

His chewing brakes: *I ain't thought of that; I only thought of you sitting next to me so long your body feels pumped with anesthesia, eyes still open, parched for anything but light.* "I suppose we could watch just this one for today, then."

Eden peeks her head in, a long pause before she speaks, and I can see in her eyes she studying the distance between me and Cotton, wondering if my legs pressed shut with effort. Disgust in her voice: "I'm goin' to the mountains."

And my gut tightens with what's unsaid. Miss Louise going to say: *That girl you got want somebody gone* and then *She using my magic to make a bad into a good.* I want to chase after her, tell her to please stay, but I stay seated. Lean into the brightness on the wall, this three-hour documentary on wild horses in Spain.

Halfway through, after they finish talking about trimmed manes and beet pulp, I ask, "Did the family raise Andalusian horses?"

His attention kept on the mare bounce-trotting in a pasture. "They owned one for a few months when their deceased daughter was young."

"It was Andalusian?" I ask.

"Probably." He reaches for more popcorn, fingers tapping against the empty bowl. "But this will make for good conversation padding, nevertheless."

When the credits roll, my head thuds with beating hooves. I don't expect Cotton to let me go; it's been one more thing all day. I don't move from the couch.

He rises, reaches to a stack of note cards. "Expanding your vocabulary will be helpful as well."

He holds up a card printed in bubbled script: turgid. He says the word with a soft *g*. I repeat. He flips the card: 1. Swollen or congested. 2. Pompous or bombastic. The next card: tumescence. He pronounces, I repeat. Again: 1. Swollen or becoming swollen (think erectile tissue). 2. Pompous or pretentious.

"Do I need both words?" I ask.

"You never know," he says. The next card: Quark. 1. Any of a number of subatomic particles carrying a fractional electric charge, postulated as building blocks of the hadrons. 2. A type of low-fat curd cheese.

We go through the thick stack one at a time, then cycle through again and again—me guessing the definition before he flips the card to reveal: *No, silly girl, you have read the definition of bibelot for innominate; you just ain't right.*

We finish. I wait with every ounce of dread, hoping he dismisses me.

He yawns. "That's it for the day. More for tomorrow."

I rise, go to the door, and before I can check my phone for the time, he says my name.

"You did great today."

My thanks: a nod, pressed lips, one more second of lingering to let him know I mean it. Then through the hall, down the stairs, patting my pockets—phone, cash, Miss Louise's instructions. Outside, the sky's edges swirl, pink and violet. Clear of clouds besides those plane trails, crossed thin, looking like stretch marks. It's only eight o'clock. I'll make it before close. On my way, I text Eden: *How's Miss Louise?* She sends me a picture of them slumped over cigarettes. In the background, Rowdy's flipping off the camera. No mention of my phone call, my request for witching help.

In the store, I walk up to the first worker I find. Short white man with gray hair thin as tissue. "You know where I can find asafetida?"

He scrunches his face like I'm trying to shovel pea mush in his gummy mouth. "I can ask a manager."

I tell him ain't no need, thank you. Shuffle on to the candle aisle, phone out, I search for substitutes. Scribble out asafetida, write garlic powder, onion powder. No black candles. The one closest sits dark blue in a jar, Midnight Rain. The scent's so strong of lilies it makes me clear my throat. In the basket it goes.

Now to the spice aisle. I add to my basket cayenne, chili; out of garlic powder, so I settle for garlic salt, onion powder.

The next item on my list: a wasper's nest. I ain't poking and prodding at a stinging thing's home. Instead, I go to the office supply section and grab a pack of thumbtacks.

One last thing: soil from a graveyard. I ain't thieving from the dead, ain't taking crumbles of their home. Miss Louise said when I go for the dirt, it'd be smart to walk in backward because spirits are gossipy as robins, and if they catch sight of my face, they might want to know who I am, what I'm up to, and follow me home. I find that same worker and ask, "Y'all got potted plants?" I could take from whatever wilts.

He walks me to the garden section: only fake plants. I got to go to the graveyard. I got to walk on bones. If I don't, Cricket will only speed up Mama Brown's end. Keep ripping into her like she a cut of good meat. A rush to the clothes, pick the thickest shirt I can find—a purple fleece hoodie—to cover my face. In the basket.

A hurried checkout. Then out into the night, down the sidewalk. A couple blocks past the funeral home. New moon, the only light comes from passing spotlights of cars, yellow streetlights.

The wrought iron fence locked shut. A historical marker with bronze statements about senators and congressmen laid to rest. I put on the hoodie and circle the property until I find an opening in the fence. Hickory roots—twisted around the iron, making it sag. I leave my bags on the other side. Hoodie over my head, I tug on the strings until my face is hidden. Off the perch of fence, to the ground. A warm breeze makes the old hickory's leaves whisper: *I been here so long, so long, how I get to be so knotted and stretched?* Ahead of me in shadows, men on horses—and I know they only statues of gun-toting men—but I can hear them, almost, galloping and gargling, bullet-rattled breathing, asking: *Who is that woman? Who is that woman with no face cupping soil? Who is that woman leaping over that fence?*

Back on the sidewalk, I dump the soft dirt in the bag and

flee, wiping the mess on my jeans. A run up the side street, feet pounding on litter, and I still feel those eyes on me. Eyes with a watch that got a lotion seep. A little more light on Broadway. Across the street, St. John's Lutheran Church. I ain't notice it earlier—stained glass haunted with holy men. The church bell rings, strikes a different fear in me. Sends me into a lunging flight.

That sense of being stalked goes away in the parking lot of the funeral home. Up the stairs, I hear Eden's violent retching. Can't hear Cotton's softness, but I know he in there holding her hair back, pamphlet-fanning her face. Straight to the kitchen. In the pantry, behind a sack of flour, waits my poppy seeds. Just a little peace before clawing at the plum skin called time. Heat high, water boiling in the pot. Off the heat, dump the seeds in. A spoonful of sugar. I take the teacup, almost overflowing, to my room. Clink it on the nightstand.

I unroll a pair of knee-high socks and toss one to my bag by the bed. Sitting on the floor, back against the mattress, I slam back the tea. Ain't as sweet as Miss Louise's. Legs spread, I light the candle, push it to the edge of my feet. Each ingredient gets emptied into the sock: chili powder, cayenne, onion, salt of garlic, a handful of thumbtacks, a prick of my blood—accidental but can't hurt—graveyard dirt, and the froth of my spit for good measure. Miss Louise said I got to set my intent with this hot foot powder—either put it in their shoes or in a bottle with their name on it. Since I ain't got either, I settle for both. My sock, tied at the end. In red lipstick, I spell his name with care like I picked it myself. And my body feels like sleeping, my body feels like rest. But I got to keep going.

Cotton's footsteps creak the wood, no more gagging. He stops by my door, probably tempted to knock, to creep into my sleeping hours, then heads on down the hall to his bedroom.

I keep my demands inside my head. Not a drop of sound coming out this room to make him turn around.

Cricket, you a nasty bug. You go on and you get. What princesses you got locked in that Bible? What if Jezebel was good. Leave Delilah alone. No, you leave my Mama Brown alone. How she falling apart and you been gone decades, still salesman-walking with pluck. I don't want to know. I hate you. You going to wander for the rest of your not-life. Damn your burning feet. You don't want to see Mama Brown. No more. You find somebody different. You find somebody different with enough to give. My mixing hotter than the hell you deserve. See this mean mixing. Know it bites. Know the teeth strong from a bitter nursing. I said my piece. One, two, three.

Miss Louise said I should take it to a river, let the current carry my words. But every muscle in me soft as butter, and every movement feels like a prologue to melting. The toilet eats up everything but the thumbtacks and sock. I drag my feet to the kitchen garbage 'cause I can't stand the thought of snoozing near his name. And if Cotton asked why I'm throwing away a good piece of cloth, something meant to be hammered, I'd just say I'm sleepwalking 'cause that's close enough to the truth.

In bed, my prayer: *Good night, Mama, can you feel the healing?* and *Good night hollow teacup, you got an acid kiss that I can stand to love.*

20

One week since cursing Cricket, and I ain't seen Mama Brown. I tried everything—standing in front of the mirror and slapping my face until I see the Big Dipper, staring at that blood bloom on my mattress and almost giving in to seeing that child, saying: *Let me see you, you whining thing.* Even bought more poppy seeds hoping she'd be so pissed to see I'm flirting with something like death she'd come to scold. It don't work. Just ends with me floating between awake and asleep. Head lolling all easy. But I know she ain't gone-gone. I can feel her.

I sit in bed and reread the next case, sent in an envelope sealed with wax.

Cotton and Eden Productions:
In the package you will find home videos, pictures, and personal items of Savannah Foster. Savannah Foster was born November 17, 1989. Her younger brother, Ryan,

can be seen in the videos. She was Irish-Catholic. She held loyalty close in all she did. Daily, she wore Yves Saint Laurent's Black Opium mixed with rosewood oil. Her favorite color was periwinkle. She was last seen in Paris, France, on July 24, 2012.

Best,
Arnold & Shirley Foster

The family will be here in a few hours. Cotton taught me about horses, about the history of Paris, the importance of the candelabra. Nothing about what makes their insides turn, what makes them tickle. From the internet, I learn more about Savannah, that the police say they suspect someone close made a drunken mistake. No arrests, no search warrants. Last night, Eden and Cotton and I watched the videos they sent: Savannah caressing her violin in a dining room, jumping rope in a cafeteria-size garden. Butlers serving her birthday cake.

Eden knocks on my door, then steps in, jeweled up and blushing, looking like Meryl. "Giddy up."

I push the case files from my lap and bring a picture of the butchered socialite. Eden pins up the picture and smears moisturizer into my cheeks.

"How you feelin'?"

I close my eyes to her massaging touch. "Nervous."

"I can't blame you. We got an hour 'til the family gets here. I got somethin' to get you feelin' like a socialite."

Her fingers lift from my face. "I don't—" I open my eyes. She ain't in the room. She steps out her bathroom with a cupped hand and drops a pill on my thigh.

I stare at the blue tablet on my skin: a grain of sea in a desert. "I'm okay."

Her nerves show: brush bouncing with her thumb, shifting legs. "I ain't sayin' I ain't got no faith in you." The bristles swirl in gold powder. "I'm just sayin' we got a lot of money on the line. And I sure as hell couldn't do what you're fixing to." She leans over me, shades my eyes. "Playin' the living dead on camera's one thing, but a party—"

Cotton walks in without knocking. I cover the pill with my hand.

"Let's do a run-through." His eyes, wide and looking for comfort.

"Give the girl a break." Eden streaks concealer down the bridge of my nose. "All through dinner last night it was: *Are you sure you understand? What perfumes did she like mixin'? Round like an* O." A glob of foundation dumped on the brush. "Hell, I could play the woman at this point."

He tosses me a stick of unwrapped bubblegum. "Let me hear it."

"Can't you wait 'til I'm finished?" Eden asks.

He yells, a new anger he keep right below the surface: "Either she kills it tonight." Don't want to say it out loud. "Or—"

Eden sighs, slams the foundation brush on her vanity. The cream flecks the mirror.

Talking to Eden like I ain't even in the room. A part of me wants to give him back his twine. If he fired me right now, I'd have no place to go and a worn cushion of mostly spent rent money. My heart got a hummingbird beat. I pop the gum in my mouth and chew until it stretches like taffy. I speak in my best film noir voice: "Hello, Papa. Dear Mother. Water and oil are a racing picture."

Cotton points to his mouth, opens and closes like a minnow gulping algae.

Eden says, "Shit fire, her mouth is round enough to deepthroat a lamp. She's got it." She waits for him to leave. He don't.

I work my words into the gum, into my jaw. "Water, Papa. Hello, Dear Oil Mother, look at my racing picture."

Cotton crosses his arms and nods. "And what do you call your little brother?"

"Ry-Ry," I say.

"And what if he happens to make fun of you? What do you call him?"

"The Kid," I say.

His mouth opens: teaspoon, tablespoon, quarter cup. "Move your lips like a fan." He opens and closes, opens and closes.

"What in the shit does that mean?" Eden pushes him out the door. "You're stressin' us. Get."

He pokes his head back in. "And what don't you mention?"

"Cause of death or suspects."

Eden's weight against the door makes Cotton pull his face away to the sound of a clicking lock. She hunches over me, blending in the makeup. "Don't you listen to him. You're staying here even if the party goes to shit." She don't mean it. A tone of pleasure hides in her voice—she got a want to see a split, to see the slutty girl kicked out to the streets. And even if she did want me to stay, the only power Eden holds in those manicured hands is the key to the hearse and pills.

"You got water?" I ask. I swallow the pill.

My hair: clamped between the heated plates of a straightener, clip-in extensions. That bare-knuckled fight with the waist trainer until I'm squeezed thin. Don't bother me as much now. I wiggle into a tight dress, black and tempting as midnight. Pearls strung around my neck. The red bottoms gone, a different pair of high heels lifting my soles.

Between Eden's fingers, the clasps of the heels tighten. "These were hers, you know."

"Who?"

"Savannah's. Family sent them with the package."

My toes squirm in the grip of lilac leather. Eden takes me by my for-now white arm, tugs me to the dining room where Cotton walks the length of the table, shut mouth, pointed finger bobbing over every teacup quiche, every cucumber sandwich, each slimed oyster. Wineglasses line the edges: three already puddled with merlot. Eden hands me one and sips from the other.

Cotton don't look up from the spread he stalks. "Twenty minutes." He rushes away, down the hallway, shouts from his study: "Where is my twine?"

Let the man panic.

Eden shuffles her feet. We both caught his jitters. I got on a dead woman's shoes. I got to look this family in the eyes and make them believe I ain't me. Make them believe I known and loved them all my life. Make myself believe it wasn't Mama Brown pluck a bug from my curls, but Arnold and Shirley Foster. And it wasn't a bug in the forest. It was pigeon shit; it was hot Manhattan sidewalk. A twinge, a bright heat in my gut. Mama Brown knows I'm trying to blink her memory away, just for a little. She should understand. She done some shit, too. If I mess this up—if my mouth ain't round enough when I speak, if my spine ain't debutante-rigid, what then? I seen anger at a losing scratch-off, anger at buried men. I seen anger at people stooped in big, shining buildings. But all that mad came from the same dirt I stomp. Cotton and Eden's anger, that's different. Their anger buys houses and ups the rent. Their anger pulls strings with prosecutors.

"Be back." I rush to my room, to my bathroom, all while cradling "my" with steady hands on the inside. When I look in the mirror, all my worry slips down the drain. This face ain't mine.

I am Savannah Foster. I am at a party on a big, fancy yacht. We dance and sing along off the coast of France. Everyone here got on bikinis and pearls. A man comes up to me on the dance floor. He say: *You sing like it hurts.* He say: *That means you mean it.* He takes a step forward. I dance, hypnotic sway of hips, all the way to the railing. He presses into me. The cool metal of the railing bumps my spine. The man say: *Sing a song for peace.* And suddenly I don't got a voice. His promise for peace is demand in disguise. The way his eyes beg, he wants to take from me. *Go on, sing.* And right before he can take what's mine, I take it for him. I leap from the edge of the yacht. The fall rushes up my tummy. The fall is dark. When I crash to the water, it don't even hurt. Because I am home in mesh of kelp; I am churning seafoam.

A prickle shoots up the soles of my feet, around the knobs of my ankles, up, up my legs and thighs. That prickle twines around me like wisteria. I walk, giddy, back to the dining room.

Eden stands, mid-pour. Cotton's piercing eyes focus on thick wedges of gouda. His hair's a forgotten nest. "Magnolia, have you seen my twine?"

"I haven't."

A long sigh through bunched lips. "Goddamn it."

My movements flittering, outstretch a glass. Eden pours. The grin on my face is right and good. I got on a dead woman's shoes.

"I want to dance," I whisper.

"That means it's workin'," she says.

"I need to go down. They're arriving soon." Cotton's nails click on the face of his watch. "One more time."

I straighten my back, roll my shoulders. "I am an equestrian drinking water and oil. The taste is turgid. Is that not a riot?"

He checks his pockets again and again like the meaning of life sits in them with balls of lint. "You keep that up." He makes it to the stairs, turns around, and calls, "And don't smile so much. They'll think it's bullshit."

Minutes pass. Eden and I down our drinks until the first bottle of wine is hollowed. I want to dance. I want to run and shed my clothes. Voices in the lobby: murmurs, neck-tie chuckles, Cotton's welcomes. Footsteps creep up the stairs.

"Should I sit?" I ask.

"Talk to me until you see them." We clink glasses. "They're friends you ain't seen in a long, long time."

The feet reach the top of the stairs, enter the dining room: Arnold and Shirley.

"Mommy. Daddy." I toss my hands up; the wine in my glass flirts with the brim.

Shirley touches her face—cheeks, eyebrows, temples—like she got to make sure she real before she know I am. "Vannah," she says.

They wrap me tight in their arms. I feel all my stickiness and hope Eden's setting spray locked the color in. After they release me, I scan their clothes. A smudge of foundation at the root of Shirley's thumb that matches her skin, almost. Barely noticeable.

A tall man with blond hair dripping to his shoulders brushes by, mutters, "This is so fucked."

Arnold and Shirley study my face, eyes big and popping, like they waiting for a diagnosis.

"Did The Kid lose his ascot again?"

Rowdy laughter, a slap on my back, they guide me to the crowd gathering around the table. A hand grips my wrist. A woman, all edges—pointy elbows, collarbone jut, a grin that stretches too wide for her small face. She got on a short dress. Burgundy, taffeta. Margot, the best friend.

"Let's find the bathroom," she says.

Leading her through my room to the bathroom, I pretend I'm lost. She closes the door. Out of her pocket, she offers a thin bubble of plastic full of tooth-white dust.

"Tell me about Paris, bitch." Her hands steady, scraping lines on the marble sink; she snorts.

"The men eat good pussy," I say.

"No. Say the men know how to lick."

I echo her words. She smiles and taps my ass, urges me with her eyes to breathe in the stuff. "I hit a line before you came," I say.

Pouting, she reaches for the door. "You've gained weight, Sav."

"Margot, know a joke." I plant my nose on the line and sniff. The burn floods my head and flickers out to numb.

She lifts herself on the sink, swings her legs, chews her lip. "I have a secret."

I let out a breathy laugh, soft and from the throat, and feel like I'm at a sleepover. After popcorn and prank calls. At the point of night whispers and laughter that can't be bottled.

"Spill your guts."

"No. Say, split your ends."

"Split your ends."

"Later." She leaps down and smooths flyaway wisps in the mirror, pushes up her tits. "We're missing a show. Christoph is here."

"You're kidding." I ain't sure if Christoph was the gardener or the ex. I clench my jaw.

"Maybe you'll get it tonight. Not of Parisian pedigree, but." A shrug, the flash of a sprite smile, she flings the door open. We whisper and laugh our way to the party. The room full of people now.

At the back of the crowd, against the wall, a man watches me. Body hidden by well-dressed men, but I'm sure his suit just as Italian and just as silk as the rest. Lapels high. The way he stretching his neck to get a view of me. It's his face I don't like. White as cornstarch, cracked with too much time. Liver spots. Eyes so deep set the brow bone hovers, gives shade for overseeing. The type of elder only the rich get. Skin saying: *I got more years than I got money, and I got a lot of money.* I bet he the patriarch. And he don't stop looking, holds me in his stare.

At the other end of the table, Margot joins a chiseled man pointing at my shoes, and nods.

"There's the princess." A man choked by neck fat and a silver tie chuckles, his face red as strawberry guts. He squeezes my shoulder.

The tiny woman next to him gives him a gentle slap. "Oh, Bert, you're drunk."

"Uncle Bert." My lips twitch, want to lift to greet the stranger I got to love, but they don't rise. Smiling means bullshit. I look over my shoulder, pretend to look at all the guests who traveled here for me, and see his pudgy fingers wiped away the foundation. To cloak the truth, I brush my hair. Mama Brown's fingers of dread poke me, but I'm too giddy to care. My heart got a new beat. "Where's Ry-Ry?"

"Sulking somewhere, you know." Uncle Bert's voice booms in his wineglass. He picks a cucumber sandwich, chews. Soft bread gummed to his teeth. "Your cousins couldn't come."

The aunt chimes in—either Sandra or Sarah—with pride. "They're on a mission trip."

"Where?"

The uncle and aunt glance at each other, then at the bottom of their glasses.

Cotton taps my shoulder, winks at the couple. "Mind if I steal her?"

Uncle Bert waves us away. We go to a corner of the room, alone, divided by a sliver of wainscot. Across the room, that old man still watches.

"How am I doing?"

He scratches his chin. "Ease up on the follow-up questions. Be a real bitch." Cotton begins to turn away.

"There's a man that keeps staring at me."

"That's kind of the point," he says.

"There's a problem," I say.

He keeps his feet planted. I move my hair from my shoulder and reveal the blurred orbs of Uncle Bert's smudging. "They keep touching me."

A considering silence. His knuckles drumming on the pale

wall. "If it becomes noticeable, go straight to Eden, or find me. Whoever's closest. Be a bitch." He goes over to the table, prods at the food, trying to act like he under control, but I know what he thinking: *I dropped the twine on a platter; it's somewhere in the hummus, somewhere under pickled onions.*

By a platter of cubed candied melon, Arnold and Shirley stand, antsy. They eye me. I join them, expressionless. "The chandelier is gaudy," I say.

"Like a hooker's earring," Arnold says.

Her lips plumped by surgeon's needles, Shirley says, "We have a surprise for you."

I ain't sure if *What is it?* counts as a follow-up question. I settle on a light head tilt and chew my lip like Margot. When they don't speak, I lift an eyebrow. The silence between us swims and swims. "Oh, tell me."

Arnold and Shirley nod their heads to the chiseled man next to Margot. I see how Margot leans into his words like she just got to taste every syllable. He look at her like she been fried in peanut oil. If they ain't already fucked, they will soon. "Oh, Daddy, no," I say.

"I felt that way about your father." Shirley strokes my hair. "Talk to him."

I cross the table to Christoph. Margot glances up and skitters away to two old men, Arnold's business partners, probably, who chatter between sips of brandy.

Christoph kisses me, his tongue dry, a touch of spearmint. He pulls away.

"Are you trying to make a scene?" I ask.

He strokes my hair. "Don't you mean bedlam?"

"Bedlam."

"You left me for Paris," he says.

"I left you for cobblestone and soft cheese."

"Artisanal cheese, you mean."

"Precisely," I say, "and you've been hopping between summer homes."

"I hope you aren't accusing me of being unfaithful. It's unbecoming." He swallows merlot. "But, you know me well." He shakes his glass. "This tastes like hell."

"Fascinating." I hand him my empty glass and walk away. Cotton catches my eye and nods with the ghost of a smile. These shoes working on me, making me grind my teeth, making me scoop another glass of merlot from the corner of the table and strut through the swarm, to the fire. I sit down next to the brother, Ryan, his legs sprawled on the shadowed sofa. Cross-legged and straight-backed, I say, "There's Ry-Ry."

He looks at the swollen cigar in his hand like it spoke, his eyes on the trail of smoke reaching up but never making it to the ceiling. "What did you eat today?"

"Water and oil," I say.

"Huh." He takes a long puff, and the sweet smoke hits my face. "You really look like her."

I take a swig of my merlot. "Don't you want to know about Paris?"

"I'm much more interested in why my mother and father insisted I fly to this dilapidated city to drink cheap wine and talk to a bad actress." He looks up from his hand to me, or maybe through me. "You make a small profit from the bad news of others."

I gaze at the tip of his nose, can't look in his eyes again.

"Those are nice shoes, but where did you buy the dress?"

"In Paris."

"My sister was butchered on vacation and cast from a yacht. Have you ever been on a yacht?"

"It's all Parisian," I say.

"You drink Dasani, don't you?" His chesty *ha ha* comes out muffled by a cloud of tobacco, black tea, cedar. "Fuck off."

I rise and waltz back to the crowd. These are the questions rich anger demands answers to: *What you smell like? Is it money? If it is money, are they new bills? Or are they crinkled soft? Are they crinkled soft because they been folded in a drawer, stuffed in socks? Do you got your scent tucked away in a vault? Tell me, has it been locked away so long, the bank feels like your granddaddy? If not, who is your granddaddy?*

The businessmen surrounding Margot chant my name and wave. "Savannah, Savannah." The dead woman's shoes carry me to their cologned half circle. The men stand bloated, their buttons ready to pop.

"Tell us about Paris," they say.

Margot takes my hand. "We need girl time." She turns her head as she whisks me away. "Daddy says hello."

On our way to the bathroom, I catch the old man's eyes again, his harsh gaze. Margot smiles behind the closed door, sits on the sink. I sit on the edge of the tub.

"Split your ends, bitch," I say.

"Okay, okay." Smiling past me, into memory. "Remember on our eighteenth birthday, when we went to Lake Como, and you told me you fucked my father?" Her words sag and blend in a slur. "How angry I was at you. How I hopped on a boat with a stranger and didn't come to shore until sunset." She shakes her head with a wide smile. "That Italian sun. My skin peeled for months after. I was so horrified. I thought I'd scar."

I nod and match her smile.

"I told you I'd get you back. But it was more than that. I promised myself. Christoph and I—"

"Margot, there are better men."

She bites her lip, looks at the ceiling, but tears roll.

"I forgive you," I say.

She hops down from the sink. I stand and smirk.

"You really are an aloof bitch, you know." She hugs me, her face wet, then staggers to the door. "Are you coming?"

"I need the toilet."

"Crass."

Once the door clicks shut, I flip the lock and twist my arms in the mirror: white rubbed to a fade. Splotches of brown. Cotton's number goes straight to voice mail. I call Eden, and before I got time to hang up, she's knocking on the door, bursting in, crystal foundation bottle clinking against the pyramid of her martini glass. "Shit fire, it's like a pettin' zoo," she says. Sponge dabbing my flesh until the tone evens out to condensed milk.

The prickling around my body now working in my chest. My ears and brain thud—hooves on packed mud fleeing a storm. "I got to go to the hospital." I press Eden's hand to my chest, every beat, my heart, a car crash.

"You're only havin' a fit."

My breathing speeds to short puffs. The waist trainer only making it worse.

"Get yourself up and out, come on."

"I ain't ever did coke before. It's fighting with that pill I took."

"Sweetie, you're havin' your first Saturday night. Congratulations."

My chest heaves. "Eden."

"I got to check on the party. You come out when you're ready."
The door shuts behind her.

I meet the mirror, mutter, "Get yourself out. Out." That don't
work. Behind the mirror, in the medicine cabinet: a bottle of
Tylenol, an empty wheel of floss, a thumbtack—pricked pinky.
The bead of blood grounds me, brings me to the now. But that ain't
enough. I rush to Mama Brown's ballerina box, take the twine and
put it in my bra. Grounded. Still jittered, I rejoin the party.

At half-past midnight, I sit by the fire. The family and friends
stand in line. Each one steps up with hushed apologies, confes-
sions. My eyes forgive; my eyes love. Ryan is the last. He hunches
over—breath burned harsh. "I pity you," he says. The crowd
trickles down the stairs, leaving behind tilted glasses, gnawed
and slobbered leftovers. Cotton ushers them out from behind.

At the thunderclap of the shut front door, I wrestle out the
dead woman's shoes. From the fire, to the dining room. The
crowd gone. A neat mess.

In the corner stands that watching man—his suit ain't silk. It's
tweed. He clutching a Bible. Thin like he got a hunger no bread
could touch. Cricket. He found me. He just gazes. Unfeeling. *I
caught you, girl. Thought you was slick.*

I run on skin to my room. Lock the door. To the toilet. My
insides beg for purging. The exorcism of Savannah goes like this:
up my stomach, out my throat, spit from my tongue. The last of
her floats in the bowl. That wine-muddy pool of acid.

Moving feels slow and fast all at once: wiping drool from my
mouth, touching the twine in my bra: *Yes, you still here, keeping me
sane.*

I creep into the dining room. Only Cotton and Eden. The
could-be Cricket gone.

"Everybody left?" I ask.

Cotton don't answer, starts cleaning the table.

"Yes," Eden says, "on to finer things."

"Did they have a preacher here?" I ask.

"Lord, hard to tell." Eden shakes the empty bottles on the table. "So many people." She goes to the kitchen, and I know she going through the pantry, to that drinking cove. That watching man was probably just a guest who had a curiosity about what I looked like without the makeup, wanted to stay after and watch me transform. Or maybe someone from off the street wanted to crash this funeral party, steal some food and glances. Whoever, it wasn't Cricket. The hot foot powder worked.

I leave Cotton to his muttering and wiping, shower and crawl to bed.

I can't sleep, too many thoughts. Cotton threatening to fire me. One way to get on his good side is by teaching him something about death. Searching the internet for facts could maybe help. *Hello, Cotton, what a lovely day. You are more likely to be killed by a champagne cork than a venomous spider.* Or maybe I'll walk up to him with a limp wrist, chewing gum, say: *Did you know that each year doctors' sloppy handwriting kills thousands?* No, I'll take him by the hand and give him a wink, whisper: *Soon after the heart stops, when the blood pressure's good and gone, eyeballs flatten. Popped balloons! Party over.*

My thinking still comes in swirls, pushes me through Wikipedia tunnels: the dancing plague of 1518, a list of deaths by coconut, lawsuits against God.

The 10 percent battery warning shines on the screen. I close the notification and watch news bloopers. Journalists swatting bugs, naked frat boys running in the camera's view. A struggle to keep my laughter hushed.

But then the dread seeps through the top of my skull. Down my throat. Rests in my belly. In the blurred edges of night, pipes gurgle. The bathroom door opens. A creak. The room is dark. A darkness so rich it grows and shrinks. My eyes try to make sense of it all. I turn on my phone flashlight. In the bathroom, Mama Brown propped on elbows, dragging her body: one leg flat as hit skunk, her head stuck to her shoulder like she got a crick in her neck. She inches to the doorway. Bits of her wet flesh sloughing off with every movement. In the dim orb of my phone's light, she gnashes her teeth. Her voice sounds underwater. Wavering, deep: "He coming for a piece of you."

I want to pull the covers over my face. This relief of seeing her, knowing she still around, mixing with the horror of her roadkill body. She ain't lasting much longer. She makes it to the edge of my mattress.

"Baby, lift me up, please. I hurt."

I push away the covers and scoop her up. It ain't her stench of mothballs and shit and cabbage gone bad that makes me choke. Or the wetness pressed against me while I cradle her to the other end of my bed. It's how light she sitting. All her meat gone. Now she the one asking to nestle, needing comfort. I settle her against the pillow, stuck head elevated.

Before getting back in bed, I strip my muddy clothes. Under the covers, I prop my head on my fist, and I feel too young and too old. Between us, I put my phone's flashlight, aimed at the ceiling for our sight. Shadows in the hollows of her cheeks. Her eyes bulging. Delirious.

"He do this to you?" I ask.

Each word comes out her mouth as a hard breath. "He left me be." A gasp for air. "This what time do."

"I made him go away."

"Last I seen him, he was clutching that Bible and pacing and pacing and screaming Magnolia, Magnolia."

"That ain't true," I say. "I made the hot foot powder."

Mama Brown laughs. Her teeth fall out, click together in her mouth like ate pebbles. Her hands shake while she fishes them out. That kind of tremor come from too much pain. "Seem like the more I lose the faster I go." Her words mash through gums. "Who taught you hot foot powder? Louise? That don't matter." She pushes her teeth beneath the pillow.

I try to keep my voice steady, but it don't work. "You leaving soon, ain't you?"

"You got to quit doing these drugs."

"I ain't. I promise."

She winces, and I know I'm that pain. "Don't let me lose that peace. Maybe if you see your child, Cricket won't want you."

I hate her like this, a folded, begging thing leaking and needing mercy. "I don't got nothing for him. Don't let him, Mama."

"What power I got?" She chuckles. We sit in silence. Then, she say, "Magnolia." Her voice serious. That *you-too-near-the-stove-eye* voice. The tone that say badness coming.

This room full of heat. The dread thickens in me like swallowed smog.

All around the bed, the floor creaks, moans, warns of added weight. My hand shakes the light around: Bianca, the nail tech, claws at the bed. Aria, the singer, and all the others. Jaundiced arms, bleeding arms, bloated arms. All grabbing at the sheets. All reaching out for me. I look to Mama Brown for shared panic, but she ain't next to me. Ain't in this room.

The light on my phone quits, leaving me in this hugging dark. I bury myself under the covers, wrap my body around a pillow. Rock back and forth to the sound of dead fingers scratching at the bed. Getting closer. Getting too close. When I first moved in with Mama Brown, we'd play a game. The bed was our boat, the floor was a hungry sea. And in that sea were sharks and sea monsters, wanting our blood. We'd throw pillows in that tiny room, squealing and laughing. She brought that play-pretend to me. Now she making it bad.

I slip my head free of shelter. Feel a hand grip my ankle, tug. Another hand grabs my leg. They take my body, drag me to the edge of the bed. Hot breath hits my neck.

The lock on my door twists. Opens. In the light of the hall at the mouth of my space stands Cricket. The hands grip me, won't let me loose.

"You have called my name."

I kick at the hands, the arms. Try to wiggle out. Trapped. Held.

He opens his Bible. His bookmark: a pair of scissors. He inches near me. Fingers in the loops of the scissors. He grips my head with one hand, a lock of my hair in the other. His voice come out altar ready: "And herein is that saying true. One soweth and another reapeth."

21

The relief of an amen, a bird sings outside my window. My room empty. Early light shining through the curtains.

Dawn. Unchanging dawn. Soft and blue and dewed as ever.

On the side of my head, a chunk of hair missing. Cricket's harvest. I take the twine out my bra and wrap it around my little toe; the little knot makes me feel more tethered. I put on socks to hide my steal and crawl back into bed. Weariness, sleep, finally comes.

Eden shakes me awake around noon. She got on Madonna's face. "Are you hungry?"

"No."

"I ain't surprised." She grips my chin, tilts my face. "What in the hell happened?"

"I got gum in it."

"Should've told me before you did that." Her hand moves from my face into crossed arms. "Peanut butter would've fixed it."

In her bedroom, she already got a headshot of today's case pinned by the vanity. A clean panic. "I forgot to read the case. I meant to after the party—"

"You ain't got to read these. You just got to stay still." She pulls the thumbtack out the cork and hands me the picture. A dress, pink as peonies, hangs sheathed in plastic. The makeup, curling iron, tinted lotions and creams, all cluttered in two glittering boxes. "Can you help me carry these down? Lightin's just as good."

"You mean down there."

"I figured it'd do you good to get used to it." She squats and grunts, scoops up a box. "I imagine you're full of nerves. I've laid in a lot of beds, but never one that shuts. And I won't ever. Not even when I'm dead."

I drape the protected dress over a box and lift. When we reach the stairs, Eden says, "Careful, easy." We plop the boxes down by the big doors of the receiving room and catch our breath. Eden props open the door with her foot, and I haul in the box, Eden behind me. The door slams behind us, trapping us with the choking perfume of flowers. We struggle past cushioned pews, around the pulpit's blushed crowd of carnations and daisies. Down a hall to a swinging door with blaring letters: EMPLOYEES ONLY. Funny, I ain't ever thought of Cotton and Eden holding that title. We pass through the door, down another flight of stairs, into a bright room with metal-slabbed tables, shining cabinets pushed deep in a wall. A pickled, sterile scent. Bleach, vinegar, and beneath that, boiled eggs. At the other end of the room, another swinging door forbids wanderers.

"What's back there?" I ask.

"Crematorium." She rolls a chair away from one of the slabs. "Go ahead and dress."

I play with the bottom of my shirt, eye the shut drawers. "They in here?"

Eden laughs. "Honey, they ain't concerned with us."

Lifted shirt, dropped pants. The cold of this room got a different bite. The dress cloaks me. The rough-backed chair, the shoulder pads, the polyester. I itch. "How old was this woman?"

"Twenty-five when she disappeared."

"She dressed like this?"

"She liked to play pin-up."

Eden shades my skin white as sunshine, sketches my eyebrows into severe arches. Baby wings reach from the corners of my eyes. She glues lashes and paints my lips manslaughter red. Wand heated, works the blond wig into tight curls. A downpour of hairspray to stiffen. She holds a lighter to the point of an eyeliner pencil, dots a beauty mark next to my cupid's bow.

"You look like a little Monroe," she says. "Damn. I forgot the shoes. Be right back." She jogs out the door, leaves me in the belly of the morgue with the forever sleepers. If Cotton saw me, moonlit with death, he'd beg me to slump, just a little more, Magnolia, please.

Eden will see the twine when I change shoes; I slip off my sock, untie, and slip it in my bra. But it doesn't stop the dread. Seeping down, further into me.

The banshee screech of metal-on-metal, a cabinet slides open. Mama Brown lays on the moving metal, her weight held on elbows, ready to grunt into a stand. Both knees, now crushed into bowls. She falls to the floor. The thud of her head hitting the tile, that look full of shame, saying: *I was once strong enough to carry worldly weights; what happened to these bones, these muscles nibbled on by white rats?*

"Stop with that ugly pity," she says. The jut of her bottom lip tells me she got tears coming. "I'm goddamn tired."

Jesus, how long it been since I talked to you? I'm awful sorry. Make her better. Even just a little bit. Work your healing. "I love you," I say, "I love you, I love you."

She struggles to scoot back against the cabinet, smoothing the flesh over her collarbones. "You promise me you done with the drugs." This her I-love-you-too speak. This her good-bye speak, another letter to rip open and read. Hoping she set me up just enough to be okay, to get by.

And Jesus ain't reaching his touch down to lift her up. Why fix people in the forgotten place when there's water waiting to be turned to wine. "Let me see her," I say. "Show me."

A look of surprise on her face—her toothless smile don't cover the sadness in her eyes, the fast blinking. Both of us knowing no amount of time or readied thinking could ever make our farewell light and easy. "Thank you, baby. Thank you."

I close my eyes, try to imagine shit-talking Mama Brown, lit blunt, cackling at the TV. This can't be the last of her; I can't bring myself to open my eyes.

A hand grazes my thigh. "You sittin' in a nightmare?"

I scream, flung-open eyes, but Eden just laughs. It's only us.

"Oh, sweetie." She wipes away my tears, fixes the running makeup. "You got nerves, don't you? I figured as much." She crouches with popping knees and slips off my socks, pushes my feet into the white heels. "I got something to help you stay still."

A pill from her pocket. White and round as a communion wafer. "It'll keep you from havin' another fit."

She hands me the cup of water. I swallow.

"It's a fast worker," she says.

"We got time to smoke?"

She wakes the face of her phone. "A little. But not out front, in case somebody gets here early."

On to the entrance of the crematorium. "Might want to hold your breath."

I cradle air in my lungs when the door swings open. Wide, clean space. Two black panels built into the wall, both with empty tracks that roll in the dead.

In the corner, Mama Brown sits on a pedestal with a rotted pout, rocking a pink swaddle of fleece. The face and body shrouded. No shriveled feet poke out the fabric, no little clawing fingers reaching for nurture. Broken stalactites, fleeing bats: inside me, a cave-in. I gasp. The smell coats my tongue: charred pork chops, cooking caramel. I bolt across the room to the door, welcome the outside air with shaking gulps. Seconds or minutes later, Eden joins me. We face a thin line of young birch.

"I'm so used to the smell." She smiles and hands me a Virginia Slim.

Tremoring, I bring the flame to my lips and suck down smoke. "You ever been haunted?"

She lights her cigarette, her face blurred by smoke. "What?"

"You ever seen a haint?"

Laughter and smoke come out her mouth. "Ghosts ain't real."

"I saw my baby."

She flicks ashes to the concrete step.

"I saw my Mama Brown. I saw my baby."

Eden cups my chin with a tight grip. Each word comes out slow and final, water dripping from a pipe: "Shut. Up." My gaze strays from her mean look, to the line of trees. She releases my chin. "It's your nerves, that's all. Cotton's already upset, and if he heard you——"

I heard those words before. I heard those words a lot. The first time I was told those words, I was five. Quarry had been living with Cherry and me for a month. It was the longest night of winter, and my room in the trailer felt built of frost. I couldn't sleep, so I played with limbless dolls and made them talk. Maybe I was too loud because the floor creaked, my door opened, and in stepped Quarry.

He spoke in a hushed rasp: "Who are you talkin' to?"

I covered my eyes with my hands, said, "I ain't here."

"What? Why ain't you sleepin'?" he asked.

I peered at him in the shadows. "My dolls was talking."

He shut the door and took the fairy-tale book out of my toy bin. In that moment, he was nice. He laid beside me in my twin bed. "This will help you sleep." He told me about "Jack and the Beanstalk," "The Princess and the Pea," and all the wolves that were ever written about. Painted pictures with words: tree-choked trails, and heavy dresses, and cloaked men. All that unspent energy worked into imagination. I started to fall asleep.

He gave me a good-night kiss on my shut eyes. "Ain't you glad you put down those dolls? They ain't your friend." He moved my hand to the throbbing bunch in his boxers. "You got to have a friend that can feel you."

And every night after that, this is what I heard before sleep took over: tales of scared princesses, the fast hiss of a zipper, the secret order—*Shut. Up.* Yes, I know those words. I know them well. We the best of friends. A part of me died every night with Quarry. But it ain't a forever death. It's a death that keeps happening, on time as solstice. And the most brutal deaths of the still-living happen with the taking of the body.

But before all that, I was allowed to be little.

Dear God,

I was a short thing with curls that yellowed in the summer. Woodpeckers and their hollow knocking scared me. My favorite supper food was Cherry's spaghetti. I'd put so much parmesan on that it made the sauce dry. Yard sales were my shopping sprees. Those bins of bouncy balls felt like looking at planets I could visit. Vacation Bible School felt like a theme park. I liked gluing glitter on crosses and singing songs I ain't know the meaning to. I tied June bugs to string and flew them like kites. I burned my finger on a stove eye. Water beds seemed like a luxury I'd never get. Honeysuckle killed my thirst. I ate strawberry bonbons and watched *The Wizard of Oz*. Strangers in the grocery store waved at me, the pretty girl, and I waved right back, trust all in my palm. I wanted to be a firefighter and a famous dancer. I wanted to be a penguin and to live in the snow, huddled close to a plush waddle. Once my kindergarten teacher put shaving cream on our desks and let us doodle with our fingers. Maybe it was to clean the desk, but it felt fun and good and right. That was a bright time, flush with light. That was a time when I didn't know what bad meant. But now, I'm in that pocket of space between being hurt and being better. My hurt been so constant, so normal. Why you let me get the chipped teacup living?

A letter in my mind that won't ever end.

Eden and I smoke our cigarettes to splinters. I stagger when we step inside.

In the corner, Mama Brown drops the swaddle. The fleece opens in the fall, shows me a mirror ready to break. A shatter to the floor, shards scattered like diamonds. Mama Brown nods.

The medicine makes everything in my head float. Each step feels like walking in a lake, the green water up to my hip bones. Mama Brown wavers like light, like light underwater, then fades with all my feelings. The numb comes back, and it's something like peace.

I walk on with held breath, lulled by the clicking of my shoes, Eden's shoes, on the lacquered floor. Into the morgue. I don't see ghosts of past cases in this blue chill, only feel them: in the whisper of the breeze from the vents, strands of my stiff hair tickling my neck, the scratching fabric hugging my skin. My weight tugs me down, down to the chair.

Eden's phone rings. "Uh-huh," she says. She looks at me. "You got it in you to sleep?"

I give her a tired smile. My heavy eyes gift me dimness.

She ends the call and hunkers down to one of her boxes, pulls out a clear spray bottle full of light purple liquid. The color of twilight. The color of dreams. Our fingers lace.

She must guide me to this room, but I don't remember getting here: warm lights, vanilla walls lined with caskets, a watching portrait of Jesus. My casket sits on a raised platform, open in the middle of the room. Shining and dark as blood. The inside is plush. Pearled silk. Cloudy ruffles. Eden mists the pillow with the perfume, brings a stool over, helps me on. I stare into the mouth of the casket.

She pats the swell of my ass. "Well, go on."

I hoist myself in—one arm, one leg, then all of me is swallowed by softness, the lavender coaxing me into nothing. My thinking an empty room. I ain't ever felt so relaxed.

"When you feel like you got to sleep, don't fight it." She frames my curls around my face. Tingles all down my spine. "It feels damn good to fight it, but don't."

I let my eyes rest.

"Oh, don't move. I got to take a picture. This is too good."

Cotton enters the room in a nice suit with a red face. "Have you seen my twine?"

It takes strength to twist my lips up in a smile. I try to focus my eyes on his face. They roll shut.

"Oh, hush, you did just fine last night without it," Eden says.

Cotton stammers like she just said the world is a fried egg. "Last night was a party. That's one thing. I can't do this funeral without it."

"Get out of your head," Eden says.

"I have searched over and over. Magnolia," he says. He snaps his fingers over my face. Mutters, "Bet she took it."

Eden strokes my wrist. "Cotton, go on to the store later and get a piece of twine. Shit, you can rip a piece of my dress if you want. But the family is here."

I force my eyes open, and he crumbles to the floor. His fingers deep in his curls, rocking back and forth in a tantrum.

"God almighty," Eden says.

I keep my eyes open as she rolls me toward the receiving room. We leave Cotton sobbing beneath the portrait of Jesus. I'm fighting the sleep. What good is this new calm if I ain't awake to enjoy it?

Eden settles the casket in place. I shut my eyes. Shoes almost muted by carpet, I hear her usher someone over. The person hovers over me—her rose perfume blends with the bouquets around me, the lavender beneath my head.

"Jesus wept," the woman says. I smell the honey-lemon throat lozenge clicking her teeth. "She looks just like her."

Eden speaks in a hushed tone meant to soothe. "I'll tell the others it's time."

"Is Reverend Ephraim here?" the woman asks.

Their footsteps fade. I hear a small crowd enter the room with quiet, pouting voices, hear Reverend Ephraim take the stand and say something about how mountains quake. Something about a great, big river that's all too easy to cross. That familiar light don't wash over me. I slip into a deep sleep.

22

Only this darkness lets me know I am here. I am here in this pillowed womb. I am here with these hymnal lullabies. And I am mother of none. I am too-touched child. I am not dead. I am too-touched woman. And I am not betrothed. I am ringmaster diva, ears sagging with diamonds. I am not Josephine Baker. I am the imaginary friend. I am hope scabbed over. I am a quarry to be mined. I am an early frost. No, I am a dripping cave. I am daughter of Cherry Miller. But I am not my mother. I am granddaughter of Alette Brown. But I am not my grandmother. I am a tattered quilt of all the women before me. I am a broken puzzle. I am Magnolia. I am Magnolia Brown. I am a dreamless peace. In this new-met dark, I am a sleeping beauty.

23

I been staying at this motel for about a week. The view ain't nothing to write home about. Old asphalt parking lot, sidewalk lined with a strip of grass that only baby finches appreciate. Beyond that, out of view, Magnolia Avenue. This room like any other cheap motel. Stuck in the 1980s, with a bathtub I got to wear shoes in to stop mushrooms from sprouting out my toes. I ain't got a problem with this borrowed living for a little bit. Sometimes at night, when sleep is running late, if it's quiet enough, I squint until I'm almost blind and pretend this room is my house. I picked out that painting of the lavender field, bought that TV with my last check, and I got to mow the lawn tomorrow because the grasshoppers real bad this year, and that's good news for copperheads. A dropped soda can or a shut car door always jabs through the cloth of my fantasy. That's fine. That painting as ugly as dentist office art, and I hate mowing. It always gives my nose a trickle.

Mama Brown had the same problem, always came back to the house in her shuffle-run after cutting grass, straight to the box of tissue. I miss her. I still see her sometimes. In the mirror, if I twist my mouth just right, there she lives in my body, making the same face she'd make when somebody showed a part of themselves without meaning to. When I suck in my cheeks and lower my brow, I'd swear she's there, sorting through the mail. Her thoughts on to-do lists.

I got my own to-dos now. Sitting on the table pressed against the motel room's wall, compact mirror in my palm. I dust my cheeks with blush. My job interview in an hour. Flight attendant. I'll get this job because I got to. I figure I got enough practice walking and talking like I'm made for living midair. I will go into the office, and I will say: *Ain't this strut ready to coax people through clouds? Please, let's fly.*

A few minutes left before I got to head to the airport. Today's newspaper by my side—before I see the classifieds, I scan through the obituaries. Holding this new wish—to see Sugar Foot's face, or Cotton's, or Quarry's, block-lettered script saying he passed in his home peacefully, of natural causes. And in my wish, I'm the only one who'd read those words and know what it really meant. That slurping down a stew peppered with the starry flowers of mountain laurel just as natural as any cause can be. The jobs posted today don't call my name like I'd like—phone bank, night cleaning, and all the customer service representatives.

I been flirting with the idea of saving enough to move to New York City or maybe Los Angeles. All the places out there for me to grab. Feeling like I'm an acrobat just before gripping the next rope, suspended. Whatever I do next, a life ain't forever, and forever ain't a life to want.

The alarm on my phone rings, always set for interviews in case I get sucked into a daydream. Out this always-dim motel, into the bright sunshine. The taxi takes me just outside Knoxville, down the interstate, to Alcoa. In the airport, my heels click on the glossed floor, and I'm important. I'm business. I can almost hear Cotton's shoes on the tiles.

It's been a week now. I stole out the funeral parlor at the darkest minute of night. I knew I had to get out when after the crowd cleared, Eden silk-stroked Cotton's back. Him sputtering and blustering, snot-clogged: *My twine, my twine.* Doing all but fumbling his way to her tit and greedy-sucking. Eden, her hands soft but her shoulders honest, leaning further and further away from her offered gesture of mothering.

It was an easy wait. Didn't take long for Eden to eat a pill, for Cotton to liquor-swill his eyes into dozing. So I packed my things in paper bags and got ready to leave.

But when I got to the head of the staircase, I stopped. Whisking myself away when they slept tucked-in felt like I was granting them a wish. Like: *Oh heavens, we ain't even need to call pest control, that cockroach left of her own volition, what sweet splendor.* They would have loved my exit to be a press-lipped hunker, knees trembling. The house had that stillness that only come when everybody in this pocket of the world sleeps. That silence was mine and mine alone, and in that moment, anything I wanted was mine. I asked myself, how many goddamn swallowed thoughts can a woman take until her insides rupture? Those words were mine, even the little inkblot at the bottom of the question mark—and the makeup bag, propped on my folded clothes, that was mine, too. The ghost of my footsteps, quiet and balanced on my toes, was mine, and it stayed mine, even as I crept into Cotton's room.

Past the door, the wood only moaned under my weight once. Cotton scrunched his brow, and I stopped, ready to make no excuse at all. He stayed asleep. At the edge of his bed I loomed, and I wondered if his mind sensed me, conjured me up to perform in his dreams. I took out the eyeshadow pallet—Dreams of Amber—and my belly held a thrill like I was pranking at a sleepover, and if he woke up, if I got caught, if, if, if. When I smoothed the foundation on his face, I claimed that nose freckle. The sweep of contour—bone structure all mine. Glittering eyeshadow, the shade named Crystallized, right on his lids. Darkened eyebrows, tinted lips, a dotted-on beauty mark for good measure. My heart turned hummingbird when I glued and balanced the lashes on, but not a peep from him, not a stir. When I finished, I kept by his side just for a second. Wondered about his peace. *Dearly beloved.* The twine I took and slipped under his pillow. *Dearly beloved, we are gathered here today.* I turned one more time before I left his room, hand on that brass knob, and I knew he was only sleeping, but I could've sworn my line of sight hardened him to stone.

When I went down the hall and neared the staircase, Eden came out the kitchen. She stopped, new cocktail in hand, and I saw her. She had just taken a bath. Her face was clean. Makeup scrubbed away, she'd shapeshifted into an ogre. All the flaws she cloaked pushed right to the front: nose crooked without the contour, cheekbones vanished, glow gone. All my things were in clear view; I thought she might try to stop me from leaving. Thought she might want to grind my bones for bread. But no—she'd been too convinced of both her largeness and smallness, as if I was concerned enough to walk on her. She hid her face behind her hands and ducked into her room. But I saw her.

My first step out that funeral parlor, I knew nothing could

make me turn on my heels. I sucked down air, a real deep breath. Tennessee summer still in full bloom. And I felt the way newborns must feel—spank of a gloved hand, lungs flushed with swirls of wind. Stunned.

ACKNOWLEDGMENTS

This book began as a short story called "The Stand-In," which I wrote in a scramble for an undergraduate fiction workshop at the University of Tennessee. Thank you, Chris Hebert, for not laughing at the stiff characters of that early draft and for reading the grown-up version years later; thank-you to La Vinia Delois Jennings for laughing. Thank-you to my other undergraduate mentors: Laura Hoffer, for offering the space to smash plates; Marcel Brouwers, for helping me wrangle in my lyricism; Margaret Lazarus Dean, for encouraging an ethic truth; Rebecca Gayle Howell, for making class feel like home; Richard Hermes, for making a career in writing seem realistic; Bill Larsen, who probably made it into heaven, for being witty and the right kind of mean.

Kim, the librarian at my hometown's local library, prayed over my application to the MFA program (and after, I sped to the post office while her faith was still fresh), and I am still mostly certain this explains the reasoning behind my acceptance. Thank you.

Acknowledgments

Amber Albritton and Catherine Dartez, for cocktails and food, for all the summertime conversations in which we've loved each other and scolded the fools, for the drive up from Tennessee to New York, thank you.

My Syracuse mentors: Arthur Flowers, literary father, thank you for my first Syracuse-winter coat, for telling all students to write a novel over the summer, for reading each of my stubborn revisions before the breakthrough; Dana Spiotta and Jon Dee, thank you for opening your home and for your steady guidance on story, for feeding us, for all the advice when the future was a hazed mystery (and additional thanks to Dana for helping me become more confident in my voice, for helping me accept that, while *hazy* is the correct choice, I will always choose *hazed*); George Saunders, thank you for your incredible emails and for each revelation you gifted in workshop; Sarah Harwell, for your wonderful humor and your hybrid class, in which I wrote the opening of this novel. Thank-you to my cohort for workshopping this novel, and for all the parties we had and missed. Extra, extra thanks to Jonah Evans for Shifty's and cabins, for writing to me on *House of Cotton*: "Your shit is bangin' though, and the writing is tits." And because all the in-betweens of drafting make the work whole: love and thanks to Neil Brian Cooney, for being an early reader and for karaoke, karaoke, karaoke; Leila Renee, for sharing drunken surrealism, for always reading with care, for your sisterhood; Brian Holmes, thank you for speaking in poetry, for being an inspiration, for dancing and meaning it; Leila and Brian, I'll do your makeup anytime, babes.

Terri Zollo, thank you for making the institution of academia less confusing and less scary when all I wanted to do was write.

Amy Stuber and Maureen Langloss and *Split Lip Magazine*,

thank you for my first printed publication, for your continued support.

Eli Heaton, thank you for being an eager reader of this book's roughest draft.

Claire Dippel, my number one fan, thank you for ushering me into the publishing process with your warmth and excitement.

To my agents, Hafizah Geter and PJ Mark, thank you for taking me back after I said no (!!!), for always fanning my enthusiasm, for reading and seeing something special in the characters' lives.

And my editor, Nadxieli Nieto, thank you for your poetic collaboration, for the gorgeous buildup of showing me the novel's cover in Philadelphia, for helping me reach the vision of the final whittlings. Kukuwa Ashun, thank you for keeping me grounded in the logic of the narrative, for your constant kindness. Y'all are my haunted book doulas, pure light in this lachrymose world.

The Flatiron family: Claire McLaughlin, Katherine Turro, Marlena Bittner, Megan Lynch, Nancy Trypuc, Nikkia Rivera, and all others who I have not met but who have helped make this book physical, readable—thank you for helping breathing life into what only existed in my head; I am forever grateful.

Grandmother—thank you for believing in me and making sure I knew before you went on.

Mom—thank you for telling me all the stories when I was itty-bitty, for making me afraid of the dark, for singing your love.

Baba—thank you for your funny hyperbole, for convincing me that squirrels laid eggs, for motorcycle days.

Mamaw—thank you for all the dress-ups and made-up games, for *The Wizard of Oz*, for spoiling me rotten.

Baby brother Dimetry, thank you for dreaming along with me so that my dreams never seemed silly; Baby sister Ariel, thank you for listening to my on-the-spot bedtime stories, the best practice in craft.

And finally, thank you to mamaw's dog, Cookie, for sitting so sweetly beside me each time I cried over the uncertainty of this novel's earliest drafts. We did it, girl! I wish you could read.

ABOUT THE AUTHOR

Monica Brashears is an Affrilachian writer from Tennessee. She is a graduate of Syracuse University's MFA program. Her work has appeared in *Nashville Review, Split Lip Magazine, Appalachian Review,* the *Masters Review*, and more. *House of Cotton* is her first novel.

www.monicabrashears.com